Tales of the
Sunrise Lands

Anthology of Fantasy Japan

Tales of the
Sunrise Lands

Anthology of Fantasy Japan

Edited by

David Stokes

GUARDBRIDGE BOOKS
ST ANDREWS, SCOTLAND

Published by Guardbridge Books, St Andrews, Fife, United Kingdom.

Contents

To my Grandmother and step-Grandfather,
who introduced me to Japanese art.

The magical world lies all around us, often lurking just out off sight. Dear Reader, join Mayu in stepping from our mundane world onto a journey of discovery...

Hanabi To Kitsune (Fireworks and Foxes)

Kirstie Olley

Mayu knew love was a battlefield. She was only one of many girls with their hearts set on Arima-senpai and her small advantage of having caught his eye and received a compliment from him at the Sumida River fireworks festival could be easily lost. That was why finding the perfect yukata was critical.

"You look lovely in that yukata, Mayu-chan. It's quite the striking pattern." Arima-senpai's words echoed in her memory as she looked at the quick selfie they'd taken together with her phone before he'd rushed off to meet-up with his friends. The familiar way he'd used -chan was as thrilling as the compliment. That he'd spotted her in the bustling crowds of one of the biggest festivals of summer, mind-blowing.

The first stumbling block in her plan to catch his eye a second time was that the yukata she'd worn that night was her only one. The second blockade was her total lack of money to buy a new one. Her friends had been all too eager to lend theirs, but they only had common patterns and prints. If she wanted to impress Arima-senpai again she'd need something that ten other girls at the shrine wouldn't also be wearing.

When despair had seemed at the door her mother had commented, almost flippantly—as if Mayu hadn't spent the last week freaking out over the issue—that *her* mother had several old yukata and kimono stored away. For the small price of helping air out the futons and buying some tofu and fish for the miso stock, Mayu gained access to her grandmother's attic collection.

Shuffling through the random junk looking for the clothes, Mayu wondered why her grandmother still lived alone in this house. Grandfather had passed in an accident so long ago Mayu barely remembered his face. Most other grandparents would either move in with one of their children's families or invite one of them to move into their house. Mayu had two uncles and an aunt on her mother's side, so it wasn't like her grandmother didn't have choices.

Before the whys could be pondered Mayu spotted some tatoshi in a drawer. With care she slid the paper packets out, carefully removing them to look at the items within. The first contained a yukata with a cherry blossom pattern; beautiful, but banal thanks to the fact every second girl had one, not to mention wearing a spring theme to a summer festival was a no-no by the rules of kitsuke that governed kimono-wearing. The next was magnolias. Mayu couldn't help but think *ugh, flowers*, and fold the paper back down. The next surprised her slightly, fireworks in a night sky. The thread even glittered. It was beautiful, but the embroidery and quality of the silk made it formal, perhaps too much so for a fireworks festival.

Reverently, she set that one aside to consider should there be nothing more casual.

The next she opened was a beautiful blue kimono with radiant red goldfish swimming on it. It would have gone in the closer inspection pile for sure except for the fact the yukata Arima-senpai praised had also been goldfish patterned.

Maple leaves floated burnished orange on midnight purple, and though it was beautiful Mayu had a feeling she still hadn't found the treasure her heart told her was hiding here.

The last carefully wrapped bundle contained a crimson kimono with golden ginko leaves strewn across it. Mayu didn't really like how she looked in red, so set it back in the drawer with a small sigh. As she carefully flattened it to ensure no creases, she bumped the back of the drawer with her knuckles. It bounced up slightly at the touch.

"Huh?" Mayu gave the back of the drawer a second prod and saw it rise up.

The secret partition was hard against the end of the drawer and it took several tries to slide it out. Two tatoshi wrapped packages flopped out once the false back was far enough removed. Mayu almost snatched them up, her skin tingling. The larger packet was light, so must be a summer yukata. The smaller packet petite enough she was sure it would be a hanhaba obi to match.

With all the restraint she could manage she unwrapped the paper packaging to look at the design beneath. The blue cotton was so pale as to be pastel. In soft, darker blue waves a river was simulated and cavorting beside the river was an orange fox.

Unfolding the yukata with reverence Mayu viewed the complete design. Eight foxes cavorted stream-side upon the design.

"Suehirogari," laughed Mayu softly, referencing the shape of the number eight, wider at the base than the top—a symbol of growth.

She'd never seen a yukata like this before. If unique was what she was looking for this was it. Combined with the lucky number eight, the foxes could also be seen as a nod to Inari, whose shrine the festival honoured.

Yes, this was the perfect yukata. But Grandmother had clearly hidden it, she would probably not be willing to lend it. Mayu chewed her bottom lip. Should she ask and risk refusal, or just borrow it?

The playful foxes seemed to smile at her from the fabric,

their cheek infecting her. Mayu needed to wear this gorgeous, unique yukata. With care she tucked it into the fireworks kimono, thanked her grandmother and left.

Mayu peered amongst the crowds bustling around the stalls lining the shrine paths. Her best friend Rinko had spent more than an hour artfully curling loose strands of hair from the elegant bun she'd put atop Mayu's head. They'd found a ribbon in exactly the same shade of colour as the hanhaba obi and taken advantage of the match. Twisting the ribbon into a flower shaped bow they attached it to the braid wrapped around the base of the bun. Mayu herself had spent that time working hard on her make up, ensuring it looked as natural as possible—an endeavour which always took far more time than any boy ever thought it would.

Putting the yukata on was easy enough with Rinko's help, but they had agonised over the obi after having watched a TV show where the stars had gone obi-less with their yukata and some fashion bloggers had touted it the 'Heisei-style', a natural progression of kitsuke. Ultimately, Mayu hadn't felt confident enough to try pulling off something so cutting edge. That and she secretly felt the obi and the yukata were truly meant to be together.

Considering the hours of effort spent on her look Mayu wasn't about to despair that a whole hour had passed and she hadn't glimpsed Arima-senpai even once. No, she'd never give up. She walked past the prize lottery and ring toss, though she made note of where the kingyo sukui stall was—she would guide Arima-senpai that way so she could show him how good she was at goldfish scooping. After all, she still had the two fish she'd caught last year. She moved past the food stalls too without so much as a glance, her eyes scouring the crowd for his gorgeous face. Even though the takoyaki smelled amazing enough to make her tummy rumble.

After the third time passing the same takoyaki stall though, she gave in and bought some—if only to try and distract herself that she still hadn't spotted Arima-senpai.

Chewing her takoyaki to one side of the thronging people—she had to stop because the last thing she'd want was to stumble in the poor lighting and crowd and splatter the yukata with her food—Mayu pondered if she should try standing still, seeing if Arima-senpai wouldn't simply come across her. This was a much smaller local festival after all, so her chance of bumping into him was much higher than last time.

Still, her eyes raked the crowds, refusing to let a single face pass by unscrutinised.

"What are you hunting this night, Little Fox?" a deep voice asked, coming from just behind Mayu.

She jumped, turning to see who was talking.

An older boy—no actually he was probably in college—more a man than boy stood there. He wore a grey yukata so dark as to look black. He'd belted it with a burnt umber and blue obi. Either this guy really knew his kitsuke or his sister was on point. He stood quite close, such that Mayu was able to make out the fox shapes embroidered in the same colour as the obi fabric, fine and subtle, so as not to be seen from a distance.

"Hunting?" Mayu asked.

"You're clearly on the trail of something," he said with a toothy smile.

Maybe it was because she was bored by almost two hours of doing nothing but searching for Arima-senpai. Maybe it was because a sense of familiarity was born from the fact they both wore foxes. Maybe it was because the playful foxes on her yukata had instilled some of their mischievous spirits in Mayu. Either way, Mayu found herself jovially replying, "I'm hunting a boy, Big Fox."

"Ah, of course, what else would a cute little fox like you be doing." He tossed his head back. "Is it a specific young man, or any handsome fellow?"

"Oh, a specific one. You know we foxes are faithful."

"Oh, definitely. The tale of Ono and his kitsune wife is proof of that."

Mayu remembered the legend her grandmother had told her of the steadfast fox spirit wife, who returned to her husband's side each night though his dog would chase her off every morning. "Kitsu-ne, come and sleep," she whispered, smiling.

"Ki-tsune, always comes," Big Fox finished for her. He smiled more broadly then. "So what lucky boy has captured your devotion at such a young age, Little Fox?"

"A handsome one, Big Fox, a year older than me at school," Mayu confessed without hesitation. Then, like it was fated, Arima-senpai came into view. "Ah! There he is." Mayu tried her best to point him out clearly, without being too obvious in case Arima-senpai looked over and saw her pointing.

Big Fox's face fell. "Oh, Little Fox, no. That one is not a wise choice."

Mayu paused, surprised by the genuine regret on Big Fox's face. "Why?" Her voice cracked as she asked.

"Follow me and I'll show you." He moved forward with casual grace and Mayu suddenly felt awkward on her geta as she followed, sticking close to his side like a little sister to her big brother.

Big Fox trailed Arima-senpai, and before long Mayu noticed he was holding hands with the girl in bejewelled jeans who walked beside him.

"Oh," she whispered, shoulders slumping. "He's actually chosen a girl." Arima-senpai was almost famed for not having chosen a girlfriend, but holding hands at a festival like this was an unspoken commitment.

"Not just that, Little Fox," Big Fox continued. They lingered as Arima-senpai and his girlfriend stooped by the water yoyos.

When his girlfriend took a hook to try and scoop one of the colourful water balloons as they bobbed in a floating circuit he let go of the girl's hand, making an excuse that couldn't be heard through the crowd and heading away while she set to catching one.

They followed Arima-senpai to a stand where corn cobs roasted on a grill, the sweet and charcoal smell beckoning to Mayu. There Arima-senpai stepped close to a girl Mayu recognised from school, Michiko-san. She was a lovely girl in the same year as him who half the boys in Mayu's class looked upon in the same way the girls looked at Arima-senpai. Arima-senpai took a little silk pouch from his pocket and handed it to Michiko-san. Inside was a ring. It was a trinket ring from one of the stalls, but nonetheless she looked as if she would have thrown her arms around him if they weren't in such a public place.

Mayu pressed her lips together in a firm line. Then scolded herself. No, maybe she had misunderstood. The girl Arima-senpai had held the hand of, perhaps she was his sister. Mayu knew she held her brother's hand in crowds so as not to be separated sometimes.

Before long however, Arima-senpai was on the move again, leaving his pretty classmate eating some corn on a bench, trinket ring on her finger. Arima-senpai slipped through the crowd. Pausing to grab two servings of yakisoba in small cardboard trenchers, he brought them to a girl waiting on the river bank, her spot staked out to view the fireworks.

He sat close to her side, far too close for the implications to be unclear. As Mayu clenched her fists at her side she tried to give him the benefit of the doubt. But after only a few moments with the riverside girl Arima-senpai was making excuses and heading back to the yoyo catching stand, where the first girl waited with a brightly coloured prize and a smile on her face. She showed off her catch, beaming and Arima-senpai praised her. Subtly he guided her as they walked until they were hidden slightly by the gnarled shape of a wisteria and its trellis. There, amongst the green leaves whose flowers had only recently been shed, he stole a secret and passionate kiss from the girl.

Mayu clutched at Big Fox's sleeve in shock, then let go quickly, surprised she would grab at the young man who was essentially a stranger to her.

"You see now he is not worthy of your devotion, Little Fox. I'm sorry to show you this." Mayu looked at the deep creases in his brow and knew he wasn't lying.

"It isn't your fault, Big Fox," she sighed, no longer feeling as playful as when she had first called him Big Fox.

"Don't frown though, a pretty face like yours isn't made for sadness. Come with me, this party is cool enough, but I know of a much wilder one." His teeth flashed in the biggest smile yet, but Mayu now felt more wary of men in general.

"I'm not such a fickle girl as to fall for you like that," Mayu said, snapping her fingers.

Big Fox laughed. "Not like that, Little Fox. I only want to cheer you after having hurt you. I promise, I'll try nothing like what you're thinking. I only want to show you something fun."

Mayu considered. So far Big Fox had been genuine. And he had saved her effort and heart break. Not to mention her curiosity was piqued. What did he have to show her?

"All right," she conceded. "Let's see what you've got."

Grinning, Big Fox took off, swift and agile, darting through the crowds. Where before they had been subtle, sneaking, edging between people, now they moved boldly. Yet somehow he never hit anyone in the crowd. Mayu struggled to keep up, other's shoulders thumping into hers, having to dance awkwardly around immovable groups of people on her geta.

Only when the crowd thinned and they began walking away from the shrine did Mayu finally catch up to him. As they drew further and further from the festival, a little worry snuck back into Mayu. Was she safe with this man? She didn't even know his name, and if things went bad, running was almost impossible in yukata and geta.

At the moment when her doubt and worry built up to the point that it was about to escape her lips in the form of an excuse to head back to the shrine, Big Fox turned to face her.

"Here we are, Little Fox."

They were on a normal suburban street. Thin, multi-storey buildings wedged up against one another, most with their fronts hidden from view by high walls. No lights appeared to be on in any of the houses within view. Street lights cast shadows aside regularly, and potted plants clustered together here and there to keep things green.

"I thought you said—" Mayu began.

Big Fox placed a finger over his lips silently to shush her. Mayu clamped her lips shut with an obedience that surprised her.

A dog barked in the distance.

The shrine was so many twists and turns behind them she couldn't even hear the hub-bub of the crowds.

Silence stretched out. It started to prickle at Mayu's skin. Just as she opened her mouth to speak again she heard it though. The soft *chang* of bells being rang, just one short shake, but many together, perfectly timed.

Grinning she took a small step forward. Another *chang* sounded, a little closer than before, and she thought maybe she could hear the footsteps too.

A parade! Perhaps a mikoshi being carried to the shrine? Though Mayu could swear they hadn't had a mikoshi at this festival any of the previous years. She moved to the cross street, peering down to where the bells could be clearly heard. Big Fox moved at her side.

Paper lanterns hung from poles to light the mass, but they were still too far away to make out clearly.

Slowly the figure out front became distinguishable. It was a short man in a resplendent silk kimono. He moved with sophisticated grace, well used to his fine formal attire. As he grew closer Mayu could see he was an old man, wrinkled and bald.

Flanking the old gentleman were two tall, broad shouldered men. They wore the mostly white garb of yamabushi monks, and red noh masks with ludicrously long noses. On their backs large black feathered wings were folded. Mayu immediately recognised them as tengu and looked back at the man between them. Even closer now she could see his bald head was strangely shaped, elongated at the back, like a gourd.

"Nurarihyon," Mayu breathed the spirit's name. A grin broke out on her face. A group of college students had banded together, dressing up as terrible yōkai to enact the Hyakki Yagyō, the night parade of a hundred demons.

As the procession came closer Mayu marvelled at their costumes. The tengu had made their wings with exceptional detail. Nurarihyon did such a good job in his acting she could sense his commanding presence which made even house heads bow to him in their own homes.

Behind them a pretty young woman in a lovely kimono glided along, a silk handkerchief disguising the lower half of her face. Mayu knew enough ghost stories to be certain underneath would be a cut-open mouth. She wondered if the woman had gone so far as to use a prosthetic like in the horror movies in her cosplaying of a kuchisake onna.

The lantern on the pole that hung over the kuchisake onna wasn't a plain old paper lantern. Goggling eyes were set on it and a ragged tear symbolised a mouth. A rubber tongue flopped out of the gaping hole. The way the lantern bobbed on the pole gave it the appearance it was a real, moving chōchin-obake, tongue swishing around in the air.

Mayu laughed, grinning. They'd put so much effort into their costumes and props. So fantastic. Big Fox had been right, this had cheered her up. A sudden thump nearby made her jump slightly. She looked up to the roof of the house beside the footpath.

A large lumpy shadow stood out from the roof. It seemed like a gigantic shaggy dog. Reflecting the light of the street lamp two large eyes glowed. In the weak light Mayu thought she could see two massive, out-ward curving fangs from a face like a komainu statue's. Before she could make out more details the shadow flew over head, jumping the road to land on the roof of the house on the other side of the street.

Heartbeat temporarily frozen Mayu gaped. The shadow leaped again. Could that have been...? No, no, there was no such thing as an otoroshi. This well-prepared Hyakki Yagyō these college students had put together had her seeing things.

Turning back to the cosplay parade, Mayu's pulse leaped to double time. Directly in front of her were three women, giggling and smiling, faces painted geisha white, lank black hair loose. Their long snake-like necks coiled and stretched, keeping their heads easily two metres from their otherwise unremarkable bodies.

Another chōchin-obake swung into view, this time flapping close to her face. A single eye blinked out of the top tear in the paper at her, its tongue lolled wildly, shrill laughter bursting from its gaping mouth.

Mayu latched onto Big Fox's yukata, shrinking behind him, gasping, but trying her best to not make a sound that might draw the demons' attentions to her.

Big Fox laughed softly, looking at her from over his shoulder. Behind him a folded down paper umbrella with one goggling eye and a long tongue like the chōcin-obake's hopped along on its one leg that protruded from the paper folds of its fan as if from a woman's skirt. Big Fox didn't even blink at it.

"Did you want to join in?" he asked.

"Won't they steal us away?"

Big Fox laughed louder. Mayu wanted to push a hand over his mouth in case he caught the parade's attention. "I guess if we were silly enough to be too obvious they might, but if we just slip in, pretend we belong, we can probably go a few blocks with them. How many opportunities are there to be part of the Hyakki Yagyō?"

He was right. It was terrifying, watching a hawk-faced tengu—much more bird in appearance than the two who had stood with Nurarihyon—race by, side by side with a ball of fire which held an old woman's face in its centre.

"Can we really, just... blend in?" Mayu whispered, still clutching fistfuls of Big Fox's yukata.

"Look," he pointed to two rather normal looking people in the procession. They wore stately silk kimono and noh masks of incredible beauty and detail. The wood had been carved to symbolise oni faces. Mayu shuddered slightly at the gleaming red blood detailed on the fangs. She was quickly distracted by something being put in her hands by Big Fox.

In her hands was another noh mask, just as beautiful but nowhere near as ancient. It had been stylised into the pointed face, slit eyed semblance of a kitsune. Looking up at big fox she found him already wearing his. She could easily believe him a real fox spirit, with his fine yukata and mask.

Pulling her mask on quickly, she followed him into the street. They waited for some bakeneko to totter by on their hind legs, mewing as they bowed politely in greeting to the two seeming kitsune joining the procession.

Beside Mayu walked a pretty young woman wearing trendy clothing who would have fit in perfectly in Harajuku or Shibuya, except for the eight, long spindly spider legs extending from her back in the distinctive black and orange of a golden orb spider. She watched the jorōgumo from the corner of her eye tentatively, licking her lips and clutching Big Fox's hand tight in hers. His thumb gave her hand a reassuring stroke and he walked confidently on, eyes forward under his mask.

Two beautiful blue-white orbs floated past Mayu. She gawked at them as they danced forward together, weaving amongst the yōkai, their movements elegant, but a little sad—like when cherry blossoms fell at the end of the season, beautiful because they were brief-lived. Mayu knew they had to be human souls. Had they been taken by the Hyakki Yagyō? That was the legend after all, that anyone who saw the parade would be taken by the yōkai. It was possible, hitodama were supposed to appear around the recently deceased. Mayu gripped tighter to Big Fox's hand and he gave her a reassuring squeeze back.

Something sticky brushed against her leg. Goosebumps exploded all over her body, but Mayu bit the scream back. She glanced down to see the mold-coloured body of a foot high creature, vaguely human in shape, but with spindly arms and legs, its greasy hair only out-grossed by its slimy skin. The creature continued scurrying forward, stooping briefly to wipe its tongue hungrily over some gum left in the road. Gagging, Mayu recognised the little goblin as an akaname and hoped she hadn't caught any diseases when the filthy thing had touched her.

A shadow flew overhead. Mayu tried not to flinch, but looked up, sure it was another otoroshi, jumping from rooftop to rooftop over head. When Mayu looked back down, she saw walking alongside the bakeneko was a dog dressed in ceremonial robes. It was hard not to stare.

She wanted to ask Big Fox why good creatures were part of the Hyakki Yagyō as well as the demons. Would he know? He seemed to know more than most other people, after all he'd known where to find the parade and came prepared with the masks.

Mayu decided when they broke from the procession she would ask, but for now, since they appeared to be safe, blended in with the yōkai all around, she would just look at everything she could.

And she did. Spirits floated by over head, smaller creatures scuttled around their feet, and those that walked alongside them moved forward or fell back and were replaced with others. Mayu soaked all the strange sights in, holding tight to Big Fox's hand with her own sweaty one to make sure they weren't separated.

For how long they walked, Mayu had no idea, but all of a sudden she realised they weren't surrounded by Tokyo suburbs any more. They were in a misty, tree filled area, a great mansion in the traditional style stood before them, and the procession seemed to be heading in, past the shoji screens and into a feast hall.

Though the mouth-watering smell of roast meats and seafood tempted her, Mayu's step faltered, bringing Big Fox to a stand still too.

"What's the matter?" he asked, turning to her. She didn't see him though, only the steps leading up to the household.

"We can't go in there," she whispered.

"Eh? Why not?"

"If we go in there we have to eat, and if humans eat yōkai food they're trapped in the other world forever."

Big Fox laughed. Mayu scowled at him. He did that a lot. Then she frowned at herself. He wouldn't see her glare under the mask.

"We'll be fine, I promise."

"We're lucky we made it this far."

That was when she noticed. In all the wonder and fear she hadn't seen them: the tawny ears sticking up from behind his kitsune mask.

She took a step back, dropping his hand. She could see his bushy tail now too. She took another step backward quickly and turned to run.

A hand clamped over her wrist, snapping on like handcuffs and she froze.

"Why are you so afraid?" asked Big Fox. It took a moment in the sudden whirling of the world, her heartbeat thundering in her ears, for Mayu to register the genuine worry and confusion in Big Fox's voice.

"Y-you're a kitsune," she answered, unable to look anywhere but at his ears.

The smile could be heard in his voice. "Of course I am. Why is that scary?"

Mayu looked around, ensuring no other yōkai were close by before whispering. "Because I'm not."

Big Fox removed his mask, letting go of Mayu's wrist to do so. "What do you mean, Little Fox?" he asked.

Mayu's stomach writhed. Her feet itched to run. Their conversation back at the festival could have been viewed very differently from his perspective. It was easy to see how he'd made the mistake. Now though, Mayu had to decide, was Big Fox only a good person towards her because he believed her a kitsune too, or was he genuinely a good creature? When his mistake was made clear would he help her back to the mortal realm, or would their tie be severed by their being different species?

There was no other option, she couldn't find the way back herself. So she had to tell him. She swallowed hard against the lump in her throat and leaned in to whisper in his ear.

"I'm not a kitsune. I'm human. This is just a beautiful yukata I found in my grandmother's attic, and all our talk—it was just happenstance, I wasn't saying the same things you thought I was."

Big Fox's dark eyes stared at her widely, then a smile broke out over his face. "Then what about these?" he asked, and tweaked her left ear.

It took a moment for Mayu to realise his arm was raised much higher than it should have been. It was almost over the top of her head. Like how his fox ears stood up the top of his skull.

Mayu remained frozen a moment. Then, testing the theory with a strange, squiggly feeling in her stomach she used her muscles in her ear to flick it and shake his hand off. Her ear pulled itself free of his fingers easily.

Staring upward, though she knew there was no way she could look up to visually confirm, Mayu reached her own hands up. Velvety soft fur met her fingers.

Slowly she breathed out, not letting her ears go as she stroked the shape of them with trembling fingertips.

"I think I'll take you home for now," Big Fox said. "And I suggest you speak to your grandmother—the one you nicked this yukata from."

"How did you know I took it without her knowing?"

"Because she would have told you about this yukata and its history, and what it means to your family before she let you out on a festival night wearing it." He gave her a slight smirk. "And don't worry, the ears and tail should fade when we return to Tokyo."

"Tail?!"

Mayu almost laughed at her grandmother's shocked expression when she opened the door to Mayu in the yukata with Big Fox behind her.

She gestured them in, but Big Fox bowed low in the doorway. "Sorry for what I have done tonight. I have returned your child to you." His sudden formalness made Mayu cock an eyebrow.

Grandmother looked between them quickly, and for a moment Mayu worried her grandmother might misinterpret the relationship. Instead her grandmother leaned forward, squinting at Big Fox. Her nostrils flared as she sniffed at the air. A slow smile spread on her lips then.

"I didn't realise there was another family near by," Mayu's grandmother said.

"I don't live near by, I'm travelling."

"Born...?"

"Hokkaido."

"Shrine child?"

"Yes, but also with the true heart bloodline on my mother's side."

Grandmother nodded and smiled. "Good. You may come

in."

"Are you sure, Oba-chan?"

"I wouldn't have said so otherwise," she winked and grinned. She looked to Mayu, gesturing to the couch nearby.

Seated she continued. "I see you found a yukata you liked. It was hidden for a reason."

Mayu hung her head.

"But I'm happy to tell you why it was hidden if you will listen."

"Of course, Grandmother." Mayu ducked her head, clutching a small fistful of the yukata in one hand.

"The yukata you're wearing now is an heirloom. Woven by my grandmother's grandmother. It was passed to the first child born of each generation that was kitsune." She waited a moment, letting the words sink in, though Mayu had already experienced half the revelation. "It was hidden because none of my children showed any signs. I never thought to look at any of you grandchildren. The chances of a kitsune being born to two human parents—even with kitsune somewhere in their bloodlines—is infinitesimally small."

"Lucky me," whispered Mayu under her breath, somewhat surprised to find she actually meant it.

"Yes, lucky," her grandmother said, a wide smile creasing her cheeks. "I feared the bloodline would die out with me. I'm so glad..." with deep creases still on her face, Grandmother's eyes misted over. After a short while she brushed her tears away with a tissue. "I have much to teach you. I think I will finally move into one of my children's houses to help facilitate your education." She looked over to Big Fox and back to her granddaughter. "But tonight it is too late to delve into these matters. You should see your friend off and go home for tonight." Her eyes fell on Big Fox. "I trust you will take her safely home."

"Of course," he replied with a deep bow.

"I will see you tomorrow, Mayu-chan. I hope to see you

again, young man, but if not, I wish you safe travels."

"Thank you." Big Fox bowed again then left, Mayu following. Outside they waved to Mayu's grandmother until she shut the front door, then they wandered the streets.

For a while they were both silent.

"I'm sorry for tonight, I didn't realise you weren't aware," Big Fox began.

"I can see how our conversation and my yukata led you to believe I knew, I don't blame you. It is strange though. Before tonight I thought yōkai and spirits were just stories, and now..." Mayu stopped to laugh at herself. "I never introduced myself. My name is Mayu, using the characters for 'genuine' and 'evening'."

"How apt on a night like tonight, where the truth is revealed to you."

"Are you implying I was named just for tonight?" Mayu arched one eyebrow, but flashed a smile to assure him it was all in jest.

"You'd be surprised how these things work out. I'm Yuuta, using the characters for 'distant' and 'to soar', a travelling name. Names can be magic spells. You might find it's easier for you to discover the truth at night."

"What, like a super power?" Mayu paused a moment then locked eyes firmly with him. "Do kitsune have super powers?"

He laughed. "We have some of the powers the stories mention, but not all of the stories are real, some are just human imagination."

"How weird," Mayu held her hands in front of her, fingers splayed and turned them over and back again. "I'm not *human*. That's so weird."

"Does it bother you?"

Mayu flexed her fingers into fists, then released them. "I don't really know how I feel yet." She looked back up at him. "Will you—"

A sudden blaze of sparkling crimson exploded in the starry

sky, cerulean searing it in close succession.

"Huh? Is it really still so early?" Mayu marvelled as the fireworks burst through the air.

"Time passes differently when you're touching the other world." He shrugged, utterly unfazed by the whole idea.

They both turned to face the sky's fleeting new decorations.

"You're staying, right Big Fox? Not forever, but at least for a bit. While I adjust to things."

He looked down at her as the air crackled with fizzling golden bursts. "Of course I will."

In Shinto, the *Kunitsu-kami* are deities of the earth, in contrast to the heavenly *Amatsu-kami*. While the Amatsu are officially worshipped by the Imperial family, the Kunitsu remain respected by the general population. Kunitsu brought welfare to humanity, and many shrines throughout the land honor these spirits. And sometimes, they travel the country...

Frogwater and Iron

TS Rhodes

Ou was traveling across the mountains, searching for a Frog.

Ou was an Ox Kunitsu, and not especially clever. The Ox totem did not give the gift of great cleverness, or swiftness of thought. Ox gave size and strength, and when it was very pleased with a Kunitsu, it gave the gift of horns. Ou could look easily over the head of any human or Kunitsu that he had ever met, and he was graced with curving horns of great beauty. He was adequately strong. But he was not clever.

For this reason he was going off to see the Frog Kunitsu, Shino, who had some renown as a philosopher. There were questions he wished to ask concerning the connections between the three planes of existence. In addition, he had not heard the singing of a Frog Kunitsu in some time. Ou had been raised by a Frog, and he wanted to hear frogsong again.

From time to time, his travels brought him to a human village. Humans were very respectful of magical creatures such as Ou, but they were often confused about the nature of the Kunitsu.

Ou did his best to be helpful. When a samurai offered him sake to drink, he did not merely refuse; he explained that it was not the custom of Kunitsu to drink alcohol. When cash was offered, he explained that Kunitsu did not use money. He accepted gifts of rice and vegetables. When healing was requested, he used what skill he had. He had some talent in using finding spells, and this aided some humans.

Often he worked in the fields. This he enjoyed.

Ou was not quite sure where Shino was living at the moment, but felt that by moving northwest he would find the Frog by autumn.

At one point Ou moved along a human road, and came to a town. There were large houses here, and a Temple-of-the-Gods, and the shops of merchants. Ou felt shy, entering such a place, but the road ran through the town, and to climb over the mountain would take much longer. He considered becoming invisible, but decided not to do so. Invisibility was for small children and weak creatures. He was no longer a child, and he had nothing to fear from the humans. He walked in along the road.

The humans stared at him. He pretended not to notice. Business on the street stopped, but no one approached him. It would be very pleasant if there were no humans in this place who needed his help. He would walk through the town, and into the next valley, and he would eat wild grasses for his supper, and sleep under the stars.

But, as so often happened, a group of children came up, pushing each other and giggling, and when they were too close to be ignored, Ou looked at them, and then they bowed to him, and then politeness required that he return the bow. After that there were questions. These town children did not even seem to know what a Kunitsu was, and Ou stared at them in mild surprise.

It was not appropriate that a Kunitsu should come into a human place, and then walk out again, leaving humans who did not know a single Kunitsu story. So Ou put his katana aside, and sat down with the children. He told four tales, about the Demon Wars, and the brave Kunitsu of the elder days, who had killed the invading Demons and saved all the humans in the land.

Ou was not a good storyteller, but the children sat with rapt attention, and asked for more stories. Ou glanced at the sun. It would be evening soon, and he wanted to get out of the village. He shook his head. "But remember these stories," he said. "Tell others."

"Sir! Sir!"

Ou would submit to being called "Sir," by a child. He looked and nodded.

"Sir! Where are the Demons now?"

"They are dead."

"But... But, if the Demons are dead... If all the Demons are dead, what do Kunitsu do now?"

That was a question which Ou did not quite know how to answer. He looked at the child, and said, "Many things," and thought for a moment, then added, "Sometimes we tell stories."

That made the children giggle, and Ou liked that sound. He smiled and stood up, putting his sword back into his sash. Sometimes work with humans was pleasant, and this had been a pleasant afternoon. He stretched a little and began to look for the best route out of the town.

A male human came hurrying up, from the direction of a group of large houses, and bowed profoundly before Ou. The human seemed very surprised when the Ox returned his bow, and stammered a bit before managing to say, "Mighty Sir, my master. Saratoma-sama, asks if you are truly a Kunitsu-from-the-mountain, and respectfully requests your company for dinner in the garden this evening."

"My name is Ou."

The man stood staring. "So sorry, Mighty Sir, what was that?"

"My name is Ou. It is not 'Mighty Sir'." Ou looked at the

sun going down on the mountain, and sighed. "I will come to your garden. Is there a place where I can bathe first?"

The human directed Ou to the town's bath house. Ou bathed and washed his clothing, then dressed himself again. He was rather ragged, but clothing in his size was hard to come by. Lastly, he knelt in meditation, raising his body temperature until the clothing was dry.

The human servant was waiting for him, and showed him the way to the samurai's house. It was a beautiful building, set away from the others, and raised against floods, with a tile roof and a wide porch of dark, polished wood. Ou was directed to the side of the house. A garden nestled here, lit with lanterns and flickering with the lights of fireflies. Low, dark green peony bushes bloomed lusciously, and the air was rich with their perfume. From around the corner of the house came the song of a nightingale.

The samurai sat on a side porch which overlooked a small stream. They rose and bowed when Ou approached, murmuring greetings. "I have the honor to be Saratoma Minoru. May I present my older brother Saratoma Keitaro, the owner of this village?"

Ou said his name, bowed and sat with them. The cushions were of silk, and a low table stood nearby, with sake and small foods. Ou did not eat or drink. He was feeling self-conscious, but grateful that there was no roof, so that he could move comfortably. He waited for the samurai to do something, but they were quiet, and the deepening twilight felt peaceful. Cicadas droned. The fireflies made their tiny lights. Ou relaxed gradually. The samurai did not seem to want anything.

The younger samurai offered to pour the sake, and when Ou shook his head, a female servant offered tea. Ou shook his head, and whispered, "Water." He did not want to break the quiet.

Hot water was brought. Ou watched the samurai pour sake for each other. The servant came back with lacquered trays of food. Ou's nose liked the smell of the food. He took up the chopsticks at once. The samurai were watching, and it seemed that Ou had broken with some custom, but they did not protest, so he ate.

The food was good. First, seaweed. Next, tiny fish filled tiny, exquisite bowls. Ou did not like to eat living things, so he waited. Next came soy soup, and vegetables cooked in oil, and pickles, and ginger. Finally came a great deal of white rice, enough, even, for an Ox Kunitsu. Ou ate slowly, and savored all the good things. The samurai ate, and toasted each other, and toasted Ou. Ou did not like the smell of the sake, but the rest was good, and he was a polite guest. At last the food was gone, and the servants had taken the dishes. Ou felt the mood change.

"Kunitsu-san..."

"Ou."

"Ou-san."

Ou sighed, but did not argue again.

"Ou-san, we are very pleased that you have chosen to grace our humble town with your presence. May we ask how long you will be with us?"

"Tonight."

The samurai exchanged a glance. "Tonight only? How unfortunate. We had hoped that you would be willing to stay with us for some time. Do you have an urgent mission?"

Ou considered. "I am on a mission."

Minoru nodded sagely. "Surely. Surely. But, perhaps, we could entreat you to remain for a short time. We are in the midst of a difficult situation, and we would very much appreciate your wisdom in dealing with the matter."

"What situation?"

"This town has long harbored a group of *eta* outcasts. They live just to the north of us, downwind. Certainly, they are filthy, but they have been somewhat useful in digging graves and other unclean tasks. They also..." Here the Minoru paused to glance at Ou's horns. "They also slaughter oxen and tan the hides.

The samurai went on. "Just lately, we have received a message. A condemned criminal has moved in with them, and begun to stir them up. They are requesting... no, they are demanding, access to our town's spring. Of course, this is unthinkable. Besides the stench that they produce, and the danger of disease, there is the spiritual uncleanliness of these people. We were hoping for your assistance in the matter."

Ou chewed a little, and thought. He had not eaten grass, so there was no cud, but still he made the motion, for it aided him in thinking. Finally he asked, "What would you have me do?"

The two samurai looked at each other again, and this time the older brother spoke. "We are not quite sure. They are an affront to us, and impudent, and they deserve to be killed."

"Samurai have no difficulties in killing."

Minoru looked pained. "But there is the ritual uncleanliness. Our swords would be dishonored, to touch such creatures. Perhaps there is some other way."

"I will think on it," said Ou, and got to his feet. "If I am going to stay, may I sleep under your roof tonight?"

The samurai were most accommodating. They showed Ou to a beautifully appointed room. He asked politely that he should not be disturbed. There was more here than these people were telling him. Ou was not good at asking questions, but he had exceptionally keen ears.

He listened to the sounds of the house's many servants. He listened to the samurai pouring sake for each other in the garden. He listened to the creak of the roof. Eventually he heard Keitaro say to Minoru, "Will it work?"

"Yes. They are reputed to have terrible tempers. The Hawk Kunitsu that grandfather told me about was involved in many duels. When this creature sees the ox hides he is sure to go mad. Tell Hediyoshi tomorrow to have the smith come at once."

They said no more of importance, and Ou lay and looked at the ceiling and thought. At last he got up and let himself out of the house. He was absolutely silent.

These humans were not telling him things. There were things he needed to find out. Ou considered what he had heard as he wandered through the town. Who was Hediyoshi? That was part of the question. Ou could not read, but he knew some small bit about the business of humans. The samurai had not used the honorific 'san', so the person they were referring to was not samurai. The name did not sound like a peasant. Perhaps it would be a merchant. Ou walked, and thought. A dog barked at him, and he looked at it until it went silent and crawled away. At last he found his way to the merchant's quarter. He stood, looking, and chewed thoughtfully.

The samurai were going to instruct this person to send for a smith. Was this person a smith himself? No. But he would know of a smith. Perhaps he was a metal-seller of some kind.

He walked and looked for a long time. At last he found a shop with a sign, characters and a picture of a bell. It was not a temple bell. Ou thought that this person must sell metal objects. He went to the side of the building, and found a good place where he could listen. Then he sat down and was invisible. He slept for a bit.

When dawn came, the merchant's apprentice opened the front of the shop. Ou woke up and waited patiently. As he had suspected, a servant came from the samurai house very early. The messenger was admitted all the way into the merchant's home. The message was, "Yes we will have it soon." Then the servant went out, very quickly. Ou got up and followed, but remained invisible.

He followed the man to the Temple-of-the-Gods, and listened very carefully. The Temple was built solidly of stone, but he could hear the tone of the human voice and the sharp click of coins passing hands.

The samurai had not told him the truth. Something was missing.

Ou sat and thought. He did not wish to go to a place where oxen were slaughtered. He did not wish to see ox hides stretched out to cure in the sun. But he had an obligation to help humans, and he felt strongly that something was not right. He began to walk off in the direction of the *eta* village.

The path was very rocky. It wound up the side of the mountain, taking the easiest path. A wounded animal could make this journey. Ou looked very carefully. This was the proper place to put a home for animal slaughterers.

He could smell the place long before he arrived. There was the stink of old blood and death, and of the tanning, which was very foul. As he grew closer, he could smell stagnant water. Nearer yet and he could smell sick humans. The mountainside was steep, and there was not enough room for proper tilled fields. Tiny patches of millet were carefully eked out between the rocks.

The *eta* settlement was a group of small huts made of grass. A dusty path wound through the center of the village. Beside it ran the bed of a stream, but it was dry. No children played. Ou saw one child sitting in a doorway, but it was not moving. He passed a hut and smelled human waste and heard a woman moaning. Other noise rose up ahead, between the rocks a little further up. Ou followed the sound.

It was a funeral, or an attempt at one. The body was wrapped in rags, and laid out on a bamboo platform between two rocks. The humans were moving back and forth, gathering sticks and grass for the pyre, but they moved very slowly. There would never be enough fuel at this rate. The body would rot first.

Ou stood and looked at the humans as they moved slowly back and forth. He crossed his arms and stood on a rock where he could be seen. After a while, one of the humans looked up. That person bowed, and then lay face down in the dirt. The others saw and did the same. Ou came off the rock.

"Who is in charge here?"

After a while, one man said, "I am." He did not raise his

head.

"Get up and look at me."

The man got his knees under him and looked up. He was dressed in rags, and was very thin, as all the humans were. One of his hands had been taken off at the wrist, but it was an old wound. The man looked at Ou, and there was no expression on his face, neither fear nor hope.

"This place is filthy. Your people are sick because of the dirt. What is happening here?"

"The water is gone, Mighty Lord." The man's face held no expression.

Ou thought. Everyone was very still. At last he said, "Show me."

The man got to his feet. He did not brush the dirt off of himself. He went down the trail to the place where the stream had run, and began to climb.

They climbed well above the village. Ou heard running water. The *eta* stopped short of the sound of water, and pointed with his remaining hand. "The stream came down through here. But last moon, the samurai from the village sent men, and they built a wall, and dug a new path for the stream. We are not allowed near. There are guards. If we come too close, we will be killed. But the water is gone, so maybe we are going to die anyway."

Ou looked. He could see how the mountain had been disturbed. He thought, and turned back to the man. "My name is Ou. Do not call me 'Mighty Lord'. I am a spirit of the earth, and the earth is under everyone's feet. What have you been drinking?"

The man bowed. "Greetings, Ou. I had a name, but it is gone now. That is my own fault. Now I am called Kuza. We have been drinking from the lake, but it is dead now, too." They went back down, slowly, because the man was weak, and they were following the rocky stream bed. Ou could smell the dead lake.

It might have been lovely once, but it had shrunk very low. Ou could see where the water had been. Now the reeds stood, dry, and the stagnant lake was filled with algae and stank of dead fish. There were ox hides on frames, on the lower side, and Ou looked away from them.

The man spoke, humbly. "It is hard to be clean when the water is like this. We were boiling it, but the fuel is running out. I was very bold, and went to ask for our water back. They did not kill me, but they chased me away with stones."

Ou stood and thought for a very long time. Finally he asked, "Why did the samurai have the water moved?"

"I do not know. Perhaps only so that we should die.'

Ou thought for a long time again. He walked through the village, and looked at the huts, and the sick people. He walked up and down the bed of the stream. He stood looking at the lake for a long time.

There was something here. Something that the samurai and the merchants wanted. Something that they could not trade for. Something that would be here after the people were dead.

At last he walked out into the mud of the stagnant lake. He looked at the mud very carefully. He followed the stream up and looked under the rocks. Then he went back to the funeral.

There was a little more fuel under the corpse. Ou began to help. He was much stronger than the humans, and he was not afraid to go farther from the village. He gathered great piles of wood, and dead grass, and carried them back. The humans bowed gratefully. One of the men asked, very shyly, "Will you pray?"

Ou shook his head. "My people do not do this. We go back to the earth." But he knelt respectfully while Kuza said some words. The fire went up, throwing hot light on the human faces. They all waited until the pyre had collapsed. Then the humans went back to their village.

Ou went with them, and found a yoke and a pair of wooden pails. He took them and went to the place where the stream had been turned. It was dusk now, and it was easy to be invisible, and to take the water. He carried it back.

The humans in the village hurried to drink, though there was hardly enough for all of them. When the buckets were empty, they sat and looked at him. Ou shuffled his feet, but he needed to speak, so he did.

"There is black sand in your lake. It can be made into iron, and iron is valuable. It is the stuff that katanas are made from. But the samurai will not take iron from an *eta* village. And they will not defile themselves by killing you."

"But they will wait for us to die," said one of the villagers. He did not even sound bitter.

"There is another way," Ou said. "We can move your village."

They stared at him.

"You know this area. Where is a place that no one else wants?"

The humans were silent. Finally one of the young men, hardly more than a boy, said, "There is a swamp in the next valley. No one goes there. It is supposed to be haunted."

"Haunted?"

"There is a monster of some sort."

"Monster?"

"None of us has seen it. It is supposed to be terrifying. No one goes into the swamp, now."

Ou nodded to himself. "I will go and speak to this monster. Pack up the village. We will move it before dawn."

Kuza stared at him with wide eyes. "But, Lord Ou, it is a long way to the swamp, and if we do not take the big tubs to tan the hides, we will starve anyway. And, Lord, we are not as strong as we were.'

Ou looked at them. "It will be all right. Put a sled under the tubs and get drag poles. You are not strong, but I am. You will have an Ox to help with your move."

Ou turned and went out of the village. He needed to get to the swamp quickly. He ran.

It was very dark when he came into the swamp. Night birds were calling. There was only a sickle moon, but the swamp-smell was good. If made him think of frogs. He could hear the little peepers from between the reeds, but he did not have time to enjoy the sound. He broke the night with his bellowing call. After a while, a stirring moved through the tall swamp-grass, and something came out. It was man-sized and covered with scales. A ridge ran along the center of the head, spiked, and baggy neck-wattles hung under the chin. Ou bowed when it came out into the pale light.

"Master Midoro," he said. "It is a pleasure to see you again."

"Ou! What are you doing in my swamp?' The Lizard Kunitsu blinked at him with pleased surprise.

Ou smiled and nodded. "I had heard of a monster here. I need to bring some people to the swamp. I came to ask your permission."

"People? Humans? In my swamp?" Midoro blinked at him again. "What are you up to?"

Ou told about the *eta* village, and the black sand, and the samurai, who wanted to sell the black sand to the merchants. Midoro listened very patiently. At last he shook his head. "I see your point. I see what you are trying to do. I have no objection to your *eta,* as such, but this tanning business is different. My swamp is already in distress. The humans have diverted two streams from it, and it is falling low on water. I have been caring for it, and I believe it will survive, but this tanning does terrible things to water. I cannot bear it now. Do you think that the humans could come, and not do this thing?"

Ou shook his head. "No. It is their work." He paused and asked, "Two streams?"

"Yes. The first was nearly three years ago, when I came here. I have worked with the swamp, and we were doing quite well, but now a second stream has been diverted. My frogs are headed toward a crisis."

Ou felt a great concern for all the little peepers. "Please," he asked, "Show me where the first stream came in."

Midoro led him to the place, and he was able to pick out the fine, steep sides of a narrow but very old stream. He nodded to the Lizard, and began to follow it up. As he suspected, the empty banks came meandering down from the town.

Ou climbed a convenient hill, and stood, looking. He thought of the soft trickling of water between the samurai's flowers, and about the thirsty frogs and the thirsty humans, and he was angry. But anger had never solved anything, and so he calmed himself. He would have to think this through. But first, he would talk to the *eta*.

Back up the stony slope to the *eta* village. The humans did not own much, but the things were wrapped in carrying cloths and laid out in the path, and the people were assembled. Ou saw the sick woman, and three children, who were asleep in the path, and he was very sorry for his plan. He sat down near Kuza. The man asked him nothing, and Ou was silent for a bit, and finally said, "I am sorry. The monster in the swamp will not allow you to come."

Kuza nodded, and beside him, another man got up and walked away without speaking. Kuza whispered, "We thank you for trying, Ou." Then he handed the Ox a bowl. In it was a small amount of parched millet. "I am sorry," he said, "This is all we have to offer you. There was not enough water to boil any food."

Ou did not wish to eat food that would do more good in the stomach of a hungry child, but he did not wish to give insult, either. He ate, and then sat, and then the people drifted back to their meager homes. Finally he stood and stretched.

"Will you leave us now?" asked Kuza.

"Yes. Keep everyone away from the stream for a bit. I am going to send the water down again."

Kuza's eyes grew very round. "But... The samurai..."

Ou smiled, a little grimly. "They will not kill a Kunitsu."

He followed the streambed up again. Dawn was breaking, and the birds had begun to sing. Ou could not feel lighthearted, for the task ahead was difficult, but he was settled in his mind, and determined.

This time, when he came close to the dam and the guards, he was not silent. This time he made a great crashing in the bracken and bellowed a little as he came. When he came out of the bush, the guards were standing, swords drawn, but the whites of their eyes showed, and they were shifting nervously.

Ou did not draw his own sword, not desiring violence. Instead he stood above them on the slope, letting them see his size and his horns. He stared at them until they knelt and bowed to him, and then he told them, "Go home. I order it. I will deal with your masters later." Then they were happy enough to go.

When he had seen the last of their heels, Ou looked the dam over. It was solidly built, but not perfect. He found a log to pry with, and he used his strength. Eventually the dam groaned, and finally it began to leak. The water did the rest.

Ou rested while the dam fell to pieces. Now he must go down to speak with the samurai brothers. This would be difficult, for he was still shy, but it must be done. He worked out the words inside his head, but did not speak them aloud.

This time the samurai were in their house. Ou opened the door and came in without asking. The servants fled, too frightened to cry out. Ou looked about. Saratoma Minoru and Saratoma Keitaro were together in the main room of the house. They were wearing their swords. Ou felt his horns scrape against the ceiling, and lowered his head, then stood, blowing. The samurai put hands to their sword hilts, but they did not attack. Ou looked at them a little, but they did not cower like dogs. They faced him. Now was the time for Ou to say the words he had practiced on the mountain.

"Saratoma Minoru. Saratoma Keitaro. You have moved the water on the mountain. You have disturbed the swamp in the next valley. The monster there is my brother, and he is very angry. What will you do to appease him?"

The samurais' eyes were as round as rice-bowls. They looked at each other, but did not speak at once. Finally the younger brother, Keitaro, spoke. "Ou-san, we did not wish to cause difficulties with your brother. Please, sit with us and have tea. We will speak together like gentlemen, and reach a civilized conclusion on the matter."

Ou was a little confused by all the words, and he did not have time to work them out. He did his best to continue looking stern. "Tea will not appease my brother."

"But no offense was meant. Surely we can come to some concurrence!"

"You have offended the mountain. You have offended the swamp. You must make amends."

The samurai still had hands on their sword-hilts. Ou remembered, quite suddenly, that these people often settled matters of honor with blood. He had not drawn his own katana in years, but he put a hand to his own sword-hilt, just in case, and went on looking stern. "It is no use to argue with me," he said. "You must make your apologies to the mountain."

They looked surprised at that, and took their hands off the sword-hilts. Ou relaxed a bit. He continued to glare at the samurai. "You must not trouble the stream further. You must help it in its work."

"Help the stream in its work?" asked Minoru faintly.

"Yes. The stream comes from a spring. You must go to the spring. You must dig it out. You must enlarge the stream bed. You must cherish the water and let it flow where it will. Then the spirit of the swamp will be happy." There. It was a lot of words, but he was finished now. He hoped that these people would believe him. He waited.

The samurai looked at each other. At last they bowed. "It will be as you say," said Keitaro.

Minoru looked distressed. "But..." he murmured. "Ou-san, is the swamp-monster not offended that the stream flowed through the *eta* village? Perhaps the stream should be moved?"

"No!" Ou replied, quite firmly. "The stream knows what it wants. Let it choose its own path."

The younger samurai looked defeated. He bowed again. "Yes, Ou-san."

Ou nodded, and restrained himself from bowing in return. He turned and walked out of the house.

It was a long way out of the town, and back into the wild mountains. Ou moved as quickly as he was able. He was very tired, but his heart was light. The breeze was fresh, the morning birds in full song.

Ou finally stopped to rest when the sun was in the middle of the sky. He ate his fill of grass. He lay down in the shade.

The samurai might not care if they killed everyone in an *eta* village, but they would care about offending the nature spirits. They would do as they were told, at least at first. The black sand in the lake had not come from nowhere. It had been washed down from above. It had come out of the earth, washed by the spring. If the samurai's laborers worked diligently, they would find more black sand. There would be work for the smith. The stream would flow through the *eta* village.The samurai would be rich. The swamp would be full. Ou sighed in contentment.

As he drifted off to sleep, a question came to him, concerning the relationship between metal and water. He thought on it, but could not imagine an answer. Ah, well. He would have to ask the Frog, Shino. After all, he was an Ox, and not very clever.

A hero does not always see the fruits of bravery.
This story originally appeared in the Canadian magazine, *On Spec* in 2001 (issue #45). It was a finalist for the Canadian Aurora Award in 2002.

The Red Bird

Douglas Smith

Asai first saw the Red Bird the night the soldiers burnt his village. Fleeing in terror through rain and flames and killing, his parents dead in the mud behind him, the boy heard his name called above the screams of the dying. Called from on high.

He looked up. Aflame against the black sky, a hawk of burning plumage hovered over the forest entrance. A voice cried in his mind. *Asai! To me, to me, Asai!*

Asai ran toward the trees. A mounted rider, gleaming katana raised, burst from a smoking house to block his path. A ruby light flashed from the hawk, striking the sword and swordsman. Exploding into flames, the soldier fell screaming to the ground. Oblivious, the man's horse bent a leg for the child to mount.

Ride, Asai! Fly with me! the hawk called.

Once in the saddle, the boy clung with bleeding fingers as the horse thundered through the streets past soldiers and the dead. At the forest edge, Asai dared a last look back. The village priest stood before the burning shrine. A rider bore down on him, spear lowered. Hands crossed on his chest, the priest closed his eyes. The look of peace on his face burnt into Asai's memory. The boy turned away, blinded by tears.

They rode on through black woods lit only by the hawk's bloody glow. Trees surrendered to scrub grass then to sand and crashing surf. Just as Asai felt he would fall from the saddle, the horse stopped before the Temple of the Hidden Light.

At the base of steps rising into the darkness of the sea-cliff waited the Warrior of the Red Bird. His gaze from beneath his visor was both warm and chill. His armor began to glow with a ruby light from above. A flutter of wings came, and the Red Bird settled with the grace of beasts onto his shoulder.

The Warrior spoke to the hawk. "Is this the one, Master?"

Yes, Ikada.

The Warrior lifted the child from the horse as easily as a bird carrying a leaf and bore him into the Temple. Servants tended his wounds then bathed and fed him. That night, alone on silken sheets and feathered bed, Asai dreamt of the Red Bird and the look on the face of the priest.

The next day, Ikada, Warrior of the Red Bird, Defender of the Temple of the Hidden Light, began to teach Asai the *bushido*, the Way of the Warrior, and of the Hundred Deaths.

Each day, as the sun first set fire to the cliffs above the white Temple walls, the man and boy would rise and enter the Chamber of the Silver Blade. There, sitting on cushions of carmine silk on a floor whose mosaic tiles told of generations of Warriors, Ikada taught Asai. In those first mornings, Asai had many questions.

"Who is the Red Bird?"

Ikada looked around before answering. "The scarlet hawk is the spirit of this place. It is He that we serve."

"What is this place?"

"The Temple of the Hidden Light." Ikada spoke the words as if they might frighten something away.

"What is the Hidden Light?"

Ikada looked away. "That which we defend."

"But what is it?" the boy persisted.

Ikada turned back. Asai first saw the sadness that he would come to realize lived in Ikada always. "I do not know," he said.

When the sun was high, they sparred on the Thousand Steps, where each stone riser but the two topmost bore a Warrior's name.

"Are there other warriors of the Red Bird?" Asai asked, avoiding a foot sweep as he had learned just that morning.

Ikada paused a step below Asai, leaning on his sword. His long braids danced as he shook his head. "The Red One's warriors have been many, but at any time only one wears the name."

"How many have there been?"

"You, Asai, will be the thousandth defender of the Temple." Ikada looked at Asai, a sad light in his eyes. "And the last."

"Why must there be a last?"

With a solemn expression, Ikada leaned very close to Asai. "We've run out of steps," he whispered.

Asai stared back dumbly until Ikada threw back his head, roaring with laughter. "A small joke on my small hawk," he said when he could control his merriment. The tears streamed from his eyes, but Asai could still see the sadness.

"But why?" the boy asked again.

Ikada shook his head. "One day, but not yet."

As the sun kissed the sea at dusk, they sparred on the sand, weaving their *kumite* among rusted weapons and bleached bones.

"Who were these men?" Asai asked as he moved back from an attack, stepping over a gleaming rib cage poking from the sand.

"Soldiers of war lords who thought to plunder the Temple." Ikada lifted a skull, a tarnished circlet still on its brow. "And some war lords themselves. Eh, Kiyomori?" He grinned. "You came to kill Ikada, didn't you Shogun? Well, many have come." He dropped the skull. "And many have died."

"Why do you serve the Temple?" Asai asked.

Ikada blinked. "Why, because I was chosen. There is but one chosen in each generation. The honor is great."

"How are the Warriors chosen? How were you chosen?"

Ikada smiled down at the boy, the wind off the sea whipping his braids behind him. "As you were. By the Red Bird."

"But why was *I* chosen?" Asai now had a home, and Ikada was like a father, yet Asai felt a fear he could not explain.

Ikada again shook his head. "Only the Red Bird knows."

Somehow, the answer disturbed Asai more than the question.

Asai looked forward to the evenings, when he put aside martial arts for other studies. The temple library was a huge domed room tiled in blue ceramics. Towering wooden racks jammed with parchment scrolls lined the walls. Asai would sit at a low table while Ikada read or taught from diagrams and maps.

Once Asai learned to read, he devoured every text he could find. He spent every spare hour in the library and had servants bring scrolls to his room to read before sleeping.

Ikada worried at this. "Asai, you have fought hard today and studied long. Take time to relax, to dream."

Asai smiled. "For me, to read is to relax, and these," he said, sweeping his arm past the scrolls, "these feed my dreams."

Not all days were so. On some, the temple bell thundered its call through the halls and down the steps. Then Ikada stopped whatever he was doing and called, "Asai! The Blade!"

Asai would run to the Chamber of the Silver Blade to take down the weapon from the wall. Made by a sword master to the first Shogun Yoritomo, its steel was folded a hundred times, polished to a silvery sheen. When Asai returned, Ikada would be dressed in his battle armor, a red sash around his waist.

Ikada would sheathe the blade on his back and stride to the crest of the Thousand Steps to survey the sand below. Most days brought but a solitary challenger or a small band.

On this day, Asai stood beside Ikada, staring down at rank after rank of soldiers arrayed on the beach. Asai had never seen so many people. Ikada grinned. "Shugon Antoku seeks to impress us." He descended the steps, humming a tune, Asai at his side.

"What is happening, Sensei?" the child asked. Shugons were local warlords, servants to the Shogun.

"Antoku seeks entrance, but the Red Bird finds him unworthy. This Shugon is famed for his cruelty. I will fight his champion, Harata, the tall one in front—a great swordsman."

"What of the army? Why does Antoku not just attack?"

Ikada just smiled and looked up to where the Red Bird circled the beach. No other answer came, and Asai fell silent. They reached the bottom step, and Ikada walked out to Harata.

The two warriors bowed and stepped back, drawing their blades. Harata lunged. Holding his stance, Ikada raised the Silver Blade, handle high and point angled low, as Harata's sword stabbed at his throat. Harata's blade slid off Ikada's, missing its mark. Ikada thrust, and the Silver Blade's point pierced Harata's chest armor. Before the man's body hit the sand, Ikada had turned to walk back to the steps, his sword sheathed again.

A gasp escaped the ranks of men. Mounted on a gray mare, Shugon Antoku raised his sword, screaming "Attack!" Twenty cavalry broke from the larger body. Asai cried a warning, but

Ikada just smiled and kept walking. As the riders neared Ikada, the beach erupted in fire, and Asai choked on smoke and heated air. When his dazzled eyes could see again, Asai gazed out on the charred bodies of twenty men and horses. Overhead, the Red Bird circled, its outline still glowing against the sky.

"Only one may challenge," Ikada said, as they climbed back.

"What if another wishes to fight you now?"

Ikada looked hurt. "Asai! Even Ikada needs his rest. One challenge a day is all the Red Bird allows."

They were not alone in the Temple. Ikada granted access to the library to visiting Jodo Shin priests. In return, the holy men gave the dharma or recited sutras for the dead. The Temple also housed servants who tended to chores and the two warriors' needs. As Asai grew, he became aware of a new need of his own.

The Temple servants included the Warrior's concubines. Although his father had told Asai of the ways of the flesh, knowing of it was far removed from feeling it. Ikada was not blind to the change. On the night Asai turned fourteen, Ikada sent his favorite concubine to the boy's bedchamber.

Neither spoke of it the next morning, but a smirk played on Ikada's face throughout the day. After that, Asai took a woman most nights, sometimes just to avoid being alone. Other nights he did not, just to be alone. The boy was tender and gentle, much loved by many of the women, but he never chose a favorite. Nor did he talk with them of much beyond his studies and Temple life. He knew this bothered Ikada, but the Warrior said nothing.

So through all the days of all the years, Ikada would teach and Asai would learn. The orphan learnt well. Asai turned eighteen as Master of the Hundred Deaths, save one.

One day as they sparred on the sand, Ikada stepped back, calling, "Yamate!" sharply. Asai lowered his sword, glad for a break. The sky swirled in gray humor, and a wind off the waves stung his eyes. Ikada stared past him up the Thousand Steps.

Above the cliffs, brilliant against the bleak sky, circled the Red Bird. Asai felt a strange dread as the hawk spiraled lower. A ruby beam burst from the bird to dance on the top steps for two breaths. Rising, the Red Bird vanished into the clouds.

Asai turned to speak, but Ikada's face choked off the words in Asai's throat. Ikada walked past him, never taking his eyes from the summit. Reaching the steps, he climbed with the gait of a man going to his own execution. Asai followed in silence.

Near the summit, Ikada stopped. Asai came to stand beside him, staring at the next to last step of the Thousand. The name *Ikada* was burnt now in Kana symbols into the stone.

"Sensei," Asai began, but Ikada raised his hand. Turning his back on the step, Ikada gazed at the sand below. Asai looked down too. A sole rider sped along the surf's edge, black armor, weapons and saddlery, a dragon's tail of sand in his wake. Ikada watched for a breath then began his descent. Asai followed, unable to speak of the fear in his breast.

At the bottom, Ikada drew the Silver Blade from the sheath on his back. He raised it to his lips then laid it on the bottom step. "Asai, give me your sword," he said quietly.

Asai glanced at the Silver Blade but said nothing. He handed Ikada his katana, a true but unremarkable weapon.

Ikada sheathed it. The black samurai now stood waiting. Ikada's voice was soft. "Asai, today the Red Bird will know how well Ikada has taught you." Grasping Asai's shoulders in both hands, he smiled. "You have been a fine student and a better friend. I love you as I would my own son. Good-bye, Asai."

Without another word, Ikada strode across the sand to his

challenger. Both bowed and in an eye blink drew their blades and stepped back into fighting stance, swords vertical in a two-handed grip. The samurai moved in at once, feinting a head cut but shifting to slash across the ribs. Parrying, Ikada slid his blade along the other's, nicking the samurai's neck. The man retreated, but Ikada closed again, pressing his attack.

Many times, Ikada came within a hair's breadth of ending the battle but could not deliver a death cut. Bleeding from a dozen places, the black samurai now fought with his blade in his left hand, right arm hanging limp at his side.

Then Ikada, blocked on a vicious downward cut, dropped into a crouch to execute a perfect reverse spin. His blade slashed under the man's guard, slicing a thigh. Grunting, the samurai fell to a knee. Ikada closed, sword raised for the final blow.

And slipped—on something in the sand. Something round and white. His blade swung wide from its *kamai* position. Still kneeling, the black samurai thrust upwards. As the point entered Ikada's throat, Asai's own throat gave his scream life.

Asai ran onto the sand, Silver Blade over his head. The samurai stood and grinned, no doubt at the sight of a man-child warrior. The two engaged, and the grin vanished. Asai attacked with such fury that the samurai could only parry and retreat. The black warrior stumbled. Asai beat away a feeble slash, and the man's sword flew from him.

"I beg mercy!" the samurai cried, on his knees before Asai.

"Beg to the demons!" Asai spat. His sword sang across the neck of his foe. The helmeted head spun lazily in the air, drops of blood shining in the evening sun, to land in the sand.

Asai stared at the Silver Blade in his hand, unable to remember picking it up. He stumbled to Ikada, feeling for a pulse that he knew he would not find. Tears streaking his face, he picked up the object that had tripped the Warrior. A skull, a circlet of metal still attached, grinned back at him.

From above came the beat of wings. The Red Bird settled

on Ikada's chest. Lowering its head into the liquid pooling at the wound, it then touched its dripping beak to its feathers, repeating this until it glistened with blood. The hawk began to glow in the dim light. The glow died, and the bird's plumage grew a deeper shade of red. The bird leapt into the air again.

"Is this how you honor one that served you?" Asai shouted at the hawk circling above, the pain inside him overcoming his fear.

Such is the final test for each of my Warriors. Asai felt the misery in those words, a black pool of infinite depth. He looked into that pool and drew back in fear from its edge. Drew back from something he was not yet ready to face.

Asai watched the Red Bird disappear into the darkening sky. He then carried Ikada up the Thousand Steps. In the Vault of Heroes, he prepared the body. He opened the next-to-last sepulcher and laid Ikada on the bier. After reading from the bushido, he closed the sepulcher, snuffing out all candles but one. He left the vault, the Silver Blade on his back.

That night, Asai lay awake thinking of things left unsaid.

The Red Bird came the next day as Asai did kata before the waves. The sky was gray and the wind chill. The hawk landed on a skeletal hand grasping at the sky from the sand.

Ikada is dead. You are the Warrior now.

Asai felt anger again. "You could have saved him, bird."

I could not.

"Why?"

It is not the way.

Fury erupted in Asai. "What is the way? Why must we die to serve you?" He flung the Silver Blade to stick in the still-red sand where Ikada had fallen. "Why am I here, you bloody crow?"

The Red Bird was silent, and fear tempered Asai's anger. Then the hawk spoke. *You must seek the Hidden Light. You are the last. The last hope for your people.*

"Why am I the last?"

The sands run out.

"Where is the Hidden Light?"

The bird looked at him. *It is here.*

"But what is it?"

That which you must seek.

Asai's anger built again. "And what if I fail, crow?"

A thousand years of misery for your kind.

His fear returned. "Why?"

War dogs gather. The light dims. You must pass the test.

A thought flew to him. "Who must? I or my people?"

Something in the hawk's gaze recalled the look Ikada would wear when Asai had mastered the next Death.

Wisdom begins. Opening its wings, the bird leapt into the face of the sea breeze. Asai watched it vanish in the clouds.

She came to him on the anniversary of Ikada's death. As the temple bell rang, Asai descended the steps to face a small figure clad in what seemed the castoff armor of a dozen warriors. A slim hand removed an ill-fitting helmet, and he first looked on her face. "My name is Sawako," she said.

"I do not wish to kill you," Asai replied, staring at her.

"Then we begin well for I do not wish to be killed." Taking off the rest of her armor and untying a sash at her waist, she pulled her dress off over her head to stand naked before him.

Asai stood transfixed for several breaths. Then sheathing the Silver Blade, he walked to her and pulled her to him in a long kiss. After what seemed a lifetime, he broke off the kiss, scooped her into his arms and carried her up the steps into the Temple. Overhead, the Red Bird cried unheeded.

That night after their lovemaking, Sawako told her story. "My village lies two days to the east. When news of Ikada-san's death reached us, Antoku, the local Shugon, promised to bring the Shogun the Temple's secret. Two moons ago, he chose a swordsman of my village to challenge the Warrior. To challenge you."

She looked away. "The man did not return. In his wrath, Antoku sentenced each first son in the village to die. I begged that we be given another chance to do Antoku honor, that I would bring him the secret. He laughed and was going to give me to his men. Then a Jodo Shin priest told him of my birth."

"What of your birth?"

"The priest said that on the night I was born, an omen appeared in the sky above our village."

Asai felt a coldness grip his belly. "What was this omen?"

Sawako turned back to him, snuggling her head into his chest. "A great red hawk, whose plumage glowed as if on fire."

The next morning, Asai showed Sawako the Temple. As they walked, she told more of her bargain with Antoku. "I did not promise to defeat you, only to find the secret. Antoku has given me one year. If I fail, he will execute my entire village." She laid a hand on the silken arm of his robe. "Show me the Light. You need not surrender the Temple but you will save my people."

Asai looked into her eyes. "Sawako, I cannot. I defend what I do not know. No Warrior has ever discovered the Hidden Light, and I am the last." He told her of the prophecy, and Sawako seemed to fall into deep thought. They walked in silence.

Later they sparred on the beach with wooden *bokken*. The

village samurai had taught her well. She was quick with fine form, but he had the reach, strength, and years of daily study.

Resting on the beach after, she spoke again of the Light. "You must find it or misery will befall our land. I must learn of it or my people die." She turned to him. "Let me help you."

Asai laughed, leaning on an elbow beside her. "So a woman-child will succeed where a thousand Warriors have failed?"

Sawako shrugged slim shoulders. "I can hardly do worse."

Asai scowled. "How could you help me?"

"The priests taught me to read and write." She pulled him close, and he felt her warm breath, smelt its sweetness. "And I can help you as I did last night. You are far too serious."

Asai felt his face grow hot. "What if we fail? What if a year comes, and the Light remains hidden? What then?"

She stood with her bokken. "Then to me, you will again become the Warrior." She turned away. "And I must kill you."

Sawako stayed, and their lust grew to love. Each morning, they sat close together in the library, reading and discussing the great philosophers. Their hunger for the secret that remained hidden lived with them each minute.

Sometimes, Asai felt he had found a great truth and sought out the Red Bird. The hawk always knew of his need and came. Explaining what he had learned, Asai would wait for a reply.

When it came, it was always the same. *You grow wise.*

"Is this the Light?"

No.

One such morning, when Sawako had been with him for about two months, Asai stood on the cliff edge, the hawk beside him. After receiving this answer again, Asai exploded in fury. "Why do you play this game? Where is the light?"

You grow close. Closer than any other.

Asai hesitated. "You never speak of Sawako, never asked me of her. Did I do wrong? Have I violated my duty?"

You alone can judge that.

"What of her birth omen? Was that you, Red Bird?"

Spreading its wings, the hawk leapt off the cliff. Asai called after it, but the only answer was the cold wind. That night, Sawako told Asai she carried his child. The next day, he took her as his wife.

She named the boy Shirotori. It meant "White Bird." When Asai asked her of it, she said "This world has seen enough of red. White is the color of peace."

And the shrouds of the dead, Asai thought but said nothing.

Asai had never known the joy he felt with his wife and child. Yet, as the year wore on and the light stayed hidden, he felt the sands of happiness slipping through his hands. On the first day of the twelfth month since Sawako had come, Asai found her dressed again in her armor, doing kata by the sea.

"Why do you do this?" he asked, his voice breaking.

"Because I must," she said. Her face was wet—with tears or sea spray, he knew not which. She turned back to her kata, and he turned his back on her.

On the eve of the anniversary of Sawako's arrival, Asai stood on the topmost Temple step, dripping with sweat, Silver Blade in his hand. The hawk settled onto a dragon statue beside him, glowing blood red in the night. *You train hard.*

"To kill the woman I love, the mother of my son." No reply came. Asai turned to the hawk. "Why must she die, crow? What does it serve?" No answer. "Over two hundred in her village will die with her. Why? What good is in this?" His rage built. "Is it the blood you need, death bird?" Still no answer came, and Asai could hold his fury no longer. "Then I give you blood!"

He swung the sword, and the hawk sprang into the air. The bird was too fast, but the Silver Blade clipped a tail feather. As the hawk vanished into the dark sky, the feather floated to land on the top step, where it seemed to melt. Touching the sticky puddle, Asai drew his finger back. It dripped blood.

He drew a line on his forehead with the blood. "Is it not fitting that I wear this mark?" he asked the night. He slumped to the steps. "If I win, she dies and two hundred more. And with her dies my love, my reason for life. No, our son would live but with no mother. What do I know of raising a child?" He stood to gaze at where the moon silvered the surf below. "But if I die, no other dies. Only Asai. What loss is that?"

The wind whispered his name. He smiled sadly. "Asai, just Asai. No loss in that." Turning from the sea, he entered the temple. That night he made love to Sawako for the last time.

They rose early and in silence. He watched her dress then walk to where he sat on the window ledge. She kissed him long and deeply. Then picking up a scroll from her table, she left not looking back. He watched her go, her tears cool on his face.

Asai stayed at the window until he saw her descend the Steps. Then he dressed and broke fast lightly. He visited each servant, saying his good-byes without saying so. In the nursery, he held his son for a long time, singing in a low soft voice a song that Sawako sang to Shirotori each night. He left special instructions with the servant who cared for the child.

In the Chamber of the Silver Blade, Asai knelt at the low table where Ikada had taught him the Way. On it stood a vial of green liquid. His studies had brought knowledge of herbs and potions. Sawako was a fine swordswoman, but Asai knew she was no match for a Warrior. His reactions were too instinctive to trust the outcome to his intent alone. The poison would work slowly, at first to impede his movements, finally to stop his heart if her blade had not done so. He raised the vial—and drank.

He stared at the top step, still blank above Ikada's name, and called to the hawk circling overhead. "Why is my name not written here, crow? You knew Ikada would die! Do you not know that I die today?" The hawk continued to circle. "So be it," Asai cried and slashed at the stone with the Silver Blade. Again and again he swung, until his name stood carved above Ikada's. With a last glance skyward, he descended the steps.

She knelt on the sand facing the sea and did not answer when he called her name. He stumbled over shifting sand, the poison burning in his muscles. He was about to call her name again when he saw the blood and the blade point protruding from her back.

His throat choked a cry that tore his heart as he ran to her. He wrenched the sword from where she had thrust it in her breast. Her face was cold as he took it in his hands. "Why?" he cried to the wind, knowing the answer even before he saw the scroll beside her, before he read the words she had written.

> *Dearest love, I will say do not grieve yet know you will. Know that I loved you and was sure of your love. I saw no other way. The Light stays hidden. I failed my people and cannot live while they die. I could never harm you but feared you would work your death to save me. This is my answer to the question we lived with this joyous year. Raise our son with the love you gave me. Forever, your Sawako.*

His sobs became spasms as he lay her on the sand. "We die for nothing, my love," he cried. No, he thought, I can still save her people. Lifting her sword, he turned its point to his breast. "If I die by your sword, Sawako, you have won the Temple." He threw himself on her blade, falling beside her. As he lay dying, her face recalled to him the doomed priest's look of peace the night the Red Bird first came to him.

The Red Bird settled on the fallen Warrior's chest and dipped its beak into the wound around the blade. Painting itself in the man's blood, it hopped then to the woman's body that lay beside him, adding her blood to its red sheen.

A glow touched its feathers then burst into brilliance as the hawk leapt into the air aflame. Fire burned away the scarlet coat, and from the center of a winged sun emerged a great eagle, with feathers of burnished gold. The eagle spread its wings. From each wing, a feather fell to land on the two lovers. The feathers became white flames, and fire consumed the bodies. From the smoke flew two white doves who circled first each other and then the eagle as all three disappeared into the sky.

Shugon Antoku and his army arrived at Sawako's village to find it deserted. Traveling monks told of two white doves who led a band of people eastward. When Antoku reached the Temple of the Hidden Light, Sawako's people were encamped on the sand. A shimmering wall of white light separated them and the Temple from Antoku and his men. Antoku ordered the villagers slain.

As the first soldiers touched the white wall, their bodies burst into flames and blew away, ashes on the wind. Those behind fled in terror, screaming of demons. Antoku cursed them as cowards but was left alone on the sand, his promise to the Shogun unfulfilled. He regarded the white wall for a long time, then drew and fell on his sword.

When he turned eighteen, Shirotori, son of Asai, son of Sawako, began to preach the Way of the Hidden Light. Villages fell under his protection and his teaching. His followers grew and the Way spread. Armies deserted any Shugon who raised arms against him. Soon his reach extended to the Shogun's palace.

On the anniversary of his parents' deaths, Shirotori stood on the steps of that palace as the Shogun broke his sword and bent his knee to the boy.

Shirotori's rule was just and kind. The people said that truth and love rode with him always, in the form of two white doves on each shoulder. He was known by many names. The Prophet. The Truth. The Loved.

But most called him *Kashoku*, which meant...Bright Light.

The *Komusō*, or 'monks of emptiness', were a group of the Fuke school of Zen Buddhism. They wore a woven reed head covering, representing absence of ego, and played a *shakuhachi* bamboo flute for meditation, alms, and healing. In the Edo period, they were respected and given extraordinary permissions to travel. However, their outfit was used by spies to mask identity, and so wearers could be challenged to prove their authenticity.

Jatsi and the Hollow Monk

Harry Elliott

The leaves of the shimmer tree were alive with firelight. As they rustled in the night-time breeze they carried the flickering light across their silver faces, like a shoal of shallow-water fish, or the flash of heated steel. In the lee of this tree sat a monk, his back snug in the curve of the trunk, its branches spread above his hooded head. At his feet a small fire dined upon dry twigs and fallen leaves. As the gathered leaves of the shimmer tree curled and blackened in the flames they sent up glinting motes on the rising smoke, like tiny stars travelling skyward.

In the ember-orange firelight the monk appeared to be in repose, but his hood hid the truth of the matter. He was awake, staring out through the slits of the reed-woven hood that enclosed his head. It was a strange item of apparel, like an upturned basket, its lip resting on his shoulders. It ought to have been ungainly, but he wore it with the sort of familiarity that comes only with practice.

His body was swathed in a kimono of thick black silk, and a white stole was draped across his shoulders. There were two loops stitched into the kimono's waist, and a pair of bamboo flutes were fastened there. His right hand lay upturned in his lap, fingers idly toying at the ends of the flutes. A hollowed gourd flask was held in the other hand, and a long straw rose from its rim and disappeared into the shadows beneath the reed-hood.

The night had brought with it a cosy tranquillity, a blanket drawn across a land coaxed to slumber. Beyond this knoll where the lonely shimmer tree was hunched, the valleys and wooded hills were washed with midnight blue, their details lost to distance.

Yet the monk was awake. He was not alone in the dark. From beyond the reach of the firelight, something drew near. The monk did not start. A shape resolved out of the night and stepped into the edge of the fire's glow. It had the look of a new-born, but over-proportioned. Its head was too big for its body, and its skin was raw and pudgy with too much flesh. It was dressed in a kimono of elaborate and beautiful detail, spiralling traceries of silver worked into the blood-red fabric.

And it had no face. Where there ought to have been eyes, a nose and a mouth there was only a sheet of skin, drawn tight over some lumpy and misshapen bone-structure. It stood there on the edge of the firelight's reach, swaying slightly and regarding the monk with its lack of eyes.

"Shall I play a tune?" said the monk, his hood betraying a slight inclination of the head.

The faceless creature teetered on its tip-toes as though it might topple over. The monk gave a small shrug and drew his right hand up over one of the flutes. Then the faceless creature was gone, as if the night had opened some secret maw and swallowed it whole. In its place there was now a raccoon dog, a tanuki. The small animal padded around the fire and sat beside the monk. It stretched its paws out and arched its back, relishing the gentle warmth of the fire.

"Must you?" asked the monk.

'As long as you persist in being so tediously stoic, yes, I must,' said a woman's voice, though it was spoken with no mouth and heard only by the monk. 'It's a matter of pride and I won't stop until the day I see you jump in fright.'

"Then we will both be dissatisfied for the rest of our lives," said the monk.

The tanuki sniffed derisively, a peculiarly human gesture for an animal, and then looked out into the night, as though some small movement had caught its attention.

"You were right, weren't you?" asked the monk quietly.

'I was. Something has awoken in the north-east,' said the woman's voice, 'ah, yes, under the chin. The neck! The neck!'

The monk had put down the gourd and had started to stroke the tanuki's head. The animal nuzzled its head into his palm.

"Is it something we can handle?"

'Who knows? Either way, I don't think it's something we can ignore,' said the woman's voice, the tanuki's voice, the voice that spoke with no mouth.

"A problem for the morning, I think," said the monk, and laid his hooded head back against the bark.

'On that,' said the tanuki, curling up in the monk's lap, 'we agree.'

A magnificent dawn woke the world. The sun climbed up from behind the mountainous horizon and scoured the night from the hillsides and the valleys. Where shimmer tree forests grew in the basins between hills, their swaying silver canopies flashed and glinted in the daylight, like pools of metal come alive.

The path north-east was taking them ever higher. The monk and the tanuki had found the remnants of an old foot-beaten trail and were following it deeper into the rising hills. There was wildlife in abundance here, green pheasants with their vibrant plumage and herds of spotted deer. The antlered heads of stags rose up to regard the monk and his companion as they passed by.

"It is peaceful," said the monk.

'Did you expect otherwise?' said the tanuki's voice in his head.

"I expected some sign," replied the monk, "the edge of a ripple that we might trace to the source."

'A terrible omen perhaps? Four crows staring you in the eye?' laughed her voice.

"Don't mock me with superstition," he said.

'You realise the significance of where we are going, don't you?' she asked.

"I do."

'The God of Metals has taken up residence in the north-east, the unlucky direction, where he is powerfully imbued.'

"You are very dramatic."

'It is not a thing to laugh about,' scolded the tanuki. 'The last time this happened the north-east was proclaimed *kimon*. When settlers returned there after a hundred years they found the villages and towns abandoned and the streets full of restless spirits.'

"*Kimon*. Demon's gate."

'Yes, the unlucky direction through which evil spirits pass.'

"And you are sure of this? Sure that the north-east is *kimon* again?" he asked.

'I will be sure when we are there.'

"So there is a chance that we might turn up and everything will be alright?"

'That would be something of an anti-climax.'

"Don't play games. What exactly is it that you know?"

The tanuki stopped so abruptly that the monk almost trod on it. His hood tilted as he looked down at the animal.

'I have felt a bad energy. It is like a wound in the world's *ki*, a tainted vitality. The violence of it disturbs my own energy. If you were as sensitive to it as I am, empty monk, you would feel it too. As much as I am repelled by it, I am also drawn to it. An itch that yearns to be scratched.'

"Then we should not delay," said the monk and set his feet back on the path.

At the foot of the mountains, vast pillars of stone dotted the landscape for as far as the eye could see. They were so tall that, close up, one had to crane their neck all the way back in order to see the tops. Their breadth was such that the largest pillars took three or four minutes to walk all the way around.

The monk was sitting by the path with his back against one such enormous pillar when the tanuki came bounding down a hill to meet him.

'There is a town on the other side of this hill,' she said, 'it would be good to stop there and ask around. Warm food wouldn't go amiss either.'

"These pillars," said the monk, tapping a knuckle against the craggy stone, "they are too big for men to have built."

'What? Why is this relevant?'

The monk shrugged. "I have heard a myth. I am sure you know it."

'We hardly have time for this trivia, don't you think?'

"Indulge me," said the monk.

'I really don't think—'

"I am sure you know the one. How does it go? The last time the north-east was called *kimon*, it is said an army of *oni*, great ogres with terrible strength, marched down from the mountains, crushing the villages and eating up the farmers as they went, and that when they reached the foothills they put up these pillars to mark the borders of their kingdom."

'They also say,' the tanuki replied scornfully, 'that had the God of Metals not been appeased and encouraged to leave the north-east, the *oni* would have stolen the mountains out of this material realm, leaving a great hole that the rest of the world would have been swallowed into. It is hard to separate fact from fiction these days, I agree.'

The monk stood up. He made a rattling noise as he did, the boxes and amulets tied about his person clacking together when he moved. "Good. So there is no chance of us running into any *oni* up there?"

'We don't have time for this!' snapped the tanuki, and began bounding back up the hill.

The town was made distinctive, even at a distance, by the squat rooftops of blue and green ceramic tiles. The eaves extended over the wooden walls of the houses so much that the lip of one roof almost touched the lip of another.

A festival was taking place. Throngs of people crowded the streets and almost all of them were wearing masks that bore the likeness of a monkey. Those without masks held up little monkey-shaped statues, or bore amulets with inscriptions. As the monk and his companion got closer, they saw that people were throwing handfuls of soybeans from their windows and shouting chants or hanging sprigs of holly on their doors.

The pair came up the path in between the terraced slopes where rice, barley and sweet potatoes were grown. When they stepped onto the streets of the town proper, their presence did not go unnoticed. The first people to notice them went quiet and still, but as more and more of the townsfolk became aware a ripple of excitement spread. Soon the festivities and chants began again, but now the people were parading around the monk, ushering him down the street.

A child held up her monkey talisman to him, tottering backwards on her tip-toes to keep ahead of him in the tide of bodies. He took it with a nod of his head and the child squealed with glee before disappearing back into the crowd.

'If I get trodden on, so help me, I'll...' said the woman's voice, heard to no-one but the monk.

"Be nice," he said quietly.

'Hah,' snorted the voice, and the tanuki leapt up on to the monk's back and scrambled its way to his shoulder, where it clung tight.

They were brought to the town square, where a large monkey statue had been raised and garlanded with wreaths of holly and strings of amulets and talismans. The crowds parted and they were presented to a group of men. These men were wearing red outer garments over their grey kimonos, wide-shouldered robes that were loose at the backs like capes. The monk took that to mean these were the town's ruling council.

One of the council members seized upon the moment with surprising vigour, climbing up onto the dais of the statue and raising his hands.

"A hollow monk has come to aid us in this time of peril! He who is without ego will take on the troubles of the beleaguered as if they were his own! We are saved!"

A great cheer went up amongst the crowds. Soybeans were tossed into the air. They made a sound like hail as they clattered back down.

"I know that you have eschewed all manner of identity in order to better serve the people, but by what name can we call our saviour?" asked the council member of the monk.

"Well, the tanuki is called Jatsi, if you like," said the monk.

There was a swell of laughter.

"Very well then, you are the hollow monk and his travelling companion, Jatsi the raccoon dog. We rejoice at your arrival!"

Another round of applause went up. The council member clambered down from the dais and came over to them. "Come, we will speak."

The monk was led up the wooden steps of a broad-faced building and under the eaves of its curved roof. Behind them, the festivities resumed with renewed vigour.

They were given a warm meal, both the monk and Jatsi. Bowls of rice and a soup made with fermented soybeans were presented, along with side dishes of fish and pickled vegetables. The monk did not reveal his face to eat; instead he passed the food up underneath the rim of the hood. This caused no offence amongst the council, who sat eagerly with him, cross-legged on mats around a low table.

The monk ate quietly for a while. Jatsi ate less quietly. When he was done, the monk laid down his chopsticks and smacked his lips.

"I am here because of the trouble in the north-east."

There was a collective sigh of relief from the council, who had been politely quiet as the monk ate but clearly full of anticipation.

"Then you will go further into the mountains?" asked the council member who had welcomed them in the square. He had introduced himself as Kudo Sho.

"I will."

"You are all too eager," said a second member of the council, a generously fleshed man whose jowls juddered as he spoke. "Are we so quick to forget the danger in trusting this stranger? How do we know this nameless apparition is truly a hollow monk and not some imposter, some enemy sent to spy on us?"

There was a murmur of concern amongst the council. Kudo Sho held up his hands for quiet.

"The concern is a fair one," he said and turned his eyes on the monk. "I mean no offence by this, but perhaps you could play your flute? To prove to us that you are who you say."

"Are you sure that is what you want?" asked the monk, his fingers straying to the instruments. The tanuki sat up sharply, its ears pressed flat against its head.

"It would put to rest our fears," said Kudo.

"As you wish," the monk said and drew the shorter of the flutes from its loop.

'Monk, what are you doing?' asked Jatsi, her voice fraught with panic.

The monk put the flute beneath the rim of his hood, his fingers poised over the holes. The sound rolled out into the air, sharp and clear. It distorted the afternoon light that came in through the shutters, deepened the shadows that clung to the corner's of the room. The men of the council began to sway, their eyes losing focus and their shoulders slumping.

'That's enough, monk!' yelled Jatsi, bouncing off of the table and on to his hood. He stopped playing and the council jerked as one, as if shocked from the edge of slumber.

"Such beautiful sounds," said the man with the jowls, his voice distant. Jatsi leapt down from the monk's head, kicked her hind-legs against his knee and resumed her feast.

"Yes," said Kudo, shaking his head to clear his thoughts. "Yes, that is all in order. We should proceed."

"There is a town, only a little way from our own, along the north-east road," said another member of the council, Goda Hoshi. "We have not heard news from them in several days. The men we sent to investigate have not returned. A thing like this has not happened in many years. We fear the worst."

"Yes," said Kudo, "we would be grateful if you could stop by there and ensure they are well. We had a good trade with them in fish and herbs."

"It would not be out of your way," promised Goda.

"Of course," said the monk. "I am curious though, what is the nature of the festival taking place here?"

The council members regarded one another quizzically, as though he had asked an obvious question.

"Why, it is to ward off the *oni*, of course," said Kudo Sho.

The monk looked down at Jatsi. The tanuki slowly pulled its snout from a bowl of fish and looked sidelong at the monk. It was a funny thing, to see an animal looking guilty.

Come evening, they had reached the second settlement. They crossed over an arched bridge, its red paint scuffed and flaking. The river beneath it was dark, darker than water should have been, even under an evening sky. There had been a beauty here once, the monk could tell, looking at the perfectly arrayed stone gardens, the ponds and the little water ways. That beauty was gone now, smothered by a heaviness in the air that seemed to occlude even the last of the day's light.

The reason for the town's silence was immediately apparent: there was no-one here anymore. The buildings were all shut and the streets were empty. Other than the gentle susurrating of the rivers that criss-crossed the neat pathways, there was very little noise.

"And the *oni* came down from the mountains and ate up all the villagers," said the monk.

'Don't be ridiculous,' said Jatsi, swatting his hood with a paw before leaping down to the ground and sniffing about. 'If one of those things had come through here, there wouldn't be a village left at all.'

"Then what happened here? Where did these people go?"

The tanuki put its nose in the air and sniffed, then shivered. 'It's getting late. We should keep moving.'

"Nonsense," said the monk, setting himself down on the

raised wooden porch of a nearby house. "We can afford to rest for the night and set off again in the morning."

Jatsi looked at him and then deftly leapt up the porch's framework and awning until it had disappeared over the eaves of the roof. The monk shrugged and set himself down against a beam. He pulled out his flask and set up a straw beneath his hood.

He woke abruptly. He did not remember falling asleep. Night had come properly and it was cold now, numbingly so. There was a weak light filtering through the slits in his reed-hood, the sort of light a lantern produces when shone through mist.

There was a person standing on the porch steps, he realised. Except the person wasn't standing, because they had neither legs nor feet to stand on. Blank eyes were staring at him from under dishevelled strands of long black hair. Limp hands, pale and skeletal, twitched in his direction, held outstretched from tucked in elbows.

"Really, Jatsi?" mumbled the monk, drowsy from sleep. "I mean, it's a good effort, I've never seen this one before, but it's getting old."

There was a clatter from the roof and the tanuki leapt down on to the porch.

'That's not me. Run!'

The monk scrambled to his feet and dashed after the tanuki, which was already slipping between the porch banisters. He vaulted over the parapet, boxes and amulets rattling, and landed on his feet in the street.

A dozen of the spectral apparitions turned to regard him with blank eyes. The town was awash with their unnatural light. Each of the spectres was accompanied by a pair of flames, small like that of a candle's, which circled about their heads. From these floating fires the light was emanating, and it filled the streets with a ghostly radiance.

The spectres had begun gliding towards him, muted mouths hanging slack and toothless. He turned to flee, but found himself surrounded.

'Now would be a good time for some music,' urged Jatsi, pressed against the monk's ankles.

"On that," said the monk, drawing the longer of the two flutes from its loop, "we agree."

He tucked the lip of the flute beneath his hood, fingers poised over the holes, and began to blow. The notes slipped out into the night air. They were almost visible, like ripples in water or an artist's rendition of wind in a painting. The icy chill began to give way to pleasant warmth and the misty light adopted a clearer quality.

The spectres paused in their advance. Some semblance of human expression started to return to their gormless faces. They were expressions of grief, pain and anger. Irises blossomed in their blank eyes.

'These were the people who lived here,' said Jatsi, braving a few steps towards the spectres. There was the sound of a horrible realisation in her voice. 'These were the people who died here. They have been unjustly torn from life. They clamour to be avenged. They cannot be freed from this place until they are.'

"What did this to them?" asked the monk.

'I don't know, what could have killed them all and left no mark on the town?' said Jatsi, more to herself than to the monk. Then the tanuki paused. 'Wait, why have you stopped playing?'

The flute was silent and the chill was creeping back into the air. The eyes of the spectres were misting over, as if plagued by sudden cataracts.

"I can't play all night, just run!" said the monk and swept through the crowd of stunned spectres. Where he brushed by them, it felt as though he had been drenched to the skin in freezing water. Jatsi came after him.

The street took them into a yard between houses. In the centre of the yard there was a solitary tree, its branches bare. The monk stumbled to a halt and Jatsi crashed into the back of his legs.

'What are you thinking—' she began, but faltered.

Strewn in heaps about the tree were dozens of corpses.

"What happened here," gasped the monk.

'Something isn't right,' said Jatsi, hesitantly approaching the nearest body. 'There are no wounds on them, no blood.'

There was a crack, like breaking bone. They both looked to the source. The tree was moving. Its branches were snapping and twisting, like a contortionist's limbs, and then falling slack against the trunk. From there they began to slither down to the ground, serpentine and with a life of their own. They meandered over the bodies in the direction of Jatsi and the monk.

'The branches have teeth, little mouths filled with teeth!' cried Jatsi, leaping away from the approaching feelers that were dragging themselves further from the tree. The tanuki landed on one of the corpses and became entangled in its kimono. As she struggled to free herself, she dragged the collar from the body's neck and revealed a small puncture mark in the skin.

Then she was being lifted up and away from the ground, hoisted into the air by one of the coiling branches. She twisted in its grip and caught the branch in her teeth. The feeler recoiled and released her.

Jatsi landed on all fours and fled from the tree. 'I don't suppose you've got a tune to play for this occasion?'

The monk brought up his flute and began to blow, but the snakelike branches showed no signs of stopping.

'Here,' said Jatsi, darting back to the monk. She had plucked a small knife off one of the corpses, a little ceremonial thing, and was holding it in her mouth. She delivered it into his hand and then shot off. She seemed to be enjoying herself, like a dog at play. 'I'll distract them! Do your best!'

"Do my best with what?" stammered the monk, looking

down at the little blade. Sure enough though, the branches were curving away from him, heading in Jatsi's direction, attracted to her swift movements.

He shrugged and stumbled across to the tree, careful not to disturb the dead. He lifted the knife and stabbed the point into the bark. It stuck fast. He yanked on the handle until it came free. From the small hole that it had made, a dark liquid started trickling out.

"Blood!" he stammered. "The tree is bleeding!"

'Good!' yelped Jatsi, dancing in and out of the flailing branches, which had suddenly become a great deal more agitated. 'Keep doing what you're doing!'

The monk turned back to the tree and stabbed the knife in once more. Ignoring the fact that he was attempting to stab a tree to death, he repeated the action, thudding the blade into the bark and wrenching it free. On what must have been his tenth attack, the blade snapped, so he took the savaged bark in his hands instead and hauled on it with all his strength. A chunk of bark broke free and his momentum toppled him over backwards.

A river of dark liquid began to flow from the hole in the trunk. He scrambled away, disgusted. The tree began to wilt and shrivel, its lively branches falling dead. It groaned, creaking and cracking. At last it went still, its trunk hunched almost ninety degrees. The monk released a pent up breath and slumped back.

'Look!' Jatsi's cry brought the monk out from his relief. He twisted around. Filing into the yard from the adjoining streets came the spectres, bringing with them their haunting twilight. He groaned and reached for his flute, but his exertions had left him short of breath.

The spectres clustered about the tree and then came to a halt. As one they looked from the sagging tree, to the bodies they had once inhabited and finally, to the monk.

"I understand," he said. "Go to your rest."

The spectres faded away, their ghostly light dissipating like morning fog.

He clambered to his feet and put a considerable distance between the tree and himself, only stopping once the bodies were out of sight. Jatsi trotted up behind him.

'Are you alright?'

"Can you still feel it?" asked the monk, "the bad energy you spoke of? The wounded *ki*?"

The tanuki put its head on one side, in the manner of a creature carefully listening. Then it opened its mouth, like a human might do in joyful surprise.

'It's gone,' she said, 'the violence is gone.'

"So, no *oni*? No vengeful God of Metals residing in the north-east?"

'This sort of thing doesn't happen too frequently, fortunately,' said Jatsi, 'it's easy to over-react.'

"Oh," said the monk, "that's good to know."

The next day they brought up men from the other town to help lay the dead to rest. The bodies were buried with ceremony, and the monk oversaw the rituals to ensure the spirits of the dead would pass out of this world.

There was a strange duality of emotion in the air. Sorrow, for the loss of life, but also tremendous relief, that an evil spirit had been uprooted from the world.

The hollow monk stayed after the men had returned to their village, accepting their thanks and their offer of hospitality whenever he should have need of it. He lingered by the freshly planted graves, thoughtful.

Then he turned, ready to leave.

A great bloodshot eye was staring him in the face. It was a bulging thing, as large as a man's head, set into the creases of a bloated skull. He jumped back, crying out in terror and tripping over his own feet. The disproportionate body of the horror loomed over him, its single eye swivelling down to pin him with its awful gaze.

The monk reached for his flutes.

Then the creature was gone. Where it had stood there was only a small raccoon dog, a tanuki, rolling back and forth in the grass. In the monk's head, Jatsi's wild laughter rolled on and on. Then the laughter came to him as well and it would not stop.

The hollow monk and the tanuki lay in the grass, side by side, laughing and laughing.

This story is a re-telling of 'The Tale of the Bamboo Cutter', also known as 'The Tale of Princess Kaguya'. The original was a 10th century story, considered the oldest extant Japanese prose narrative. Consider the feelings of the parents of an extraordinary child...

A Farmer's Good Luck

Alison McBain

The best time to cut bamboo was at the end of the rainy season and the beginning of the dry season. Cut too early and it would be moist and crack later on during the dry season—houses collapsed when bamboo was cut too early. Cut too late and it would be sweet as sugar and attract insects to eat it, causing many problems for the people living there. It was Take's job to determine the best season and work quickly for a good harvest. The best bamboo came from this time, and he could sell it for the highest price.

So it was nearing the end of summer when he was walking through the stand, assessing the stalks. There was a brief break in the rain; the air felt cooler as it became drier. Under the stalks, it was dark already, although out in a field, the sky still held the violet of sunset. He moved by feel and the change in the air and was lulled by the music of the plants, the loud shushing of the leaves. His eyes were useless in the dark, so he closed them and walked forward using his hands and the hardened soles of his feet, knowing the land better than he knew his own body.

Suddenly, his eyelids glowed red and he opened them to see the stalks of bamboo outlined by a powerful light, a glow so bright that he had to hold his hand before his face. He couldn't see the source of the light, but it was blocking his path home. He'd seen wildfire before, but this brightness was too strong to be flames and did not carry their heat.

He walked forward through the stalks with his heart racing in his throat. Tales of spirits filled his head, and he wondered what torment he would suffer at their hands. He knew the old tales, and a simple bamboo farmer like him, living by the plenty of the seasons, had nothing worthy to offer them. He couldn't give fine wines or meat, couldn't even offer a child of his body, for he and his wife had never had any. They were poor in all things but love.

Squinting through the shifting stalks, he finally came to the source of the brilliance. He bent down, unable to see clearly, and felt around with his calloused hands. It felt like just another stalk of bamboo, only swollen close to the ground with some hideous growth. He brought out his knife, picturing all the days of his life, wondering if this was the end for him. As he cut into the tough stalk, he closed his eyes against the glare and held out his hands.

A weight fell against his palms and his eyelids became black. The light had been snuffed with the final slash of the knife. He opened his eyes, but was blinded by the sudden darkness and couldn't see what he held.

Tsuma stood in the doorway waiting for Take. It was unlike him to be out much beyond twilight, and dinner was waiting on the table. She fanned her face in the heat, waving away the black flies.

When she finally saw movement, she knew it was him. They had been married too long for her to mistake her husband for a stranger, but she saw that he was carrying something. The light from behind her was too dim to tell what it was.

And then she heard it. The sound she had always longed to

hear, but never expected to welcome to her home: a baby crying. The light fell on Take's face like a benediction and she saw the tracks of tears down his cheeks.

"We will call her Kaguya-hime," he said. "Our bamboo princess. Our daughter."

The couple was not young. As if understanding that, the little girl proved easy to care for. She slept the whole night through, and ate the pottage Tsuma made in the morning. She did not cry at all other than that first aborted wail when brought before the light of their cottage. And her cry then had been musical and low, like the natural shush of bamboo leaves.

Take told Tsuma the story of how he had found the baby. Tsuma believed the tale unquestioned, for the child could not be a natural creature. She was too beautiful, too perfect, to be born of an earthly mother and father. And her eyes shone with a glow like the moon's, soft and radiant.

The next morning, Tsuma strapped Kaguya to her back to take her into the fields. She was quietly working nearby to Take, Kaguya sleeping on her back, when she heard her husband scream in the next stand of bamboo. *Here is the cost for my perfect daughter*, she thought and went running over to him. Her mind swirled with thoughts of a severed hand or leg, cut through by the sharp machetes they used to harvest the bamboo. Instead, she found Take sitting flat-out on the ground, staring at his two still-attached hands. She looked for blood, but there was nothing. "What? What is it?"

His palms were cupped around something and he raised it up to her, wordless. In the center of his hands was a small nugget of gold.

"Where?" she whispered.

"In the center of the stalk," he said, and she saw his dropped machete behind him and the fallen swathes of bamboo. Inside each stalk was a golden heart.

She laughed, which woke Kaguya, and the baby laughed too. Take stood up and hugged her, hard. Then he pulled the baby from the sling and spun her round and round while the child laughed and laughed.

"You are our wonderful princess! We should have called you good-luck instead," he told her.

They ate meat with every meal now, and built a grand house next to the bamboo fields. Kaguya grew up, as children do, and she became lovelier with each passing year. Take became known far and wide as a humble man with a generous heart, and he entertained visitors from all walks of life, who took with them tales of the old farmer with the beautiful daughter.

On Kaguya's sixteenth birthday, a horseman arrived bearing a sealed message. Take held it in his hands when given it, but looked helplessly up at the man in brightly lacquered armor perched far above him. "I cannot read," Take told the man, who sneered and snatched back the missive.

"The Emperor Mikado has heard of the beauty of Kaguya-hime. He will be here tomorrow at daybreak."

Take grew pale. Tsuma burst into tears. Kaguya, herself, looked peaceful and serene. Then again, she had always been unnaturally calm, even when very young.

The village turned themselves inside out to help the family prepare for the Emperor's visit. Red banners lined the houses. Children were washed and threatened with dire punishments if they got dirty again. Take bit his nails down to the quick, and Tsuma shut herself in their bedroom and didn't come out until the evening meal. Her eyes were swollen and red, as if she had been crying the entire day. Only Kaguya ate each grain of rice with gentle precision, her face expressionless. She seemed to not know the importance of the Emperor's visit, or not care.

Take and Tsuma did not sleep that night. When the sky first brightened, they stared into each other's eyes. They had been together for a long time, and had been old even when Kaguya had come to them. Now, they were older still, and the same fear was in their hearts. But they said nothing to each other, at least no words aloud.

Take's bones creaked. Tsuma's back ached. They rose and threw open their doors as the sun crested the hills and shone like a funeral lamp upon their home.

Lines of soldiers trotted up the path on matched horses. There were too many for the narrow path that led from the village, and their horses milled nervously in the small space. Their ranks parted around the house and a man dressed in golden robes came walking up the dirt path, his litter too wide to be carried this far. He was neither young nor old, handsome or ugly. And he did not smile.

Take and Tsuma dropped painfully to their knees and bowed their heads before the man. So they did not see Kaguya step out the door from behind them, nor did they see the Emperor's face when he saw their daughter. If Take had seen their visitor's face at that moment, he might have recognized the expression of a man who had fallen hopelessly in love. Or perhaps he wouldn't have, since he'd never seen his own face upon seeing Tsuma for the first time, those many decades before.

Tsuma, however, glanced up at Kaguya's face as her daughter first looked at the Emperor. And she saw nothing in her daughter's face. No expression, no greeting or recognition. Absolutely nothing at all.

After his knees failed him and Tsuma helped him stand,

Take invited the Emperor into his home and served him the best dishes, prepared by his wife with her own hands. The Emperor ate little, merely stared across the table at Kaguya. At the end of the meal, the man said, "Marry me."

"No, thank you," their daughter replied calmly. Bowing, she left the room.

The next day, the Emperor arrived with a fanfare and a chest full of glowing emeralds, strings of perfectly matched white and black pearls, and silver crowns studded with rubies. "Marry me," he told their daughter, and "No," she replied.

The days passed, and with each one the Emperor brought a new gift and the same request. However, Kaguya's answer never varied and the spring season pressed closer to summer. On the solstice would be the full moon.

Each month since her daughter's thirteenth birthday, Tsuma had noticed Kaguya grow restless on the night of the full moon. The girl would sit outside for hours, no matter the weather, and stare up into the sky. Even when there were clouds or the worst storms, she would disappear outdoors and not reappear until the moon had reached its zenith. Then she would return to the house, her glowing eyes dimmed, and take to her bed without a word.

This night was no exception. However, this time Tsuma followed her daughter out of doors and watched her. She was worried enough about the Emperor's proximity to wonder if he would dare kidnap the girl on a night such as tonight. But she didn't expect to find what she saw.

The moon glowed down from a serene sky. And Kaguya, looking up, wore the expression of a woman very much in love.

"What is it?" Tsuma asked, her old voice creaking with the weight of her years. She knew, even then, without asking. She felt it in her bones.

Kaguya looked at the woman who had raised her, at the only mother she'd ever known. And she answered, as calmly as she ever had. "My home. They are coming for me. Soon, they will be here."

Unlike the moon, the Emperor's love and patience didn't wane over the next month. He might never have realized a change was coming except that Tsuma became ill. She dared say nothing to Take, afraid his heart would break as hers was breaking under the burden of her new knowledge. Kaguya would have stayed at her bedside and nursed her, but the pain of her daughter's presence made Tsuma's health deteriorate. Finally, she sent her daughter away from her, too heartsick to care.

The Emperor visited the old woman in her bed. "What is it?" he asked her, but she turned her face from him. He was afraid of what he saw in her eyes. And so he set guards around their house night and day, leaving Kaguya and her family trapped within.

The days passed, but Tsuma knew when the time had come of the full moon, because Kaguya disregarded her edict and came to visit her. The girl took her foster mother's frail hand in hers, and her beauty was so overwhelming in its intensity that Tsuma had to close her eyes.

"I love you, Mama," she said in her musical voice. "I will always love you. But I do not belong here anymore." She kissed the old woman on the cheek, and Tsuma opened her eyes to watch her daughter walk away from her. Then the old woman turned her face to the wall.

Kaguya came upon Take, who was crying silently where he stood by the door. He put his arms around her, but there seemed nothing to grasp—she felt as light as air. "I love you, Papa," she said. He let go of her and she opened the door and walked into the night.

Three figures waited for her. They glowed so brightly that they blinded the human eyes of the Emperor's guards. When the light of their presence faded, Kaguya was gone, too.

Take joined Tsuma in their bed, and they held each other close as the night passed into day. They did not rise again from their bed, and when the Emperor discovered them both gone from this earth the next morning, as if to escape his wrath by joining their daughter, he stared at their bodies for a long, long time, seeming to age and harden as the moments passed. When he finally walked away, he ordered his guards to set fire to the house and salt the fields. When the fire cleared and the embers settled, nothing grew there, from that day until today.

Emperor Mikado returned to his capital city and didn't set foot in Dewa Province for the rest of his life. But on his deathbed, he was said to look up at the moon and murmur a name. And the look in his eyes was one of love.

A *Rōnin* was samurai without a master, a condition brought about by the death of the master, or withdrawal of his master's favour. As a samurai's status and duty was tied to that of his master, a rōnin was cast out of the social order. While some found employment as bodyguards and mercenaries, many became criminals and bandits.

The Kakashi and the Raven

Steven Grassie

Masako knelt before her kakashi, her beseeching gaze upturned to his impassive one as she waited to feel a sign in her heart that he'd heard her words, her pleas for guidance. Against the slate-grey sky he loomed over her, arms upraised forbiddingly. The light rain pattered against his coat formed from reeds, his round straw hat. His black-painted face, stark against his pale, straw-stuffed sack of a head, was as inscrutable as it was coarse. Two crude scabbards were lashed to the kakashi's left hip, containing old wooden practice swords.

Eventually, Masako dropped her head to stare unseeing at the rice cake she'd placed where the kakashi's upright disappeared into the ground. Unmindful of the dampness seeping through the hemp over her knees, she wondered at the silence of Kuebiko the Wise—the kami whose essence the kakashi held—pondered his unwillingness to impart any wisdom upon her. Was she not devoted enough? Had she offended the deity in times gone by?

At the end of each and every day, as the others trudged back through the fields to their hovels in the village, Masako would go to her kakashi—*hers* in that she'd fashioned every bit of him, in spring, with her own two hands (except the practice swords). She would kneel and offer a rice cake; yesterday's cake was always gone, no doubt pilfered by the most courageous crows. Then she would pray to the knowledge kami and ask for direction in her life, in her son's life—"Should we remain here? Should we move on?"—and the effigy would gaze indifferently over her bowed head at the dry rice-fields, at the forest skirting them.

The final thing Masako would do—as she did now—was lean forward and tenderly rest her fingertips on the soil beneath the kakashi, then close her eyes and try to feel a connection to what was buried—

A high-pitched cry cut across the field and she jumped to her feet. More voices raised in alarm reached her ears, and without thought she set off towards the village. As she hurried across the freshly-harvested soil, she spotted several figures on the eastern road approaching the village. She quickened her pace, removing her straw hat lest it escape her head by itself. At this distance she couldn't tell much about the figures, save that there were six or seven of them and that they were all afoot, and this made her very nervous: retainers on official business for the daimyō would be on horseback. Common bandits, then? No—bandits would never be so brazen to walk into a village in broad daylight. *So that must mean...* Masako's heart rose into her throat, and she broke into a run.

Rōnin.

The first thing she did on reaching the village was make sure her son Takahiro was safe. Breathing hard, she sneaked up the side of the village's biggest house—that of Benkei, the village headman, and his family—and gently knocked on a shuttered window. A moment later the shutter was opened a fingerbreadth and an eye belonging to Chima, Benkei's wife, peered out a her. "Go around the back, I'll let you in," Chima whispered.

Masako didn't move. "Takahiro?"

Chima gestured over her shoulder at a closed door. "They're all together." She had two girls—twins—and at six years old they had two years on Takahiro. Masako noticed a polearm leaning against the wall next to the front door; she hoped Chima wouldn't have to use it. Before the headman's wife could say another word, Masako edged to the front of the house.

The small band of rōnin had been confronted by the village's menfolk—all twelve of them—who had armed themselves with swords and other weapons. Masako could see that Benkei stood at the front of the group with his arms folded across his pot belly, a sheathed sword resting on his hip. Not ten paces away stood the six rōnin, all men; five were spread out behind a well-built and moustachioed man who must be their leader. All were armoured and heavily armed, though no blade or bow was drawn. Yet.

"—need not be any trouble," the lead rōnin was saying. Masako's stomach lurched at the sound of that voice: she knew its owner—known as Raven—from the time she had come to think of as Before; before the village, before Takahiro. Raven was holding his arms out to the side, palms open and empty. "The choice is a simple one, headman: let us take two full carts of rice, and without another word we'll be on our merry way. Deny us the rice and... well, we'll take it anyway and"—he glanced at the buildings either side of them—"cause some damage before going on our merry way."

"Not possible," Benkei replied, shaking his head. His voice was carefully neutral. "The drought made this harvest the worst for years. Once we provide our tax share to our Lord Daimyō we will not have enough to survive the winter."

Raven glanced over his shoulder at his fellow rogue samurai—none of whom Masako recognized—then gave Benkei a stony stare. "Our hearts bleed for you all, they really do." A few of the rōnin smiled; one even dramatically clutched at his chest and sniggered. "But I'm certain that your lord...?"

"Takeda," Benkei provided.

"...I'm certain Lord Takeda will forgive your taxes being lighter this year, considering what now befalls you."

"Then you do not know of our Lord, rōnin," Benkei replied, icy emphasis on his last word.

Raven stiffened at Benkei's tone; Masako also noticed the tiniest change in the rōnin's stance. She emerged from beside the house, announcing loudly, "There is a problem with your offer—a practical consideration, if you will." Every eye turned to her as she strode over to stand beside, but slightly behind, Benkei, who looked as surprised by her appearance as the others were. A few rōnin hands had clutched sword hilts, but now they relaxed: there was nothing in the world to be less concerned about than an unarmed peasant woman.

Masako watched Raven's expression change from a grimace of annoyance, to a frown of confusion, to wide-eyed recognition. "Masako?" he asked, and barked a laugh. "We thought you were taken in the night by a bear! Look, boys—a ghost!" His men's silence and uncertain expressions betrayed their bafflement. Masako had to assume the faces of the village men behind her were similarly nonplussed.

"Yamada Musashi," Masako said. "Or as you prefer: Raven."

The rōnin's expression darkened at being named. "Still the vixen I remember, eh?" He gestured out at the fields, at the village, and asked incredulously, "And *this* is the life you chose?"

Masako ignored the question. And although she desperately wanted to ask a question of her own—*What of Takeo?*—she kept silent.

"Well, farmer-woman," Raven spat, "what is this 'practical consideration' you speak of?"

She replied, "Your timing is poor—the rice harvest was only finished yesterday." It was a lie—the harvest was finished four days since—and she could only hope the menfolk had the sense not to correct her. None spoke up. "The crop is unthreshed." A half-lie, this one—much of the rice had been separated from the chaff.

A small frown marred Raven's forehead. His scruffy topknot wobbled as he glanced at his companions, none of whom volunteered any help. Eventually, however, the rōnin's expression changed to show he understood Masako's meaning.

"So," Masako said, "unless the six of you planned on threshing all evening and night...?" *What of Takeo?*

"She speaks truly," Benkei offered up.

Raven glared at the headman for a long time. Then, in a menacing tone, "Do not try to send for help—I've many more men around your pitiful little settlement." He considered a moment, as if something had just occurred to him. "Tell me, how many horses do you have here?"

"Only one," Masako answered quickly. Another lie; half the true number. *And Takeo?*

"One," Benkei echoed.

Raven nodded. "At dawn tomorrow we shall return." He pointed a finger directly at Benkei. "*You* will have ready what we require," he warned, turning his gaze to what must be the headman's house. With a last narrow-eyed glance at Masako, Raven took several backward steps before spinning on his heel to stride away, his men falling into step behind him.

Masako watched his retreating back. *Why did you not tell me of Takeo?*

Not long after, a spade hefted over one shoulder, Masako re-crossed the field back to her kakashi. She knelt briefly before him, more out of habit than any intent to ask Kuebiko for guidance: lack of time, if not lack of hope for answers, put paid to thoughts of any prayers.

Earlier, once Raven and his men had disappeared from sight, Masako had gone straight to see Takahiro—who was as ill at ease about their situation as his four years allowed—kissed him, then went to find a spade. Having been joined by their women and children, Benkei and the menfolk still stood out in the road. A murmur of consternation filled the air and shouted questions—"Who do you think you *are*?" "How *dare* you speak for us?"—followed her as she strode towards the fields. She could hear that Benkei, too, was receiving his fair share of demands for explanations. It was understandable: here was a woman who'd said nary a word to her fellow villagers for nearly five years, having one day appeared from nowhere; and now here she was representing them against a band of rōnin, not to mention her mysterious, inaccurate answers!

Masako was struggling to keep her mind calm and focused. Raven's appearance had wrenched up memories and emotions that had finally begun to settle. None of the rōnin with him were known to her, so he'd either been expelled from their former band or, as had Masako, left of his own accord; she very much believed it was the former, the man was abhorrent. Throughout their exchange, she had been desperate to demand knowledge of Takeo, her former lover, her soul mate, Takahiro's father. How was he? Where was he? How did he react when she'd left? What news of him? The questions yet buzzed around in her head like hornets in a disturbed nest. Ultimately, she had not enquired after Takeo for one good reason: it would demonstrate she still cared. And if there was one lesson she'd learned from her days running with masterless samurai and other, less savoury rogues, it was that the ties binding you to those you love can be used to strangle you. No one had known, not even Takeo, that she had been with child...

Masako's first thrust of the spade severed the untouched rice cake in two, her second and third obliterated it. She took two deep, calming breaths and dug more carefully: it would not do to strike that which she sought to unearth. Indeed, presently she spied the top of the wooden box she'd buried beneath her kakashi almost three years ago. Dropping the spade, she knelt in the upturned soil and used her fingers to scrape away enough dirt to get purchase on the side of the long, narrow box. The soil was reluctant to give up its bounty, but Masako persevered.

Finally, she turned away from the kakashi to lay the box down on a flat piece of earth, then reached for the spade—

—threw herself sideways, rolled and came to her feet, as the kakashi toppled face first to where she'd been kneeling. Thankfully the box had been out of harm's way.

Masako was furious with herself. How could she have been so careless? She would not have been harmed in any lasting way, but a nasty bump or gash could have resulted if she'd been struck. Her eagerness to get to the box had clearly clouded her judgment, although the kakashi had seemed so stable...

As her shock and annoyance faded, it was replaced by a tinge of regret: to see her kakashi with his face pressed to the ground, his hat knocked off despite the fact it had been tied to his head. She couldn't leave him like this, but he'd have to wait—a more pressing matter was at hand.

Kneeling again, she brought the edge of the spade's head to where the box's lid met its base, and about halfway along its length. Then she carefully worked the edge until the hardened rice paste, weakened by dampness over the last two years, gave way with a muted *crack* and the lid came off. She immediately bowed low to the box's contents, her forehead touching the soil. When she straightened there were tears in her eyes, which she impatiently wiped away.

There they were. Her swords: katana and wakizashi, in their black, lacquered scabbards. Her father's swords... until he had committed seppuku.

For these past two years, it had been like having part of her soul buried out here in the field, but it could not have been avoided. A peasant uprising in a neighbouring territory had caused an already nervy Lord Takeda to initiate a 'sword hunt' of his land holdings: his samurai scoured estates and villages, even monasteries, seizing swords and all manner of other weapons, should there be anyone else harbouring ideas of rebellion. Thankfully, news of the sword hunt travelled quicker than the hunters themselves. It had broken Masako's heart to bury her swords—she was not the only villager to conceal a weapon or two—but they were better in the ground, with hope to be seen one day in the future, rather than confiscated and never seen again. After all, these swords were her son's future, his *destiny*. Takahiro was of strong samurai stock; this life among fields and oxen and hovels should not be his.

Masako's fingers itched to take hold of those familiar worn hilts and draw the blades, but now was not the time. There would be time enough later, hopefully, to inspect the blades for rust or other imperfections, and perhaps even to remedy them. Moreover, she would need to find a long moment to reacquaint herself with the swords' feel, their weight, their *life*, as well as banish the rust from her own body.

Masako replaced the lid, stood, and hefted the box under her arm. Briefly she considered the spade, but decided to leave it where it lay; it would be needed when the kakashi was raised again.

If it was raised again.

Frowning, she moved her gaze to the fallen effigy. Her eye was caught by one of the sword hilts poking out from beneath the kakashi's reed coat. For all the world he seemed like a warrior slain...

For a time she stood utterly still, pondering, then hastened back to the village.

It was clear from the men's expressions that none of them

was pleased about Masako's position beside Benkei. Just as clear, however, was their curiosity about the blanket-wrapped bundle before her.

They were in the main room of the headman's house, sitting and kneeling around in a circle: Masako, Benkei and the village's ten remaining adult males—Kotaro had earlier ridden for Lord Takeda's castle with news of their plight. Masako knew she appeared calm externally, although within she was boiling with frustration and impatience. For what felt like most of the evening, Benkei had been asking the men for opinions and ideas regarding their predicament: each and every one of them believed the only viable option was to meet Raven's demand, that a belly rumbling all winter was preferable to a belly full of steel at dawn. Indeed, as these men sat spouting their naïve nonsense, every other able hand in the village was furiously threshing the remaining rice crop.

Finally the headman turned to her, as did the others. "Masako?"

She looked around at them: every face displayed its own shade of guarded curiosity. For almost half a decade she'd been living and working among these men and their families, yet she remained a mystery to them. They knew little of her other than what they'd seen that spring morning when she had walked into their village asking to see the headman, wearing tatty clothes and carrying nothing, if you didn't count the babe in her belly. (She'd left her swords well-concealed in a patch of forest beyond the fields, to be retrieved later.) In private, Benkei had listened to her story (she hadn't mentioned the swords) and agreed to let her stay and have her baby safely; and then, depending how useful she was in the fields, he would decide if she and her offspring could stay long-term. Now, having endured the men's ignorant discourse, Masako believed it essential that they too heard her story... so that they'd then *listen* to her.

Masako leant forward and unwrapped the bundle before her. There were several sharp intakes of breath as the men gaped at the matching scabbards. The worked, lacquered wood and the intricately wrought handguards were of a standard none present had ever lain eyes on. Masako could sense the men's desire to look upon the blades such scabbards must contain, though she had no desire to display them.

"These belong to me," she stated. "Before, they were my father's. One day, they'll be Takahiro's." There was no point in naming her father this far north, though her words suggested two significant facts: that he must be dead, and that he was a man of some import, at the very least a mid-ranking samurai. Through years of battlefield prowess and unquestionable loyalty, he'd become a trusted retainer of daimyō Lord Amago, who commanded a vast territory far to the south. But when Amago was betrayed by an unidentified member of his inner circle and poisoned to death, Masako's father and several other samurai had been obliged to take their own lives, swept up in the resulting power struggle. Soon after, grief-stricken and dishonoured, her mother had taken her own life. Masako, seventeen years of age and the daughter—indeed the only child—of a disgraced retainer, had absconded in the night with Takeo Wada, a young, low-ranking samurai who'd been secretly courting her over the past year. Aside from being tainted by her father's perceived failure and dishonour, Masako had been terribly scared, and terribly lonely... and terribly in love.

The men sat silently as she spoke of these things; of how she and Takeo had soon been taken in by a gang of rōnin, an inevitable outcome for 'rogues' such as themselves—how else to survive in such an unforgiving world? Her voice was low as she expressed her regret about the many questionable things she did or was involved in. And that brought her on to Yamada Musashi, and she told of his iniquity, his cruelty: "He's not called Raven only for his beady eyes and long, sharp nose. That man is as ruthless as he is cunning. That he ever displayed a samurai's honour is incomprehensible." Finally, Masako spoke of her shock at discovering herself pregnant, of her agonizing decision to steal away from Takeo, from that life, of her decision to travel as far north as her feet would carry her...

Silence descended on the room like winter's first snowfall.

Presently Masako said, "I believe we should send another rider to Lord Takeda, but he should go west first, then cut around." Although she was looking around the circle of faces, her words were for Benkei. "Raven and his men will be looking out for only one horseman."

The headman was quiet for a moment and then, affecting the air of a seasoned general, said to the men, "Which is of course why we'd claimed only to have one horse." Masako resisted the urge to glance sidelong at him.

"I will go, if it please you," Kazuki spoke up. "After Kotaro I am the best rider here." Kazuki was young, only a year or two older than Masako, and he indeed was a strong horseman. Masako admired his courage—he and his wife had a baby boy.

Benkei nodded. "As soon as we're done here, you may depart." Kazuki inclined his head.

"As I understand it," Masako went on, "even if Lord Takeda sends men immediately they'll be hard pressed to reach us by dawn..." She turned to Benkei and he grimly nodded his agreement. Tellingly, no one took issue with her use of 'even if', rather than 'when'. A few carts of rice taken from a small village might not overly concern the daimyō. What they must hope *would* concern him was a gang of rōnin taking what was rightfully his, not to mention what other trouble they might go on to cause on his lands.

"I believe they'd be too late, anyway: Musashi will not wait till dawn as he promised. The only promises I ever saw him keep were those involving suffering and pain." She addressed Benkei: "If you recall, he knew not Lord Takeda's name, meaning they must have not long wandered into this area... meaning they've no idea how distant our daimyō's castle is. Which is why I believe they'll be back sooner rather than later."

The headman asked, "And by 'they'll be back' you mean they'll attack?"

Masako gave that a moment's thought. "'Attack' is too strong a word; perhaps 'raid' is closer to the mark. But be assured," she added, turning to the group, "any who challenges them will feel the razor kiss of their steel."

"I don't understand," Genba said, the pallor of his face now matching the white of his hair. "If it's the rice they want..." He seemed to lack the strength to finish the thought.

"Believe me," Masako replied, "selling the rice for high profit is only half of what motivates these men. They will have whatever takes their fancy... and *who*ever." That last elicited several shocked looks.

"What worries *me*," Issen piped up nervously, "are the other men surrounding us he spoke of."

"A bluff—there *are* no others," Masako told him confidently. "If there were, they would've been with h—"

She stopped short as the room's door slid open. They all turned to see Chima inclining her head for the interruption. "Forgive me," her voice was brittle, "but Kotaro's horse has found its way back to the village." The room's temperature seemed to drop as Chima looked at her husband and shook her head.

Some of the men couldn't help but look at Kazuki, and the young man displayed immense bravery and honour as he stood and bowed to them all, ready and waiting for Benkei's dismissal.

"The night's dark can be our saviour rather than our doom," Masako said into the taut silence. "Maybe we can scare this troublesome bird away."

They stared at her, expressions ranging from sceptical to hopeful.

"First, we need to bring any remaining kakashi in from the fields."

The silence became an uncertain one, and the men threw

glances at each other. Benkei, however, gestured for Masako to continue.

"Let me explain..."

In the dimness of her hovel Masako lay on her sleeping mat, her son's head nestled in the crook of her arm. Although Takahiro's breathing had settled into the regular cadence of sleep, Masako continued to lightly brush her fingertips across his forehead, the action affording comfort only for her now.

A little earlier, she had hurriedly fetched her toppled kakashi from the field as others brought in two more remaining effigies not yet collected. Then she had gone to remove Takahiro from Chima's charge. "Only for a short while," she'd told the headman's wife, and Chima had smiled and nodded knowingly, if not sadly.

Masako was utterly exhausted, but sleep was not an option. The evening's events—the encounter with Raven, her conversation with the village men—had been enormously taxing, not least because of her revelations about herself, of her past. Now everyone knew who she was; who—and what—she *really* was, including the previous incarnations of herself. She felt exposed, vulnerable. But it could not have been helped... could it?

Masako closed her eyes to rest them. This time alone with Takahiro was essential, as much to settle her spirit as focus her mind. She had said her piece, had done all she could. Now it was Benkei's voice that needed to be heard—indeed, even now she could hear his deep voice outside, giving orders and directions.

Earlier, having outlined her modest plan to the men, Masako patiently waited for the clamour of protests and scepticism to die down. Then she'd pointed out that they had nothing to lose by doing what she suggested; that if her idea did indeed work, then it would hopefully buy them the time until dawn. "And when the rōnin return at dawn?" they had asked of her. "Well," she replied, "if no help arrives from the castle, or if it comes too late, then at least we can defend ourselves in the light of the rising sun, rather than the dead of night." At that, Benkei had sombrely asked the group if anyone would care to suggest a better way to proceed... to be met with silence.

Masako was thankful for Benkei's support. Truth be told, the headman had always been fair to her despite, or indeed because of, what had occurred between them only two nights after her arrival in the village—something she had left out of her story to the other menfolk. Reeking of saké, Benkei had let himself into the dirty hovel behind his house that he'd turned over to her, to tell her the deal was off—no, it had *changed*. The glint in his eyes told her exactly what his new terms might be. But suddenly, the point of Masako's wakizashi was at his throat, the point of her katana at his groin. The glint in Benkei's eyes dulled, and he gasped as the wakizashi nicked the skin of his throat. Masako softly suggested that she scream for help? Or perhaps *he* would like to? Benkei gave a tiny shake of his head. Masako stared at him until shame swam up through the saké to join the fear in his eyes, then she lowered her swords. And so it was that their original deal remained unchanged, and Masako had promised to overlook Benkei's indiscretion if he promised to overlook her blades.

Takahiro murmured and stirred; his mother whispered comfort into his ear and kissed his head, and so he resumed his slumber. But then cold fear flared in Masako's belly and she did well not to flinch. She was seized by an almost overwhelming urge to jump to her feet and, for the third time in her life, flee the circumstances she found herself in... But what about her plan—that which she'd suggested to the menfolk? If her plan succeeded then—*No, of course it won't succeed!* Yamada Musashi was as canny as the bird he was named for; he'd *never* fall for some foolish sleight-of-hand. Should she grab some belongings and silently escape into the night, clutching Takahiro to her breast? She could run through the dark as far as her legs and chest allowed...

No! she told herself. *Not this time.* She suspected—no, she was *certain*—that Raven would pursue her, with or without his men. She had no real notion why, and there was little point in dwelling on it, but she had no doubt that once he was done with the village and its occupants, Raven would spread his dark wings and fly after her.

Masako inhaled an expansive breath, gathered up all the poisonous doubts and uncertainties lurking inside her, and banished them in one long, cleansing exhalation. A grim resolve filled those spaces left vacant, solidifying in her belly, her heart.

Taking care not to wake Takahiro, Masako manoeuvred herself to her feet and gathered up her swords.

She lay on her belly in a hollow beside the road, peering out into the darkness. Garbed head to toe in black, like a ninja assassin, only her eyes were uncovered; her katana lay reassuringly beside her. She was glad that the light from the moon found only the occasional chink in the thick armour of cloud.

For what felt like half the night Masako had been straining her senses for signs of the rōnin, a task made more difficult by a growing breeze. Behind her, interspersed with the menfolk and strategically positioned throughout the village, were ten samurai warriors.

Or, she hoped with all her heart, that's what it would look like to an attacker.

Over the prior few days, as the harvested fields had yielded the last of their bounties, the effigies that had protected them were brought into the village and carefully stacked. There they'd lain in wait for the Ascent—two days from now—when the villagers would pay them their respects and thank them for their vigilance. Rice cakes would be placed around them, prayers would be said, and then the kakashi would be set ablaze to release Kuebiko's spirit which had inhabited them during their watch. Tonight, the villagers required of them one last call of duty.

There had been fourteen kakashi in total, including Masako's; now there were ten, adapted and adorned to seem like samurai, at least from a distance. For that's all the kakashi-warriors could be: a deterrent. Although it was necessary Raven and his men get close enough to think help had arrived, it was essential they didn't get *too* close and see through the ruse. It was a delicate balance, if ever there was one. But it *had* to be struck.

The main adaptation the kakashi required was to bring their 'arms' down: crosspieces were shortened and repositioned to be more naturally man-shaped. The vague appearance of armour was achieved by re-stuffing reeds and straw into garments and shaping them as best as possible—although Old Kimura and Ikku had some assorted pieces of armour from their days as foot soldiers in long-ago campaigns. Straw hats were replaced by helmets fashioned from upturned cooking vessels. It helped that several of the kakashi already carried weapons of their own: some had old practice swords, like Masako's, while others held worn-out bows. As evening gave way to night the villagers had worked quickly and discreetly—who knew what unfriendly eyes might be watching?

Masako shifted her position, careful not to make any noise. Her limbs were beginning to chill and stiffen, stationary as they were, and she moved and stretched them as best she could. She turned her head to glance into the village and found that some of the 'samurai' had shifted their own positions: Chima and some of the other wives, dark-garbed and hidden in shadow, would every so often turn a helmet or move a kakashi's arm to further the deception.

Her head snapped back round—had that been whispered words, or merely a trick of the wind? She stared down the unseen road, not daring to blink or breathe, her pulse beating in her ears like a battle drum.

Movement: black on blacker still. The soft scuff of footsteps on the road. And there he was, Raven, his moustachioed face melting out of the night. But he stopped, as did the half-seen figures behind him.

Masako let her spent breath escape into the wind, took another. The rōnin were a mere fifteen paces away, conversing in harsh whispers. As she watched, Raven gestured for the others to wait, then sidled further along the road. He lowered himself to a crouch and stared at the village, reaching up—as was his wont, Masako remembered—to tug on his moustache. It seemed an age before he stood and took a few paces to his right, leaving the road.

Silently, Masako pushed herself up onto her knees and picked up the three small stones she'd placed beside her. With a glance at Raven's men—who were watching their boss—she quickly threw the stones into the village: the agreed sign. Immediately, several shouts of alarm went up, followed by the muted clamour of weapons being drawn and readied. The rōnin reached for their own swords, but then one of them yelped in fright as a flaming arrow skittered past his feet; he and the others shrank back, cursing.

Raven swore at his men and angrily gestured for them to move forward, though Masako noted that he stayed off the road. But then another flaming arrow scythed through the air and he had no choice but to stalk after his retreating men, hissing curses and ordering them to wait... to no avail.

"BEGONE!" roared a voice from the village—it was Benkei's. "AND DO NOT RETURN!"

Raven halted and turned. Masako could feel the fury emanating from him, even from here. As before, he stared long and hard at the village, then glanced left and right. Abruptly his face melted back into the darkness.

For some time after the rōnin had departed, Masako stayed in her hollow at the side of the road, peering suspiciously into the murk. At first, she had made to follow them to see if they retreated fully, but changed her mind: if they caught her, especially some distance from the village, she'd be snuffed out like a candle-flame.

When she eventually re-joined the others, she was greeted by several inclined heads—including Benkei's—and a few relieved smiles, though most faces seemed to be reserving their smiles for the dawn. She couldn't resist looking in on Takahiro—who was, of course, sound asleep in spite of the recent commotion. He and Chima's twins huddled close together on their sleeping mats. From the room's door, Masako watched her son's chest rise and fall, rise and fall...

Next she sought out her very own counterfeit samurai: he was standing at the corner of the house nearest the road, so that he'd appeared to be half-concealed and peeking out. Of all the kakashi, hers had needed the least adaptation—most obviously, his hat had been swapped for Old Kimura's ancient, battered helmet. Now, as he stood there with his impassive face and his 'arms' down, he seemed dejected. Masako reached out and pulled him from the ground, then carried him behind the houses backing onto the south fields. He was more ungainly than he was heavy, and she soon had him standing in soil again, if a little unsteadily. "Where you belong," she said aloud, and the thought of him burning during the Ascent pained her.

Masako knelt. She bowed. She thanked Kuebiko for his grace. Tonight, at last, he had guided her, allowed her a nugget of cleverness—and not just for the benefit of herself and Takahiro, but for all the villagers. She rested her head on the ground and cried a little; tears of joy, of relief. She was so tired. Exhausted. She gave a shuddering sigh and closed her eyes...

...and jerked awake—stung by a wasp, in the neck.

A moment for her bearings to return... Lying face down on the ground; still dark; cold. She fell *asleep?*

"Sshhhh," came a whisper. She made to lift her head, but stopped in agony—the stinger was back in her neck, at her throat now.

"So much as *breathe* loudly..." Raven left the threat unfinished. "Kneel on your sleeves."

Masako slowly pushed herself to a kneeling position, the tip of Raven's katana never leaving her throat. She did as he instructed, pulling her sleeves down over her hands and placing her knees on them. Moving her eyes, she saw her own still-sheathed katana in Raven's other hand; he must have sliced through the sash tying it to her waist. But as far as she could make out, the rōnin was alone.

Raven nodded at the kakashi without taking his eyes off her. "Your husband, or just a lover?" His smile was cold.

Be calm—think! Masako told herself, but the image of Takahiro's chest rising and falling was in her mind, and a cold panic was growing in her belly.

"Don't worry—Takeo won't mind," Raven went on. "He's long dead." He lifted her katana high and gestured with it. Behind him, to his left and to his right, the other five rōnin emerged from the night.

Takeo... Masako's head slumped forward, her loose hair blowing about her face in the strengthening wind.

"I found no horses," Raven said down to her. "And no horses means no samurai." All the same, he sounded as baffled as he was pleased.

His men approached, weapons already drawn.

"Round them all up in the headman's house—alive," Raven told them, and they advanced like ghosts on the village. "And *behave*, at least for the time being."

Masako barely heard the screams for the rushing inside her

head. Although Benkei and the others would have kept their weapons to hand—a brief clash of steel indeed rang out—being taken unawares gave them very little chance. As his men went about their work, Raven eyed Masako the way the bird he was named for might eye a field mouse.

Soon, four of the rōnin returned. Each of them carried a kakashi, which they dumped on the ground near Raven and Masako. Two of the men were chuckling and shaking their heads. Another said, "Some of our samurai adversaries," and he at least had the grace to look embarrassed.

Raven silenced the laughing men with a look, then asked Masako, "I assume this was your doing?"

"Mama!"

Despite the sword at her throat, Masako jerked around to face the back of Benkei's house. It was too dark to see, but she knew Takahiro was at the small back window looking out at her. At Raven.

"Be calm, Takahiro!" Masako called out, then grimaced in pain as Raven flicked his wrist and the flat of his blade struck her cheekbone.

But when she looked up through watering eyes, her captor's expression was one of genuine surprise. Then shock. Then a kind of dark amusement. He said, "She's Takeo's..." Not a question. "Now I see..."

Masako said nothing. She was thankful to hear the sound of the window's shutter being closed.

"The rice?" Raven barked at his men.

One answered, "Only one cart's ready."

"It'll have to do. Toshi, go hook the horse up to it."

As a disgruntled-looking Toshi stomped off, Raven stepped back from Masako. "What to do while we wait..." he said slowly. He threw her katana to the side and raised his own to caress her cheek, then the side of her neck, with the flat of the cold blade. His men edged closer.

Masako closed her eyes, the tears that dropped from them borne away by the fast-growing wind. A choice: relent and then die, or merely die.

Takahiro...

She shot upwards—not towards Raven, but towards her kakashi. Her hand closed around the upper of the two sword hilts on the effigy's belt and, in one smooth motion, she drew the weapon and slashed around in a downwards diagonal arc, left to right. Raven had sprung forward to grab her, but he abruptly redirected his momentum to stumble out of harm's way.

Or so he'd thought. He growled in pain and placed his fingers to his chest; they came away dark with blood.

Masako stood with her wakizashi at the ready. Much earlier she had replaced the practice sword with her own steel should the fight have moved into the village.

The other rōnin moved closer, but Raven screamed "No!" and readied his sword. He had been lucky—his wound was not a debilitating one.

Masako parried the first two blows, her arms reeling with the power of Raven's attempts. The fight would not be a long one: katana versus wakizashi was a mismatch, and Masako's lack of practice with her blades would be telling. Soon she was driven to one knee by an overhead attack, and immediately Raven twisted his blade down to cut from right to left, slashing across Masako's breast. She screamed and toppled forwards, her sword hitting the ground a moment before she did.

"Pathetic," Raven spat down at her. "You don't deserve those swords of yours, you never ha—"

Sudden shouts cut the rōnin short—fearful shouts. Masako found the strength to lift her cheek from the cold earth and look back up over her shoulder. Through bleary, disbelieving eyes she saw her kakashi loom up behind Raven, his wooden katana raised high and right. The rōnin began to turn just as the practice sword struck him on the side of the head with abnormal force; the cracking noise was not the wood's.

The breath exploded from Masako's body as Raven's dead weight crashed atop her. As she gasped for air, she saw the other kakashi stir... they were rising up from the ground...

Screams and curses from the rōnin; the sounds of them fleeing into the night.

Masako's eyes fluttered closed.

In the dawn's pale light, they found her kneeling in mud and blood before her kakashi, her swords across her lap.

Lord Takeda's men had indeed come. Masako raised her bowed head to glance at the six battle-dressed samurai standing near her in the gentle rain. The warriors were gazing in silent curiosity at the display before them: the four prone kakashi, the upright one, the dead rōnin. No doubt they wondered what befell the other masterless samurai.

Benkei and several others were shuffling onto the field, but they stopped short of the scene—there were children among them. Masako's eyes sought out Takahiro: there, in Chima's arms—where else?—a blanket covering him from the rain.

"There was another," Masako said to the samurai, gesturing vaguely at the village. "The rice. He was sent—"

"Dead," interrupted one of the warriors. He nodded at her kakashi. "Beneath one of these." There was an odd note to his voice.

Masako leant forward and bowed to Kuebiko, her forehead touching the wet earth. *Forgive me—your silences were all the answers I ever needed. I was blind, but now I see.* She straightened and painfully climbed to her feet, using the kakashi for leverage. The slashed flesh of her chest seemed afire.

"I should think Lord Takeda might have a use for you," another of the samurai said.

She looked long and hard at the young man, then dropped her gaze to Raven. The rōnin was staring dead-eyed at the lightening sky, his neck unnaturally angled.

Masako walked past the samurai, towards Takahiro. "My only uses, sir, are here."

Cranes are revered in Japan, as symbols of longevity and good luck. Because cranes are monogamous, they are often used in wedding decor. 'The Crane Wife' is a traditional story, where a man marries a crane disguised as a woman. When the man discovers his wife's true identity, she leaves him. But what if there were a child from that marriage...

Cranes' Return

Marta Murvosh

The day after Nozomi buried her father, the red-crowned cranes returned to Naniwa. The flock sped through the heavy summer air as if the God of the Winds lifted their black-tipped wings. An older female led a small group to Nozomi's home, where they landed in her garden trumpeting, voices rising and falling like a dirge.

Nozomi wiped away tears and returned to weeding. Her father used to offer the sacred birds the best selections from his and Nozomi's daily meals. "The cranes bring good fortune," he had said when Nozomi's belly cried for food. Since her life lacked good fortune, she thought the sacrifice useless.

The cranes leapt to her roof stirring the thatching with their talons. She hoped they weren't harming it, for the roof leaked on rainy days. Fallen evergreen needles whispered under footfalls, pulling her attention from the lovely cranes and the sad roof. Diagorō, a fisherman newly come to Naniwa, strolled through the pines and cedar huddled around her tiny home.

Whenever she saw him in the market, Nozomi longed to

spend time with him. Normally, he possessed the grace of a crane in flight. Today, he reminded her of a fledgling before that all important first leap.

He carried a crimson camellia. Her favorite.

Where had he found such a bright spring flower when summer's sultry heat was fading into fall's cool nights? She drew in his clean scent of sea and cedar. And why bring such a beautiful bloom?

"Oh." She stood, brushing garden dirt from her skirt.

Her hands cradled Diagorō's to inspect the blossom as crimson as the crowns marking cranes' heads. The camellia's texture felt rougher than the silk of petals. The corners of her mouth lifted. He had folded rice paper to capture the essence of her favorite flower. She had not known he was among the few in Naniwa who used paper.

"Beautiful. Where did you learn such clever folding?"

"China." His tense shoulders loosened.

"You've seen such a far-away land?" Her knowledge of China came from thrice-told traders' tales and the Buddhist priests. Her father had once claimed that Nozomi's mother had turned into a crane and flown to China, one of the many foolish tales that he had told while intoxicated. "Was your father a trader?"

He shook his head. "Sometimes fishing takes you further than you expect."

He lifted a hand as if he would caress her face.

The old female crane trumpeted, flapping her wings and stalking toward them. She swished her head back and forth, her cheeks pearl-gray and her crown the same color as the flower.

Diagorō dropped his hand. To Nozomi's amusement, he bowed to the bird.

"May I visit you?"

Nozomi was unsure if he asked her or the crane.

The female crane offered a chirring purr.

"You may." A cool breeze brushed across Nozomi's neck. She shivered as if feathers brushed her back.

A few days later Diagorō returned. Nozomi's spirits soared. She thought of the paper camellia sitting on the shelf holding her humble kamidana. The blossom felt at home next to the carved o-fuda, Inari's sacred foxes, and the small wooden statuette of a crane kami with its head tucked under a wing. She admired the folded bloom every night and morning and thought of Diagorō.

He carried a small pack and a huge basket filled with salmon that smelled of the deep ocean. "I caught these fish for you."

Accepting such a costly gift was improper. But with no living relatives, she needed to be practical. Smoked, the fish would last into winter. "Thank you Diagorō."

A crane, the old female, stalked through her garden and scolded Diagorō. Did the bird object to him or did she want a bite of the fish?

When he bowed to the crane, Nozomi laughed.

Her smile faded into irritation as he scaled the sloped side of her home, heading to her roof. His open pack held twine, a knife and other tools for repairing the grass thatching. Too bad he hadn't asked.

She hefted the basket of salmon and took it inside her one-room house. He had gutted and cleaned them. A good sign. She thought of her father and his tales. Sometimes her father had told her he was gathering wood when he met her mother. Sometimes he wove sails. Sometimes an arrow struck the crane. Other times the bird sought shelter, exhausted by a storm. In all versions, too many assumptions, too little trust, and too little talking forced Nozomi's mother to leave. Her mother's absence had left her father aching as if a crane's wing beat sorrow into his chest. Rice liquor hadn't dampened that pain.

Nozomi would not have a husband who did not consult her.

Deciding the fish would keep, she went outside, tucked her skirt about her legs, and climbed to her roof.

Diagorō balanced on the roof's incline, eyeing the areas where the grass had worn and let in water. His black eyes sparkled in the late summer sun. When she joined him, he murmured, "Careful." "

Who do you think fixed this roof last year?"

"Your father."

Her brows narrowed.

"You?"

"Father was ill. The roof needed attention." Her anger at her father's need for rice liquor and his foolish decisions about finances eclipsed her irritation with Diagorō.

"That could not have been easy." His voice soothed.

A cool salty breeze glided over Nozomi's arms. What would it be like to soar over the delta of the Yodo River? When her father was alive, she had spent her few spare moments on the roof wanting desperately to leap into the air and catch hold of the wind.

This past winter and spring her father had rarely left his sleeping mat. Seeing to him, gathering firewood for heat and to sell, and maintaining the garden had left her with no time for repairs or dreams of the sky.

"I've upset you," he said. She suspected Diagorō was too polite to mention the true source of her father's illness. "Was it the reminder of your father's death?"

"No." She debated climbing down and letting him continue with his repairs because the roof *did* need fixing. She put her hands on her hips.

"Diagorō, this is my house. Would you like it if I showed up at your boat and started repairing your nets?"

"You know how to repair nets?" He cocked his head and grinned. Her mouth thinned.

He shuffled his feet, rustling the grass on the roof.

Cranes circled overhead as if chaperoning her. She envied the graceful curves of their wings and the congeniality of their avian conversation.

"I thought with your father gone, you would want help."

"I appreciate the offer and would appreciate it even more if you would ask before presuming—"

"Little Nozomi!" a rough voice called from the ground. She recognized Ryobe, an old fisherman who had been her father's friend. Though she was old enough to marry, he still treated her like a girl.

She climbed down to greet him with a smile. "Hello, Ryobe."

"How fares Osamu's little girl?"

His hands stretched out to hers and she accepted them even though Ryobe smelled of the liquor that he claimed eased his aching joints. "Diagorō was just offering to fix my roof."

He had followed her down and greeted Ryobe.

"I would offer to help but my joints are aching." The old fisherman observed to the younger man. "Nozomi, do you have any spirits to set my ache to rights?"

"I'm sorry, Ryobe. Perhaps some pine needle tea?"

Ryobe glanced up. A red-crowed crane, the older female, had settled on the roof.

"Shall I weave a snare so you can catch that crane, little Nozomi?" Ryobe's eyes gleamed. "You could sell it to the Emperor Kōtoku's magician. The gold and jade would keep you into old age."

"No!" Nozomi recoiled. She might not want to share her meals and garden with a flock of cranes but she would never steal the life of a sacred bird. It was against the Emperor's laws. Only his magician was allowed to capture one sacred crane each year to make the special potion that lengthened the Emperor's life. She realized, with the Emperor building his palace in Naniwa, the cranes that visited her garden could be endangered. "That would be wrong, Ryobe."

Judging from Diagorō's gasp and his light touch on her shoulder, he felt the same.

Ryobe's wide face turned crafty. "No one would ever know."

"Ryobe, thank you, but I don't want you to risk imprisonment for me," she said. "And the cranes are so beautiful. My father would never have wanted one harmed."

She glanced at Diagorō and was caught by the fierceness she saw in his expression, his regard for the cranes in his eyes. Her heart was caught as neatly as a fish in a crane's beak.

After trading turnips and ginger at the market for rice to pay the tax and to place offerings of rice wrapped in fried bean-curd at the Shinto shrine to Inari, Nozomi returned home.

The door gaped open. Muddy footprints marred her woven mats.

Was anything was missing? She clenched her fists and scanned her kamidana and hearth. The shrine's carved o-fuda sat untouched on their shelf. She caressed the wooden crane and patted at the rice deity's crafty foxes. Cooking implements and her good knife were scattered. The packages of smoked salmon were untouched but the clay bottle that once held liquor lacked its stopper.

Her beautiful scarlet blossom lay open, its intricate folds undone, the paper crumpled.

"Who? Why?" She tucked the unfolded flower carefully into her pocket. Perhaps Diagorō could repair it.

Screams invaded her open door from the woods.

She set her jaw and grabbed her good knife, for she knew a few people might think her father's death left her vulnerable. She plunged though her door and into the cedars, heading toward the screams.

Where the trees gave way to marsh, the dappled light revealed the older female crane. The bird bugled furiously and flapped her wings. Her talons clutched a bundle.

A whoosh of air and water drew Nozomi's attention to the bundle—it was another crane ensnared in a fisherman's net. The older crane couldn't lift it free of the marsh. The trapped crane sank lower into the watery muck. Its head slipped underwater.

Ryobe must have set this trap. The fool!

Nozomi plunged into the marsh. Water soaked her garments; mud sucked at her legs.

Would the cranes let her near? Their wingspan was wider than she was tall. A wing strike could fell her as if it were a weapon.

The trapped crane fought against the binding. A downdraft from the older crane's attempts to raise the other bird from the water forced strands of Nozomi's hair into her eyes.

The older crane bated at Nozomi and she ducked. She slid and fell. Muddy water splashed over her face and the birds.

Getting to her feet, she chided, "I can't help if I drown."

The older crane chirred and jerked her wings back.

Nozomi slid an arm under the trapped crane's head to keep it above the water. She took hold of the crane with both arms and pulled, but the netting resisted her efforts. It must be secured under the surface.

The bird's heart pounded. Nozomi tugged at the net with one hand, pulling away loose sections. The trapped crane screeched. She must have drawn the net tighter.

"Shh." She stroked its face as she held it above the water. Even covered in muck, the feathers felt as smooth and warm as Diagorō's hands. The crane calmed, heartbeat slowing.

"Thank you," she whispered.

She pulled her good knife from her pocket and carefully began to saw through the layers of netting.

The older crane helped pull a section free and flapped to

the trees. The trapped bird bated. Nozomi paused, fearing she would cut feathers or muscles by mistake. "Shh, just a few more moments."

Its black-feathered cheeks told Nozomi it was a young male. The crane's black eyes fixed on hers, reminding her of Diagorō's piercing gaze. Its muscles relaxed.

She sawed through the tough fibers, until the layers fell away. The crane gained its feet.

It cocked its head, moved into her arms, and lay its cheek upon her shoulder.

For several moments she inhaled the scent of cedar and sea. Too soon, the bird backed away from their embrace. He launched into the air.

At a chirr, Nozomi turned. The older female waded back into the water, a bit of crimson caught in its beak.

It was the red rice paper, soaked. It must have fallen from her pocket when she reached for her knife.

"My thanks." Nozomi said, and took the crimson paper.

The older female muttered and leapt into the wind.

Nozomi watched the two birds soar to the east, away from the river, away from her home. Did the cranes seek safety? Would she ever see them again? Maybe they would glide away to China or another faraway land, one she had never heard of.

Why had her mother left her father? Had his tales been right? Had they each not trusted the other? Could she trust Diagorō?

Nozomi smoothed the sodden red paper with shaking fingers and wondered how to ease the fear in her heart.

Mud coated Diagorō's everyday clothing. He leaned against her open doorway as if too weary to stand. Red welts marred his forehead and throat, the markings as bright as a crane's crown, as intense as her ruined camellia.

"What happened?" Nozomi guided him inside her home and to her messy hearth. She rummaged for a blanket, adding to the disarray left by the intruder, and wrapped it around Diagorō. After stoking her small fire, she gave him a bit of the smoked salmon and pressed a cup of pine needle tea into his palms.

"Diagorō?" She ran gentle fingers over his hands. Under the stink of mud and marsh, she scented sea and cedar. Huddling close to him, she hoped their combined warmth would settle him. Being near him drove away the fear she had carried since finding the netted crane. "Who did this?"

His voice cracked. "I think it was Ryobe."

"Why?"

"I think he wanted to take care of you."

"He thinks he knows what's best for me? He presumes to reject the man who I—" Rage rose in her like a winter storm, cold and furious. "He doesn't think that little Nozomi knows her own mind. He's as bad as my father was, never asking what I want!"

"What do you want, Nozomi?" Diagorō's black eyes sought hers, a crane sighting the sky.

She longed to lean against him, to give her acceptance of his suit, to declare she wanted a future with him. She couldn't agree, not yet. A marriage needed more than smoked salmon in the larder, more than repairs to a roof; she wanted, no needed more.

She reached into her pocket and slid the scarlet paper, crushed and muddied, into his hands. "Tell me the truth."

His fingers smoothed and folded. The camellia re-emerged, stained, but even more beautiful in her eyes for seeing his clever hands at work.

"There in the marsh, it was me who was ensnared."

She took the battered flower back from Diagorō and with it claimed the gift of his honesty, more precious than the paper camellia. She decided to leap like a fledgling into the wind and imagined spreading her wings to catch good fortune.

"I know, and I want you as my husband."

Diagorō's face radiated joy. She drew him into an embrace as close as the God of the Winds caressing the wings of a crane in flight.

Takumi are Japan's revered master craftsmen, who hone their skills through years of practice and discipline. Japanese craftsmen created clockwork puppets for religious festivals and theatres. In the Edo period, *Zashiki Karakuri* were small, domestic clockwork servants, such as a tea-serving doll, used by the richest aristocrats to entertain guests. What would happen if a master-craftsman made a fantastic Karakuri as his child...

Kuriko

Stewart Baker

Kōchi Castle, Tosa Province, 1780, Third Month

Kuriko held the rabbit tightly in her tiny, wooden arms. His fur was as white as the moonlight and softer, she thought, than the silk on the formal kimono her father had worn to visit the lord of the castle. Softer even than the whisper of the Eastern sea from the simple workshop where they lived.

"His name is Oolong," said the man who was leading her along the hallway. "Would you like to take care of him?"

Kuriko was not certain of the man, who stank of *sake* and whose eyes were unsteady, but she nodded. "Can I show him to my father?"

The man hesitated, then shrugged and led her back down the corridor and slid open the door. Inside, the lord of the castle and her father were seated as they had been when she left, the same tension in the air.

"Jiro," the lord said, "I told you not to disturb us."

"My apologies, Lord Toyochika. She wanted to show Matsutaka the rabbit."

Toyochika grunted. "Be quick about it."

Kuriko took the rabbit to her father, careful not to drop it as it squirmed, and held it up for him to see.

"His name is Oolong," she said. "They said I can take care of him."

Her father smiled and stroked him with one finger. "He's beautiful." He lifted his hand to her face and brushed it softly; she thought for a moment from the look in his eyes he would cry. But instead, he only said, "Let me wind you."

Without speaking further, he lifted her key from its ribbon around her neck and placed it in the hole at the base of her skull. She stood, stiffly formal, as he wound the springs which powered her—never before had he wound her in front of another.

When he had finished, he nudged her away. "Now be a good girl and go along with Jiro there."

She looked uncertainly from her father to the lord, who sat cross-armed with a scowl on his face.

"Go along," her father said.

The lord nodded, and she was herded from the room again, back down the hallway and into an empty room. After the man called Jiro shut the door, she sat in the dark and stroked the rabbit's fur.

"Oolong," she whispered, "I'm worried."

Once she was sure her escort had really gone, she walked over to the door and slid it open just enough to see into the hallway—empty. She looked back to Oolong, who was sitting in the middle of the room nibbling on a head of lettuce.

"You stay here, Oolong," she said. "I'm going to make sure father's okay."

Then she was back in the hallway, taking small but purposeful steps to the room where her father and the lord had been arguing. The castle was darkening along with the evening, and as no lanterns were set out Kuriko had to run her hand along the wall as she walked. She met nobody, though she could hear servants talking and laughing in a distant part of the castle.

After several minutes and a few false starts, she found the hall that led to the room where she'd seen her father. Dim yellow light filtered through the screen wall's wooden trellis-work, falling dappled across her face. Three oddly-shaped shadows in the room sent great swathes of darkness into the hall. Kuriko stood and looked at them, trying to figure out what they were.

A squat rectangular form with the upper body of a man, its head and arms moving in short, sharp gestures, must be the lord at his desk. The second was clearly a man, but he stood too tall to be her father and carried swords, his hand never leaving the long one's hilt as he paced back and forth across the breadth of the room. The third shadow was an oddly-shaped lump against the right-hand wall. It seemed to press up against the paper screen, making it bulge slightly near the floor. Kuriko could not make out what it was, so she moved closer.

Still, the men's low, urgent voices only allowed her to catch a few words here and there: mistake, shōgun, Matsutaka. Matsutaka—her father's name. Had he left, then? She remembered how happy he had been on the journey here, pointing out the cherry blossoms which bloomed along the path to the castle. Talking of the castle's lord, an old friend who had long supported him. He had not hidden the shock in his face when they arrived and learned of that lord's sudden death, of his son's rise to control of the province. She thought again of that last winding, of how upset and tense her father had seemed as he bid her go with the man, Jiro. But why would he leave without her, without even saying goodbye?

From the corner of her eye, Kuriko seemed to see the third

shadow move. However, when she looked again it was the same as before. The castle's darkness closed in; her springs felt strangely tight, her gears slow and cumbersome.

She advanced and slid the door open just a crack. She placed her eye to the crack, bringing the left half of the room into view. She could see the samurai called Jiro pacing and, just barely, Toyochika seated at his desk. The floor in front of her gleamed wetly, but she did not look closer. The room smelled of copper, with a tang like the sea.

As she pushed the door open further, it made a rattling sound and Jiro spun to face it.

"Who is it?" Toyochika asked him; the lord's body tensed, though he did not rise.

Kuriko backed away from the door,; then she froze, not daring to move as Jiro walked over and looked out.

He paled, then after a moment's pause said: "There's nobody there."

Toyochika hunched, then half-stood at his desk. "There must be someone," he said, licking his lips. "Check again."

Jiro shoved the door open the rest of the way and took a step forward. He looked to the side and then, as he scanned the rest of the corridor, his eyes met Kuriko's. She stepped towards him.

"It's th..., the doll," he said.

Kuriko took another step forward. As she did so, the samurai took a stumbling half-step back. Toyochika leapt to his feet and strode around his desk towards the door.

Kuriko took one more step, bringing her fully into the room, but could not bring herself to look at what was casting the third shadow. She felt as though the shadow was a living thing; that it was expanding, covering more and more of the room, sweeping towards her with terrifying rapidity—it would eat her when it arrived. She shuddered.

Toyochika reached her first. He brought his arm up high and slapped her across the face full force. Kuriko scattered backwards into the hall, her kimono askew and her key on its ribbon almost coming loose around her neck. She tried to right herself, her small wooden arms and legs struggling with the unfamiliar motion. Toyochika reached down and yanked away her key, snapping the ribbon.

"Jiro," he said, "take the doll back to its room and see that it doesn't get out. I will attend to our business here alone."

"Yes lord."

Jiro carried her to her room and set her kimono straight, avoiding her eyes. This time when he closed the door he sat outside, but he needn't have bothered: Toyochika had her key and the walk to the room had used most of her energy. After a while he fell asleep. Kuriko sat up until morning, watching his shadow's rhythmic sway and thinking of the soft rain of pink flowers on the field.

Tosa Province, 1782, Fifth Month

Kuriko looked out the window as the carriage rattled across the country-side. Toyochika had treated her like a daughter at first, apologetic and doting after the incident. When he determined she was undamaged, he had stopped pretending. Now whenever he looked at her she felt he was sizing her up, measuring her joints and limbs in his mind for some unknown purpose.

Jiro, who acted as her minder and companion, was the only person in the castle she really felt close to. Sometimes she felt sorry for the samurai: the rest of the lord's men looked down on him because he was kind to her. And she had heard them laugh of how Lord Toyochika picked him up on the road to Edo one year, starving, bedraggled, and furiously drunk. She had never seen him that way, though. Something must have changed him, but she could not think what.

Kuriko had become used to staying in her room and its tiny courtyard garden with only Oolong and Jiro to keep her company. The last time she could remember leaving the castle was two years ago. She wondered what occasion made today different.

"Where are we going, Lord?" she asked.

Toyochika answered without even lifting his head, leaned back against the carriage's seat. "We, little doll, are going to watch the cherry blossoms."

She thought for a minute, gears turning silently. "Is somebody important going to be there?"

He narrowed his eyes at that, but nodded. "Tanuma. I've heard he has quite a fascination with the mechanical."

"Tanuma?"

"Senior Councillor Tanuma," said Jiro. "He's the Shōgun's main advisor."

Toyochika laughed. "He's more like the Shōgun's puppeteer than his advisor. He has immense power, little doll, and can make or break a man as he sees fit."

"That's dangerously close to treason, Lord," Jiro said.

"What's treason?" Kuriko asked.

"A betrayal of trust," Toyochika said. He leaned forward now, a gleam in his eye. "Jiro could give you a good example, isn't that right, Jiro?"

She looked to Jiro, but he didn't answer; he just set his jaw and glared out the window.

The blossoms fell in small spirals, in no hurry to carpet the ground in pink. They were lovely, but stirred sad memories: Kuriko remembered the warmth of her father's back and wished she knew where he was, and why he had never returned to the castle.

Still, she had Oolong and Jiro now—she wouldn't be alone.

Lord Toyochika and his courtiers sat at the top of a small hill with an older man that she guessed must be Tanuma. Kuriko sat apart from them, closer to the trees at the centre of a blanket that Jiro had set out for her. She fed Oolong long blades of grass from a pile she had gathered and watched the drifting petals.

The rabbit had grown too big for her to carry comfortably. Jiro had given her a small cage with wheels that she could use to pull Oolong behind her when she left her room at the castle. Its workmanship reminded Kuriko of her father, but when she asked Jiro whether he had gotten it from Rinsou, the samurai seemed troubled and would not answer. When she had pressed him, he made excuses and left.

Jiro now sat at the corner of her blanket, taking occasional sips from a flask of heated *sake*. When she asked he would wind her, but otherwise he was still and silent. Toyochika and his courtiers had been drinking steadily all morning. As the hours drew on—and the servants were twice sent back to the baggage train for more *sake*—they grew more and more raucous, singing bawdy lyrics and laughing and acting out political scenes with the exaggerated stiffness of satire.

After the noon meal had passed and yet more *sake* had been served, one of the courtiers stood, a small *shamisen* in one hand, and bowed in Lord Toyochika's direction. The other revellers slowly quieted, and when all was silent he spoke.

"I, the great poet Tatekawa Hanzou—"

The drinkers pelted him with sugared candies and jeers, but he waved them to silence and began again.

"I, the great poet Tatekawa Hanzou, have laboured long and hard since just before lunch to bring you my latest verse." He bowed once again to Lord Toyochika. "I hope that it pleases you."

He bowed one last time and then plucked a few strings, cleared his throat, and began.

> Little foreign-made girl, living in a box
> Thinks he is her friend but doesn't know a
>
> lot:
> If she were to ask him where her father went,
> He would—

That was as far as the man got, for Jiro leapt to his feet with a roar, drew one of his swords, and charged towards Lord Toyochika's party. Senior Councillor Tanuma shook his head and leaned towards Toyochika; Kuriko could see the anger on the lord's face even from where she sat. She pushed Oolong towards the trees, tipping over the rabbit's cage to spook him and set him running.

"Jiro!" she cried out. "Oolong is running away!"

The bodyguard stopped in mid-stride and swore.

"I'll deal with *you* later," he said, pointing his sword at the nobleman who had been reciting the poem. Then he sheathed the weapon in one fluid motion, turned on his heel, and sprinted after the rabbit.

The self-proclaimed poet laughed, his voice a bit shaky, plucked a few more strings on his *shamisen*, and cleared his throat.

> Grand rabbit protector, mightiest of men,
> Draws his potent weapon, sheathes it up
>
> again—

"I wouldn't laugh too hard, Hanzou," Lord Toyochika cut in, a grin on his face. "That rabbit is the only thing that stopped him from sheathing 'his potent weapon' in your drunken skull."

The self-proclaimed poet turned a sickly white, stammered, and fled towards the carriages. Though most of the men burst into laughter, Tanuma did not. Face dour, the older man leaned in towards Lord Toyochika and said something, gesturing towards where she sat.

Try as she might, Kuriko could not make out the man's words. All she could hear was Jiro's voice calling "Oolong! Oolong!"

On the ride back to the castle, Kuriko kept Oolong's cage in the seat next to her, one arm on top while she stroked the rabbit through the bars with one finger. Jiro and Lord Toyochika sat facing her, a study in opposites.

Jiro sat ramrod-straight, arms crossed and a scowl on his face. He had not said a word to Kuriko since returning Oolong to her. Toyochika, on the other hand, slouched back against the wall of the carriage, expression calm as they jolted along the road back to the castle. He did not speak to Kuriko either, but she was not surprised. The lord rarely had words for her, even when he took her along with him on visits of state or outings like this one.

"If I see him again, I'll kill him," Jiro said, suddenly breaking the silence.

"You'll do no such thing," Lord Toyochika replied.

"But he—"

"I said, you'll do no such thing."

"I will *not* sit by and let some drunken—"

Lord Toyochika, his indolence gone in an instant, grabbed Jiro by the throat, slamming him against the carriage wall.

"You forget your place, *bodyguard*," he snarled. "You *will* sit by and let Tatekawa Hanzou—or anyone else—say anything they want about you. Or was Tanuma right about you? He said you were a half-wild dog, in danger of turning on its master."

Kuriko was afraid then, afraid of the way Jiro's jaw clenched and of the way his hand spasmed around the hilt of his sword.

For a long while, he was silent. At last, though, he bowed his head and said "Yes, Lord Toyochika. Please accept my humble regrets."

"Good dog," the lord said, then sat back with a snort. The rest of the journey passed without a word.

Kōchi Castle, Tosa Province, 1783, Ninth Month

"Doll!" Lord Toyochika called in through the sliding paper door of her room. "Kuriko!"

Kuriko set Oolong in his cage and walked softly to the door. "I am here, Lord Toyochika."

He shoved the door open, nearly knocking it loose. "Tomorrow," he said, then swayed in place.

She could not smell the *sake* on his breath, but she did not need to. It was common knowledge that Lord Toyochika drank heavily, sometimes late into the night.

"Tomorrow, you will come to the courtyard early in the morning. I am going to the capital for my year of visitation, and I want to show you to some people." He paused, and for a minute she thought he was finished. "Don't bring the samurai along." He gestured to the empty spot in front of her door where Jiro usually sat.

She bowed, her kimono sleeves brushing the floor.

"You may bring the rabbit," he said, then burst out laughing and staggered away down the corridor.

Kuriko was still standing in the doorway an hour later, when Jiro returned. He started when he saw her there, then knelt on one knee by his customary spot.

"Something the matter?" he asked.

She shook her head.

"Then what are you doing out here? Come looking for me?"

"Where were you?" she asked. "I... was alone."

"Sorry about that. Lord Toyochika sent me on some fool errand a stable boy could've done. I told him you might need me, but he said not to be such an idiot. Wouldn't take no for an answer."

"Oh," she said. "I'm sorry. I missed you."

Jiro grinned. "Not your fault he's a drunken mess and won't hear sense. Let's get you to bed."

"Okay," she said as he picked her up and carried her into the room. "But wind me first."

The next morning, she was careful not to wake Jiro, sliding the door open quietly and sneaking past him with Oolong and cage in tow. Lord Toyochika's carriage was waiting in the courtyard by the main gates of the castle. Members of the lord's retinue surrounded it, going about their business. One of the men stopped what he was doing to lift first her, then Oolong, into the carriage. Lord Toyochika was already inside, eyes squinted against the light let inside by the open door.

Even after the door had been closed again, plunging the carriage's interior into a dim half-light, he seemed tense. "Jiro?"

"He's still asleep."

"Good," Toyochika said, the tension leaving his body as he leaned back in the seat. "Good."

"Why can't he come?" she asked, but the lord made no reply. She touched her neck where the ribbon which held her key used to hang, remembering with a quiver of fear the last time the two men had been together in one carriage. She did not question him again.

A few minutes later the crack of the whip sounded, with the driver's *ya!* to the horses. Lord Toyochika was asleep within the hour, and Kuriko opened one of the windows so she could look out of it.

The trip passed in silence. Kuriko spent her time playing with Oolong or watching the retainers and servants who followed them cut through the verdant countryside of Tosa. As they passed the rice paddies, filled with peasants bent over in toil, strains of country songs blew in through the windows.

> Sleeves, sleeves only
> have I dyed in crimson—
> See how red they are—
> From a hard life
> filled with toil—a ssei, a ssei ya.

Kuriko revelled in these experiences. It was not the first time she had seen people who weren't nobles or samurai—she saw the castle servants daily—but life in the castle was infinitely more muted and hesitant. She kicked her legs in time to the songs, whispering the words just under her breath.

Lord Toyochika slept on, slouched back in his seat and snoring occasionally.

Around mid-day, they stopped at a road-side inn. Toyochika stepped from the carriage, stretching and yawning, and exchanged words with a retainer.

"Come, Doll," he said over his shoulder. "We will take some tea here."

The staff of the inn stood in a line by the side of the carriage door. A man at the front of the line was speaking, wringing his hands as his head bobbed up and down in nervous half-bows.

"It would be a great honour, Lord, a great honour."

Toyochika and Kuriko were led inside and given a separate

room, while the rest of Toyochika's retainers vied for space in the common room. A serving girl came in with a large *sake* bottle in one hand and a plate of chopped carrot in the other, which she placed at Kuriko's side with a curious stare before seating herself beside Lord Toyochika. She poured him cup after cup, stealing glances at Kuriko while he drank them.

"Want a closer look?" Toyochika asked.

When the girl nodded, he slouched against her, one arm around her shoulders, and forced his hand between the folds of her kimono. She turned red and struggled, but not very much.

"If you want," he said," I can give you one."

He pulled her to the floor and then turned to Kuriko, seeming to remember they were not alone.

"Wait outside, Doll. We'll call you in when we want you."

She took Oolong with her and stood outside feeding him carrot slices, pretending not to hear the sounds that escaped through the door's wooden lattice-work. The men in the common room paid her no attention, occupied with *sake* of their own.

A voice came in a hissing whisper from behind her, "Kuriko!"

At first she thought it was Toyochika, and was surprised at his quietness. When she turned, however, she found the door still closed, the other sounds still spilling through it.

"Hsst! Kuriko!"

The voice came again, from the hallway next to Toyochika's private room. Kuriko slowly walked down the corridor, tugging Oolong's cage along behind her. She saw a figure hunched over in the shadows and stopped.

"Who's there?"

"Don't recognize me?"

"Jiro? But Toyochika said you needed to be left behind."

Jiro paused before responding, and his voice when he spoke was strained. "He said that, did he? I thought he'd just... Well, no matter."

"Jiro, what—"

"Shh." He raised a shadowy finger to his lips. "Where is he?"

"Drinking *sake* with a serving girl," she told him. "He said to wait outside the door until he called."

"You'd better do that, then. You know how he can get." He stood and took a few steps down the corridor.

"What are you going to do, Jiro?"

He stopped at a corner in the hallway, but didn't turn around. "Don't worry about me. For now, just keep it a secret that I'm here."

He stepped around the corner and Kuriko heard a door open and shut—Jiro was gone. She walked back to Toyochika's door, where the sounds were becoming more frantic, and stood waiting, feeding Oolong with pieces of carrot. The minutes stretched into hours, and eventually one of the lord's retainers approached. He stepped past Kuriko and rapped lightly on the side of the door.

"Lord Toyochika, the innkeeper wishes to know if he should prepare rooms for the night."

There was no response, and the man slowly cracked open the door and looked through. Kuriko saw naked flesh and a rumpled kimono before he coughed and shut it again, then walked back to the common room.

"The lord is occupied," she heard him say. "We will stay until morning."

The next day Kuriko and Oolong were led back to the carriage behind Toyochika. The lord looked as though he hadn't slept at all. He climbed in, stiffened momentarily, and then sat glaring at the opposite seat. A servant lifted Kuriko in and she saw Jiro sitting there, arms crossed but expression calm.

Toyochika, surprisingly, said nothing; when a retainer asked if he was ready to depart he responded with only a grunt. The carriage jerked to a start, but Toyochika remained silent until they had left the inn's courtyard.

"Do not forget, bodyguard. Wild dogs are put down."

"I apologise if I was out of line, Lord Toyochika," Jiro replied. "I thought *you* had forgotten *me*."

Both men were smiling, but there was no humour in it. Just a taut, deadly seriousness.

Edo, Imperial Capital, 1783, Tenth Month

Edo was massive. The capital dwarfed the castle town of Kōchi, and was built much differently besides. Where Kōchi had steep slopes, Edo was mostly flat; where Kōchi twisted and turned, the streets of Edo formed a grid. The capital, of course, had far more people in it as well—more than Kuriko had ever seen in one place. They thronged through the streets in a riot of colour and sound. Through the nervous whinnying of the horse and the shouts of people hawking merchandise, Kuriko could just make out the melancholy tones of a mendicant priest's bamboo flute. The carriage was forced to proceed at a pace slower than even Kuriko could have walked.

Lord Toyochika kept calling out to the driver to go faster. When this had no effect, he cursed and yelled back to the rest of his retinue to clear people out of the street by force, if they had to.

Even Jiro seemed ill at ease, but Kuriko didn't mind the press of the crowd.

She made sure Oolong's cage was properly secured, then knelt on the seat and looked out the window, taking in as many sights and sounds of the great city as she could.

After more than an hour, they turned down a side street which was less crowded, and Toyochika leaned back in his seat, muttering to himself. Kuriko stayed where she was, no less fascinated now that the people were gone. They soon came into an area where the crowded houses pulled back from the streets and were separated by dirt yards. The yards in turn were replaced with solid plaster walls topped by sloping tile roofs.

At one of these houses, the carriage came to a stop. The gates, standing open, revealed a finely kept garden in much the same style as the one at Kōchi castle. They rode down a grey gravel entranceway and came to a stop at the end, where another carriage already stood. The air was utterly silent, as though they had left the capital some time ago and were again out in the country.

"It looks like Senior Councillor Tanuma is already here," Jiro said, his tone dry.

"So it would seem," Lord Toyochika replied. "I wonder to what I owe the honour."

Jiro snorted, and the lord scowled at him. "*You* will stay here, bodyguard," he said. "Doll, come with me."

The scorn on Jiro's face quickly vanished, replaced by worry. "Lord Toyochika—"

"Enough. Stay here."

The lord opened the door and stepped down into the courtyard. "Hand me the doll," he said.

Jiro grimaced, but obeyed, then sat back in his seat and stared emptily at the wall opposite. Lord Toyochika closed the carriage door, and Kuriko could see no more of the samurai. Toyochika led her through the stately house's main doors and into a lavishly appointed waiting room. Senior Councillor Tanuma was sitting on the raised platform at the head of the room. Toyochika closed the door behind him and bowed deeply.

"You honour me too much, Senior Councillor."

The older man did not so much as bow his head. "I begin to think I do, Yamauchi."

The lord flinched and bowed again. "I had trouble on the road, Senior Councillor. The samurai Jiro—the one who chased the rabbit."

"You still retain him? I warned you once before."

"I appreciate your concern, Senior Councillor, but I've handled worse dogs than him and lived to tell of it. Besides, I enjoy the thrill of it: safe men are far less interesting to control."

"It's your own life, I suppose. But never mind that." Tanuma leaned forward, his eyes greedy. "Let me see the doll."

Without speaking, Toyochika stripped off Kuriko's kimono and pushed her forward.

She took a few halting steps forward and bowed. "How do you do."

"Indeed." Tanuma ran his tongue across his lips, as though they had suddenly gone dry. "A genuine Matsutaka. It is *astounding*. Did you know, he refused every request I ever made? I wish he had not disappeared all those years ago."

Kuriko spun to face Lord Toyochika. "Disapp—"

"Sh," he hissed, turning her back towards the councillor. She quieted, remembering the anger on his face when Jiro had embarrassed him in front of Tanuma. She stared hard at the floor: *Father is gone?*

"Indeed, Senior Councillor," Toyochika continued. "I saw him once when I was younger, and was much impressed by his ability. He visited Kōchi again after my father's unfortunate death, and wished the new lord to receive what he had intended for the old." He laid one hand on Kuriko's head.

Tanuma scratched his chin with the fingers of his right hand. "A stroke of luck. Your father would never have betrayed the inventor's trust by selling his work."

He sat back and picked up a document that had been resting on the platform next to him. He unfolded the paper and stamped it, then closed and sealed it.

"Take this to the Dutch at Nagasaki," he said. "Keep the doll hidden while you are in Edo, and depart when your year of visitation is over—it would look strange to leave sooner. I will meet you there. After they have given it a thorough examination, I will give you what you want."

Toyochika bowed again. "Yes, Senior Councillor. It will be done as you say."

Kuriko could feel the man's eyes upon her, and looked up. Before, she had only seen the councillor from a distance; up close, he was ugly, frog-like, almost physically repulsive. His eyes glistened as he examined her from where he sat.

"Can I... wind it?" he asked in a hoarse whisper.

"Of course, Senior Councillor." Toyochika took the key from his kimono pocket and handed it to the older man. "The hole is in the base of the skull."

Tanuma put one hand on her shoulder, turning her slightly away from him. From the corner of her eye, Kuriko saw his other hand, just barely shaking, lift the key into place. Tanuma wound it three times, a strong firm twist each time. He pulled out the key, but left his hand there, his fingers exploring the joint where her neck met her shoulders.

"Incredible," he said. "Just incredible."

Kuriko closed her eyes and pretended he was gone, and that her father was coming to find her.

After the councillor left, one of Lord Toyochika's retainers dressed her again. The lord sat where Tanuma had been, resting on one elbow and drinking *sake*.

"You will say nothing of this to Jiro," he said to her, "if you value his safety."

Edo, Imperial Capital, 1784, Ninth Month

Kuriko's time in Edo was much the same as it had been at home: shut away in a room with only Jiro and Oolong to comfort her. One day, Oolong slept all day. By evening, when she could not wake him, she became worried. She walked to the edge of her room, pushing aside the screen door which separated it from the hallway.

"Jiro," she said. "Oolong isn't moving."

Her bodyguard had been sitting cross-legged on the floor, picking at the bottom of one of his feet. He twisted around to look over her shoulder and into the room.

"You sure he isn't just sleeping?"

"I even stroked him and he didn't move."

"Hell." He swore softly, and she pretended not to hear.

"Can you look at him for me?"

"Of course. Why don't you... run along to the kitchen while I do that? I heard from Genzo they're making *mochi* for the lord's guests today."

She stepped out into the hall, but then looked back into the room.

"What about Oolong?" she asked. "Will he be okay?"

"I promise you," Jiro said, "he'll be fine."

Kuriko took a few steps down the corridor, but then turned once again. She could just make out the still form of her pet rabbit through the open doors of her room.

"But..."

"Here," Jiro said, turning her back towards the kitchen, "let me wind you."

When she returned, wooden fingers sticky from helping the cooks pound the rice, Jiro was standing in the garden outside the hall, looking up at the moon.

"Where's Oolong?" she asked.

"I'm afraid he's gone home."

"Home?"

Jiro pointed to the moon, which hung full and low in the sky. "Didn't you know where rabbits come from? On clear nights like this one you can see the mark of their kingdom on its surface."

He hoisted her on his shoulder and her eyes followed the

direction of his finger. "There's the rabbit," he said, showing her a series of shadows in the brightness of the moon. "You see it?"

She nodded. "But why did he leave?"

"Well, uh." Jiro set her down and scratched his head.

"Didn't he like it here?"

"No," he told her, squatting down to bring his face closer to hers. "That's not it at all. You know how happy he was with you!"

"So why did he leave?"

"Well, he has family there, you see. He misses them, and he hasn't seen them in over ten years now."

"Family?" she asked.

"Sure."

"Oh. I understand."

She stood looking at the moon for a few minutes more, until one of the windows in the lord's chambers spilled light into the courtyard. His boisterous laughter rang out over the plucking of the *koto* the women were playing. She missed her father, and now Oolong was gone as well. How long would it be before Jiro, too, left her?

"I think I would like to retire for the night," she told him.

"Of course."

Once Jiro had tucked her in and closed the door, she quietly stood up, slid open a window, and watched the moon slipping through the night clouds.

On a crisp spring morning, the carriage pulled out of magnificent wooden gates of Toyochika's Edo estate and began the long journey to Dejima—the only place in the country where foreigners were allowed. Kuriko had heard tales of their fiery beards and strange ways, but she had never seen one before.

She was excited despite herself. Lord Toyochika planned to sell her, but she couldn't believe he would go through with it.

Surely he was too jealous and selfish to give her away, even if he did think of her as a mere doll. In any case, Jiro would no doubt go with her, and she doubted Tanuma would be any worse than Toyochika—if he was disgusting and his touch lingered too long, at least he didn't drink and wasn't violent.

Jiro seemed surprised at the trip, but so far as she could tell did not suspect anything—Lord Toyochika had insisted she not tell him anything, and she had reluctantly agreed lest he hurt the samurai. When Jiro asked, Toyochika muttered something about the marvels of the Dutch and tried to brush him off.

"Did she ask about the moon?" Jiro said.

"Yes, of course. The moon. What else would it be?" The lord laughed, as if sharing a joke with himself and nobody else.

They had set off so early that it was still pitch dark outside, and Kuriko leaned out of the window until Jiro pulled her back in.

"You'll hurt yourself."

"But I want to see the moon!"

"When we get to Dejima," he told her, "you can see it through the special glasses of the Dutch."

"Oh *yes*," Lord Toyochika said. "The Dutch have such excellent moon-viewing equipment. And you, little doll, will be able to use it as much as you want!"

"Promise?" she asked.

"I promise, little doll," he said, "and *I* keep my promises."

Jiro scowled, but said nothing. Kuriko avoided his eyes.

Nagasaki, Hizen Province, 1784, Tenth Month

It took three long weeks, but they finally arrived at Nagasaki harbour in the early afternoon of a quiet, balmy day. Kuriko sneaked looks at Dejima, the enclosed island where the foreigners lived. Although it was only a few feet off the shore, it may as well have been another world. Walls topped in black shingles stopped observers from seeing in. A gated entry-house—the only way into and out of Dejima— was set at the end of a long bridge leading to the island. At the gate stood three samurai.

Even for a man of Lord Toyochika's status, entry to the island did not come easy. It took Jiro an hour before the official in the gate-house even came out to the carriage, and another hour after that during which the lord himself stood outside, waving Tanuma's sealed envelope in the official's face and calling him names. Even then, the man would have refused if Toyochika had not paraded Kuriko back and forth, lifting the folds of her kimono and saying, "You see how she is made!" in a loud voice. "She is a genuine Matsutaka—one of a kind!"

The Dutch rushed out of the gatehouse, past the stunned samurai, and surrounded the official, speaking in a stream of babble. He relented at last, sweat clear on his forehead, and they followed him across the bridge and through the gates, surrounded still by the strange foreign men. In the gate-house, the guards made Jiro hand over his swords, citing a directive from the shōgun which limited the carrying of weapons to nobles.

Jiro was reluctant, but at a barked order from Toyochika he surrendered his swords.

"No knives?" the guards asked him.

"Knives?" he replied. "Why would I have knives?"

The guards looked at one another, amused. "Not much of a samurai," Kuriko heard one of them say as they left the room.

Then they were through. The inside of the Dutch quarter looked disappointingly like the rest of Japan: there were the same cobbled streets, the same shingled roofs. Some of the foreigners even wore kimono instead of Western clothes. Kuriko had expected it to be different, somehow.

"The moon?" she asked.

"Later," Lord Toyochika told her. "Even *they* can't see it in the day. In the mean time, we will let them examine you."

Hours later, Kuriko had been stripped, poked and prodded—everything short of dismantled. She felt a little uncomfortable having so many people handle her at once, but if enduring the rough voices and hairy hands of foreigners was the price to see the moon, so be it. Their interest, at least, seemed clean: driven by an interest in mechanics and nothing else. She remembered Tanuma and shuddered.

At first Lord Toyochika and Jiro stood by, watching the foreigners work. After a while Senior Councillor Tanuma entered with several armed samurai. Jiro looked at their weapons and scowled. The foreigners stopped what they were doing and bowed respectfully.

Lord Toyochika walked over to Tanuma and bowed deeply. The older man bowed back—little more than a nod—and then embraced him, laughing.

Jiro muttered, but smiled when she looked at him.

"Don't worry," he told her. "I'm just going to talk with Lord Toyochika, okay?"

She nodded.

He put a hand on one of the foreigner's shoulders. "If she says stop, you stop. You understand me?"

One of the men translated his words into the language of the Dutch and the others nodded. Jiro walked to where Toyochika and Tanuma stood.

"Ah, Jiro!" Toyochika said as he approached. "Perfect timing. You can guard the door."

Kuriko could see that Jiro wasn't happy, but he did as ordered, standing at the door on the far side of the room after Toyochika and the others had gone through it. He crossed his arms and scowled, looking at nothing in particular.

Then she was lost once more to the poking and prodding of the Dutch. Just as she was sure they would never have enough of examining her, they split apart and left in two babbling groups except for one man who had a full dark beard—the one who had translated Jiro's words before.

Tanuma and Toyochika emerged from their room, flanked by the councillor's bodyguards. Jiro said something to Toyochika that Kuriko couldn't hear, but the lord waved him away. Jiro came over to where she was standing, redressed her and wound her up, fussing more than usual.

"The moon?" she asked.

The foreigner who had stayed behind smiled, nodded, and showed them outside; Toyochika and the others followed. The sky had grown dim, with wisps of cloud occasionally drifting across the front of the moon. The Dutch man gestured to a large basket set beneath a giant paper lantern, the whole of which was tied with thin strands of rope to a wooden stake hammered into the ground.

"In this," he said in broken Japanese, "we go up to the sky. The Moon is better to see there."

"What is it?" Jiro asked.

"We name it a balloon," the man replied. "It is a new invention in France, near by our Holland. The telescope is already inside."

He hoisted Kuriko into the basket and set her in a seat built into its side. She squirmed, eager to explore the strange gadgets at the bottom of the basket. She hoped it would be powerful enough to spot Oolong or her father.

"Is it safe?" Jiro asked.

"I certain you, it is quite safe. We will go up 300 rods, view the lady the moon through the telescope, and down again."

Lord Toyochika nodded and turned to Tanuma. "I trust you will not back out of our deal should anything happen to it during this excursion."

"I am sure that Mr. van Rheede will provide us with his assurance," the other man agreed. "I would hate for our relations with the Dutch to sour."

The bearded foreigner coughed, and spoke in a language unintelligible to Kuriko. Toyochika looked equally blank, but Tanuma's eyes narrowed, as though he could understand what the man was saying.

"It's not right," Jiro said, suddenly and loud, cutting off the stream of Dutch.

Lord Toyochika and Senior Councillor Tanuma turned to look at him, and Kuriko felt a strange excitement deep within her.

"What did you say?" Toyochika asked the bodyguard.

"It's not right, treating her like something to be bought and sold. It's bad enough what we—"

Toyochika laughed, a quick barking sound. "We? *We*? As I recall, it was *you*—"

Jiro gave a tremendous shout, pulled a small knife from inside his kimono, and jumped on Toyochika quick as a shadow flitting across the moon. The knife flashed in the dim light and the lord fell, his throat a mess of red. Jiro yanked the dying man's sword from its scabbard and tore something from his pocket, dashed past the stunned Dutchman and dropped Kuriko's key, slick with Toyochika's blood, next to her in the basket.

"I'm sorry," he said to Kuriko. "I'm so sorry."

"Jiro," she began, but he wasn't listening. "Jiro, I..."

The samurai stood, silent. For a moment, Kuriko thought he would speak again, but he just took one slow breath in, let it out, and flashed Lord Toyochika's sword through the ropes holding the balloon. Then he turned, slowly, to face Tanuma, whose bodyguards had drawn swords of their own.

"Stop her!" the senior councillor shouted.

A few of the Dutch made desultory grabs at the balloon's trailing ropes, but it was too late; Kuriko was up and away, following the moon across the still waters of the harbour.

She unbuckled the restraints and turned around in the seat. Jiro stood with his back to the wall of the building, surrounded by Tanuma's men. The flickering light of the lanterns painted the scene in dappled shadow. Jiro lifted Toyochika's sword above his head, and then the balloon was past the island's walls and Kuriko could see no more.

The balloon rose higher—the sky above mirrored by the silent sea below. She passed through a stray wisp of cloud and the moon hung before her.

Soon, she thought, she would see her father again, and Oolong. Maybe Jiro, too, would be waiting for her, in that distant, unreachable place. She held the blood-slick key to her chest, closed her eyes, and waited for her springs to wind down.

Onmyōji were civil servants, specialists in magic and divination. They studied *Onmyōdō* cosmology, which incorporated Chinese philosophies of Yin-yang and the Five Elements, astronomy, and observation of the natural world. Their duties ranged from keeping the calendar to divination to protecting from harmful ghosts. The *onmyōji* in this story also features in the author's 'Kitsune Tales' series.

Kusanagi

Laura VanArendonk Baugh

The house was not large, not fine, but it was well-maintained and clean. That made the long smear of dried blood across the *tatami* all the more startling and wrong.

Tsurugu Kiyomori leaned from behind the two lords to look over the scene. They kept their distance, to avoid defilement with nearer exposure to the death.

The murder—clearly, a murder—had happened in an outer room. The body had been dragged through the door and across the *rou*, the external deck, and then carried away, possibly in a basket to slow the blood trail. It could be followed yet, but Tsurugu waited to see how the great men would respond.

Naka no Yoritomo, ever the strategist, also bided his time. He rested his left hand upon his sword and looked at Minamoto Katanori, the *bakufu* official who had brought them to this place.

Minamoto Katanori did not see an advantage in reserve. "Search the house!" he snapped. "Tear it apart! Bring me anyone you find, or anything!"

Anything was a very large order, and Tsurugu noted that Minamoto was still unwilling to share what had brought them here. Naka-dono's men scattered throughout the house, and the sound of their tramping and overturning overwhelmed the birdsong from the garden.

Minamoto Katanori put a hand to one of the pillars and looked at the blood. "We are dead men," he said quietly.

Naka no Yoritomo was a daimyō, a warlord for the shogun, and not a man to accept death without knowing the reason. "What did you expect to find?"

Minamoto Katanori pointed to the widest stain on the floor. "That man. Alive."

Beside Tsurugu, adolescent Kaworu shifted his weight, all that he would betray of his curiosity. Tsurugu noted his restraint and resolved to compliment him on it later.

The clamor of the search faded; it was a small rural house, with little to hide. *"Tono,"* reported one of the warriors, "there is no one here, and nothing but ordinary household goods. There are papers which have been burned, but they are only fragments and ash."

"No swords?" asked Minamoto, as if the man would have forgotten to report one.

"No, *tono*. No swords."

Minamoto let out his breath in an unhappy rush.

Tsurugu finally spoke. "If you will permit, *tono*, I will ascertain whether anyone remains near, in hiding."

"The men can search the garden—"

"No," interrupted Tsurugu, more sharply than was proper, or wise with a *bakufu* official. "No, they will only disturb the energy and foul the trail. Leave it untouched until I have examined it."

Minamoto glanced at Naka, unused to taking orders from a subordinate, but Naka's face betrayed only confidence in his *onmyōji's* suggestion. Minamoto nodded. "Very well. Do what you can. We will camp near the road; I won't stay where a murder has happened."

Briefly Tsurugu wondered if an angry *onryō*, lingering after the murder, might tell them anything, or if it would be too wholly consumed with revenge. It was better to hope there was no ghost.

"I will need space and quiet," he said. "Kaworu, bring my materials."

The servant brought the bound coffers to the *rou*, and Tsurugu knelt to mark a circle with five curved stone *magatama*. *Earth, Metal, Water, Wood, Fire.* Behind him, the great men and soldiers retreated to a safe distance, leaving them alone in the house.

Kaworu knelt a step away, waiting. Tsurugu concentrated a moment and then sent a gentle questing push into the evening air. There were plenty of living things, but no humans near the house, not until their own group near the road.

Tsurugu pointed to where the bloody smear slid off the edge of the wooden deck. "Follow that trail," he instructed Kaworu. He permitted a small smile. "And there is no one to see if you do it more efficiently."

Kaworu nodded and, in a flash of kimono and fur, an adolescent fox darted off the *rou* and began nosing about in the flowers, eventually following a scent off into the garden.

Tsurugu rose and walked through the house, touching none of the overturned furniture or emptied cabinets. He did not expect to find anything the daimyō's men had missed; he was looking for other evidence. An older house, such as this one, had more residents than its human owner and his servants.

Kaworu gave a soft yip to signal his return. "Come in," Tsurugu called.

The servant entered, once again in human form, and shook his head. "It's as if he disappeared. He must have been carried away while wrapped in something to slow the blood."

Tsurugu nodded. "A basket, perhaps, or bound in cloth.

Where did it lead?"

"Across the garden, to the woods, and down to the river. There the trail disappears. They didn't cross the river."

Tsurugu nodded. "A boat, then. Good work. I'll set a barrier about this place, to know if anyone returns, and then let's go back to the others."

The others were making camp not far from the road, and Tsuguru dispatched Kaworu to work and went to Minamoto's tent to report their findings. "There is no one here, only ourselves, and I believe the body was taken to the river and then into a boat."

"Impressive," admitted Minamoto. "At least we know where the murderer fled. I have been told Naka-dono's *onmyōji* was among the most skilled, but it is something else to see it myself."

"Who has said this of me?" asked Tsurugu. It was not an idle or self-effacing question. He was very particular not to draw attention to himself, when possible.

"Most recently, one of my subordinates," Minamoto answered. "He is anxious to be introduced and wishes to join you."

Tsurugu blinked. "To join me?"

Minamoto waved at a servant, who departed. "Makino Koretoshi-sama. A distant cousin of mine."

Tsurugu noted the subtle nudge. A cousin of a Minamoto, however minor a Minamoto, must be dealt with carefully. And Minamoto Katanori might not be as minor as Tsurugu had first assumed. A potentially fatal failure implied a more weighty and impressive mission, entrusted to a more weighty and impressive retainer.

Minamoto Katanori had requested Naka no Yoritomo's aid in coming to this rural house. Tsurugu had believed it was because he did not merit shogunate troops on his own. He wondered now if it were to obscure his travel under another lord's colors.

Naka no Yoritomo's mind was also working. "Will you tell me now what we seek? If it has been carried away, we should know what we are trying to find."

Minamoto took a breath and held it, pressing his lips in thought. "The dead man.... His name was Fujiwara Morihito."

Tsurugu nodded. The Fujiwara had been close to the imperial family for centuries, bound by oath and blood, and were often the truer rulers. There were any number of political reasons the Minamoto might seek one of them.

"There are many Fujiwara. I married one myself." Naka was not satisfied. "You said we were dead men. I can hardly be blamed for failing to find what I did not know to search for."

Minamoto nodded but remained firm. "Let me keep that a bit longer. For now, we should concentrate on finding that boat. Send men up and down the river to search for landing places."

A young man entered and bowed his greetings, as a boy behind repeated the actions in a servant's posture. "*Konbanwa.* My name is Makino Koretoshi, and I have come with Minamoto-dono specifically to ask Tsurugu-sama to take me as his student."

Tsurugu was certain his face betrayed his dismay, despite Minamoto's warning. "What? No. I am not seeking a student."

Makino turned to face him, ignoring Naka no Yoritomo, and this breach of manners would have been enough to refuse him. He was young, and eager, and proud of his skill, and none of those were necessarily faults, but Tsurugu disliked him immediately. "Please! Hear my request, at least."

Naka no Yoritomo clearly disliked him, too, but as daimyō he had a simple solution. "Go and talk, the both of you," he ordered. "Tsurugu-san, if there is anything else to be learned, let us hear it."

Tsurugu bowed and retreated, with Makino dogging his heels like a hungry puppy.

His tent was ready, where Kaworu was working to prepare for the night, and Tsurugu took a seat. Makino spoke without waiting for invitation. "I have made up my mind to become an *onmyōji* for the shogun, and I have come to learn from the best."

Tsurugu's stomach tightened. He did not want this

ambitious young man, barely older than Kaworu, and he did not want the fame this Makino was claiming for him. "I have told you, I am not taking a student."

"I could be your assistant. I could be more useful than this boy." He gestured at Kaworu.

Kaworu, still lanky but hardly a boy, let his lip curl a fraction before continuing his work in silence. Tsurugu pretended not to notice. "One cannot simply decide to become an *onmyōji*. The shogun's *onmyōji* should come from a family of *onmyōji*, and your training should have started as a child."

"It did, it did," Makino protested. "Test me. I know all the ways *onmyōdō* may predict the future."

"No." Tsurugu's voice was sterner than he'd intended, but he did not regret it. "No, *onmyōdō* does not predict the future. We read tendencies, which inform us of the shapes the future may take and the probabilities of those shapes. But we do not read the future, and it is foolhardy to pretend we do."

Makino was only slightly daunted. "Of course, of course. I misspoke. But I have studied. I have read all the *Senji Ryakketsu*. Abe no Seimei was the greatest master of *onmyōdō*."

"And why was Abe no Seimei great?" asked Tsurugu.

"Because his father was skilled and his mother was *kitsune*," answered Makino without hesitation. "This gave him power beyond an ordinary man's. This is why he is the greatest *onmyōji*."

Tsuguru had hoped for an answer about great study, great effort, or great teaching. "Well, it is a shame then I am not half-*kitsune*," he grumbled.

Kaworu snorted and quickly covered it with a sneeze.

"Perhaps not, but you are a very skilled *onmyōji*," Makino said, clearly worried he had offended, "and I have determined to learn from you." He beckoned to his servant. "Orochimaru!"

The servant scurried forward, deposited a coffer on the ground before Tsurugu, and bowedbowing.

"Gifts?" asked Tsurugu.

"No, Tsurugu-sama, a man of your prestige must receive many gifts. I have brought my library to show you what I have read already, to save time in your teaching."

Tsurugu fought down an unseemly answer and kept his eyes carefully on Makino, knowing that if he glanced even inadvertently at Kaworu, the servant would giggle inappropriately and then Makino might ask for retribution. "None of this is to the point of our current charge," he said, "which is to learn what happened in that house before we arrived. How would you accomplish that, with all your study?"

Makino shook his head. "It is an unreasonable request," he said. "*onmyōdō* is about the future, not the past."

Tsurugu knew in that moment he would find something to answer Naka-dono's questions, if only because the natural world could not allow this brazen braggart to go unrefuted. "*onmyōdō* is about ten thousand phenomena, and that includes the past. We shall see. Follow me, and touch nothing."

They went to the darkened house, Kaworu and Orochimaru carrying lanterns, and once again Tsurugu walked through the empty rooms, wishing he were not yoked with the ambitious cousin.

Makino squatted to look at the pile of mostly burned pages beneath Orochimaru's lantern, surprisingly obedient in not touching. Even the surviving bits were difficult to read, and not only for their damage. "This is *wakan konkou shou*," he realized. "I can't read it."

"Only the most educated can." Tsurugu enjoyed the flash of frustration Makino betrayed, and it did not matter that Tsurugu could not read the esoteric language, either. "But there is not enough to decipher, anyway." He bent over the writing desk beside the dried blood, examining the ink-stone. "But perhaps we will not need to."

"Tsurugu-sama?"

Tsurugu ignored him and turned to Kaworu. "Go and bring

Naka-dono and Minamoto-dono. I believe we have their answer."

Daimyō Naka no Yoritomo and Minamoto Katanori seated themselves at the room's edge where Tsurugu indicated. "What do you have to show us?"

"I'm afraid we must wait," Tsurugu said. "I cannot say how long, so we must be patient—but we must be here. If I have identified it correctly, it will come as the night progresses."

Makino, sitting slightly behind Minamoto, fidgeted and clearly wanted to speak. He had nothing to say, however; Tsurugu had not pointed out the answer to him.

Kaworu and Orochimaru set lanterns to illuminate the corners beyond the light at the writing desk. They sat still, waiting.

It started with a tiny sound, like the lap of a puddle if it developed a tide. Tsurugu strained his eyes to focus on the writing desk, and there was a blur about the ink-stone. The sloshing grew louder, and he began to distinguish motion on the surface of the stone, now glistening as if newly wet for ink.

"Are those—waves?" breathed Minamoto.

"Tsurugu-sama, what is this?" asked Naka.

The ink-stone brimmed and spilled ink across the writing desk, and waves began to roll across the polished wood.

"It is a *suzuri no tamashii*," answered Tsurugu. "A spirit resides in this ink-stone, and it has absorbed the tale written with the stone."

Boats appeared on the sea of ink, all in deep black like the waves they rode. They faced one another, flying equally black flags. But even without their colors, Naka no Yoritomo knew them. "The Taira and the Minamoto. This is the battle of Dan no Ura."

The two great clans had clashed for years before meeting in

a final, brutal naval battle. In the end, the Minamoto triumphed, and Minamoto Yoritomo became the first shogun.

The ocean of ink spread and spilled off the writing desk, shaping itself on the *tatami* into the straits of Shimonoseki. The spectators shifted further back, avoiding the splash of ink against the rocks. The two fleets clashed, with tiny inky arrows flying between them and intricate warriors falling into the black sea, screaming over the growing sound of the waves.

Makino watched in fascination. He was too young to have seen it, and no telling of Dan no Ura could match the marvel of watching it unfold in horrific miniature.

Archery gave way to boarding and hand-to-hand combat. Ships sank or began to drift unmanned, and it became apparent the Minamoto would prevail. The Taira saw it, too. On one ship, tiny black figures began to gather at the edge, and these were not wearing armor but the elaborate *juuni-hito* of court women.

Naka-dono's fist tightened on his thigh.

The women began to leap into the water, pulled beneath the waves by their many layers. A Minamoto ship rushed toward theirs, but they continued to jump. One held a box, ornate even in its solid black reproduction, and took it with her into the sea. Another clutched a sword and a child in regal attire, and with a mask of absolute resolution she carried both with her into the water.

The Minamoto arrived and men swarmed over the ship, catching at the remaining women and pulling them back from the edge. Some looked over, pointing.

Then the boats blurred into the sea, merging with the waves, and the ink rolled back, leaving the silhouette of a sword drifting downward. A swimmer, tearing off bits of light armor, dove and caught it before leveling off and swimming away from the chaos. The black figures separated and shrank back, back into the ink-stone, leaving the desk and *tatami* unstained.

"The sword," murmured Naka no Yoritomo, breathless with

excitement. "He had the sword. Who is he?"

Minamoto exhaled. "That is the man we came to find," he said. "And Kusanagi."

"Tell me, Kaworu," said Tsurugu, "what personality does Makino-sama bear?"

Kaworu wrinkled his nose. "Lessons again, *onmyōji-sama?*"

Tsurugu gave him a stern look full of more humor than reprimand.

Tsurugu's private quarters often permitted a very different picture than before the rest of the household. Just now Kaworu and Gennosuke were playing at a game they had scratched into the dirt floor. Kaworu was *kitsune*, a young fox *yōkai* entrusted to Tsurugu, and Gennosuke was one of the daimyō's shadows, working unseen in silent, ruthless efficiency but concealed for this journey as a simple laborer. These three were bound by obligation and experience, and here in this private space there were no masks.

"Is his personality balanced?" Tsurugu pressed. While Kaworu was not meant to become an *onmyōji*, his education was part of Tsurugu's responsibilities.

"No," Kaworu answered without hesitation. "He is Metal. *Myou,* not *on.*" He frowned in thought. "Possibly born in the year and hour of the Horse and Rooster. That would give him the tendencies toward impatience, brash speech, and ambition, and then he has not schooled himself against these."

"There are five elements," Gennosuke said, making his move on the impromptu game board, "and then the twelve animal signs, which makes sixty tendencies, and each may be *on* or *myou,* I remember that much. But I forget the rest."

Kaworu quickly played his turn and straightened with the pride of knowledge. "There are also the five planets, the eight directions, and the twenty-eight guest stars," he began. "These all bear an influence, and together these tendencies and influences will suggest probabilities and auspicious—"

"I win." Gennosuke marked the game board and grinned at Kaworu's consternation.

Tsurugu stifled his smile and uncovered the *chokuban*, the domed divining board marked with the stars, directions, and lunar mansions Kaworu had been listing.

Kaworu, anxious to shift the focus from his loss, turned to his master. "Are you reading for the murder?"

Tsurugu shook his head. "No. Makino-sama was correct in that, at least; *onmyōdō* is not a way of reading the past. But I will read for Kusanagi."

"So they are looking for a sword? Why a sword?" Kaworu was clever in many things, but he was not always familiar with the details of human politics. "What is Kusanagi?"

Tsurugu looked at Gennosuke. "You should know this."

"I know some of it," he hedged.

Tsurugu sighed in mock despair. "See how you both have fish heads for brains," he said. "Now listen."

Susano-o had been cast from heaven for his grave affront to his sister Amaterasu, and as he wandered the earth he discovered three people sobbing together. The husband and wife explained they lost a daughter each year to the dreaded Yamata no Orochi, a great serpent with eight heads and eight tails. Seven daughters they had lost, and now they expected to lose their eighth and last daughter, the young woman who cried with them.

Susano-o thought the young woman beautiful despite her tears and asked, "Will you give your daughter to me?"

Marriage to this strange deity seemed better than certain death to the great serpent, and they agreed. Susano-o promptly began to prepare for battle. He directed the parents to brew powerful sake, eight times refined, and to build eight platforms to support eight vats.

Then Yamata no Orochi appeared, crawling over hills and valleys and covering all with his presence. He was a terrible beast, with all his eyes red like cherries or blood, and he came to where they waited, and he found the sake. Each head went to a vat and drank all, and so powerful was the wine that each head, upon finishing, drooped and fell asleep upon the ground.

Then Susano-o went to work with his magic sword Worochi no Ara-masa, and he struck off each of the eight heads. The river flowed with the blood of the dragon. Not content with this work, he went around the serpent and began to strike off each tail. But when he came to the fourth tail, his sword broke, shattering as it sliced.

Susano-o thought it very strange that his sword should break on a tail, and he opened the cut to see what was inside. There he found another sword, a great sword beyond his own magic blade. He drew it out of the serpent, and he named it Ama-no-Murakumo-no-Tsurugi, the Sword of Heaven's Gathering Clouds.

"But that explains nothing," protested Kaworu. "Now we have two magic swords, and neither of them is Kusanagi."

"Patience, Kaworu," Tsurugu said with a smile. "It is indeed the same sword. Susano-o presented it to his sister Amaterasu, a gift to settle their differences. Through her shrine it came to the legendary Yamato Takeru."

"I know him!" Kaworu exclaimed, glad for familiar ground. "He was a prince and a warrior, and he fathered an emperor, and his stories are still told a thousand years later." His face lit up with recognition. "Wait! This was his sword?"

"Yes. Why don't you finish the tale, and let's see what you remember."

"He was on a grass plain, and a rival killed his horse and set the plain afire, to kill him. Yamato Takeru in desperation tried to use his sword to cut the grass and deprive the fire of fuel, but in doing so he discovered his sword's swing could control the wind. So he used his sword instead to enlarge the fire and turn it back upon his attacker."

"And so he lived that day, and had the opportunity to rename his sword Kusanagi no Tsurugi, the Grasscutter."

Kaworu grinned, pleased at having come out clever in the end.

"Yamato Takeru, as you said, fathered an emperor, and the Kusanagi became part of the imperial regalia, proof of the emperor's divine heritage and right to rule. It was kept in the imperial palace or in Atsuta Shrine for a thousand years, until Taira no Munemori took the child emperor and the imperial regalia—the sword, the *magatama*, and the mirror—and fled from the Minamoto. When at last they met at sea, the court women meant to keep both the emperor and the regalia from the victorious Minamoto."

"By leaping overboard," said Kaworu.

"The emperor's grandmother took the sword with herself and the child. Another attendant leapt overboard with the *magatama*. A third tried to drown herself with the mirror, but the boarding soldiers seized her before she could leap. The *magatama* was in its protective coffer and floated free once the drowned woman released it, and it was recovered."

"But not the sword."

"Swords don't float. And that was the last anyone has seen of the Kusanagi."

"But Fujiwara Morihito believed he knew where it was," recalled Kaworu.

"And he is dead." Tsurugu raised an eyebrow. "Which means?"

Gennosuke nodded. "Which means he did know something, or there would have been no reason to kill him."

Kaworu frowned. "But how is the emperor enthroned, if the sword was lost?"

Tsurugu raised a finger. "Ah, there's the question. Some say the sword on the ship was a replica, and the real sword was safe in Atsuta Shrine and is yet there. But no one has seen it." He turned the dome of the *chokuban* as he spoke. "The Fujiwara have been closely tied to the emperor for centuries. If anyone were to know a state secret about the missing imperial sword, it could be one of them." He looked expectantly at his audience. "And he who has the sword...."

"...Has the imperial regalia and so the Chrysanthemum Throne," concluded Gennosuke.

"And our master?"

"Naka-dono serves the shogun," answered Gennosuke promptly, "who governs in the name of the emper—oh! Who could *be* emperor, if he could show the regalia!"

Tsurugu smiled. "Very clever."

"So someone learned the location of the sword—from Fujiwara-dono, or from the papers that were burned—and then killed to keep the secret."

Naka no Yoritomo's men found no sign of a landed boat in either direction for a long way. They did question the inhabitants of the river village which lay three miles to the southeast of the empty house.

"They say they rarely saw dealings with Fujiwara-dono," reported the officer. "They say they did not know his name, only that a great man lived here in solitude. A fish merchant had most recent trade, but that was a week ago and of course he dealt only with servants. No one knew of any boats coming this direction, no matter how we questioned them."

There was another river settlement to the west, and it likewise proved initially fruitless. But a chance comment caught Naka-dono's attention. "What was that?"

"A dragon, *tono*. A child said he'd seen a dragon in the river. We did not believe him; the weather has been fine and sunny, and no one else saw it."

Naka no Yoritomo glanced at Tsurugu.

Tsurugu shook his head. "There may be a minor dragon of this river, but if so he is not near. I could hardly fail to notice a dragon in my readings." The dragons of ordinary rivers were nothing like the dragon gods of the seas, but they were powerful enough.

Makino made a face. "If you please, I believe there are other *yōkai* to be found and questioned. Tsurugu-sama found the *suzuru no tamashii* in the ink, but I would search along the river for other witnesses. *Yōkai* are everywhere and they see much. I will trap one and interrogate it."

Minamoto-dono nodded. "That is sound. Go and look."

Tsurugu walked near the river, with Gennosuke following. Naka-dono believed him looking for *yōkai* informants, but his mind was filled with swords, gods, and dragons.

Kaworu burst from the growth, and the expression on his face was enough. "Show me where," Tsurugu said.

He followed the servant to the empty house's garden, where

a handsome man crouched in a circle of colored *magatama* and lines in the mud. His shoulders were hunched and his lips were drawn back in a feral display directed at Makino Koretoshi. Behind his master, Orochimaru squatted, his eyebrows drawn together.

"I have told you enough," growled the man. "Let me go."

Makino looked around as Tsurugu arrived, and the man in the circle moved. Immediately Makino turned back, clenching his fingers compulsively, and the man was trapped as the spell tightened again.

"I have found an informant," declared Makino.

"A *kawauso*, I see," agreed Tsurugu.

The river otter in human form glanced at Tsurugu, and his fierce expression faltered. Tsurugu made a quieting gesture. "Be at peace, friend." He frowned at Makino. "Are you trying to force him?"

"He saw something," Makino said. "Tell him what you told me."

The *kawauso* curled his lip. "I saw a snake," he said stiffly. "A snake in the river."

Tsurugu made a show of resisting rolling his eyes. "A snake, you say? In the river?"

"It was a large snake!" Makino added.

"And you think this snake killed Fujiwara-dono? Have you seen a snake bite leave so much blood?"

Makino hesitated. "I thought it might have eaten him. Perhaps he was killed, and then the snake ate the body."

"And then how does the snake help us to solve the murder?"

Makino opened his mouth, fishing for a response, and the *kawauso* darted out of the circle as the *onmyōji*'s concentration wavered. He bounded away a few strides and looked back, grinning. "I'll tell the snake you asked for him."

Orochimaru laughed, and Makino cuffed the back of the boy's skull. "It is a magic sword," he said to Tsurugu petulantly.

"The *yōkai* must know something of it."

"Most do not concern themselves with human affairs," Tsurugu answered. He turned toward the house, leading the others inside. "It is a reasonable question, but we should not be surprised when it is not a profitable one."

But inwardly he nodded to himself. Fujiwara-dono had not been carried away in a basket or boat.

"And have you a more profitable question?" demanded Makino.

Tsurugu turned to Kaworu and Gennosuke behind him. "Who would kill to keep the sword from the shogun?"

"The Taira," offered Kaworu promptly. "It was they who lost power, and allowing a Minamoto shogun to become emperor would doom them forever."

Tsurugu's insult—asking a servant to guess what Makino had not—struck its mark. Makino's jaw tightened. "So we look among the Taira," he said, as if he had deduced it himself, and as if there were not hundreds of Taira to question.

Tsurugu went into the room where Fujiwara-dono had died and seated himself near the abandoned writing desk. "How will you do that?"

"There are many small strongholds of escaped Taira; that village may be one. Those dull soldiers would not have seen it. I will go and question them in my own way."

Makino started away, disdainful of etiquette. Tsurugu gave a tiny nod of his head, and Gennosuke moved to stand in the doorway, facing Makino with an air no servant could ever adapt toward a court official.

Makino hesitated and then pointed fiercely. "I have been suspicious of you all along! A skilled *onmyōji* may have inhuman servants. But I will deal with you as you deserve!" He produced a *shime-kazari*, a wand tipped with a long zig-zag of folded paper, and began to wave it deliberately as he chanted.

Gennosuke stretched out his hand and crumpled the paper

in his fist.

Makino released the wand as if it were aflame and jerked his hand to his body. Gennosuke let the *shime-kazari* fall to the floor.

"He is not *yōkai*," Tsurugu said wearily. "He is as human as you. But he will not allow you to leave this place to scour the Taira."

Makino turned to Tsurugu. "Why not?"

"Think what will happen if you carry the story that the Kusanagi is in the world," Tsurugu said. "Already there has been death, and it has not even been found. Ambitious men will continue to kill for the mere rumor of it, and once it is located, armies will be assembled and great battles will be waged for the possession of it. The *bakufu* will collapse, as daimyō turns against daimyō, and the emperor cannot retake power, not now, not without a government." Tsurugu shook his head. "It will be like throwing a haunch of deer among twenty starving dogs."

Makino sniffed. "But what if I approached a powerful daimyō? Your daimyō, perhaps? And I delivered the sword to him?"

"And earned yourself great favor and wealth?" Tsuguru smiled. "Why not? But you must find it first. Do you think you can search without drawing attention?"

"You underestimate me," snapped Makino, his expression dark. "It will be to your disgrace. One day soon I shall return to your master, and I shall give him the sword, and he will be emperor—and you will be nothing, cast out in the dirt that you are, and I will be his *onmyōji*."

Tsurugu raised a hand in mild surrender. "Then, dirt that I am, I cannot stop you. I only caution you to take care with such great stakes."

"Men like you are always cautioning those who threaten them," retorted Makino, "to keep us in our place. But we will displace you."

They were bold words, and Tsurugu might have challenged

him for such rudeness. Might have tried once more to save his life. But Makino was determined, and so he only sighed and said, "Gennosuke, let him pass if he wishes."

Gennosuke frowned but obeyed. Makino went out the door, and they heard his footsteps upon the *rou*. Tsurugu reached and caught Orochimaru by the back of his *happi* to restrain him, shaking his head.

The footsteps continued and then paused. "Orochimaru!"

"Let him be," said Tsurugu, holding the servant's gaze. If Orochimaru were the only one, if Tsurugu could convince him—

Makino cried out, and Tsurugu's stomach clenched. Makino garbled the first few syllables of a chant and then screamed. Something heavy struck the wooden screen and then slid to the *rou*.

Gennosuke looked to Tsurugu, ready to run outside. Tsurugu shook his head, twisting his mouth with regret. "No. Not you, too."

The struggle went silent. Orochimaru looked upward at Tsurugu.

Tsurugu sighed. "Now, Gennosuke."

Gennosuke eased out the door. He returned a moment later. "He's dead," he reported. "His neck's broken."

Tsurugu nodded slowly. "He played with imbalance. An *onmyōji* should have known better."

"You knew he would die?"

"An *onmyōji* does not predict the future," Tsurugu repeated, raising a cautionary finger. "He reads the tendencies and thereby supposes the probabilities. Makino announced openly that he would defy both the emperor and the shogun. It was not hard to suppose one or the other would kill him."

Kaworu nodded, his eyes wide. Neither he nor Gennosuke were strangers to death, but they had not expected it so suddenly and so near.

"Or, that is what will be said, at least," Tsurugu continued.

Kaworu and Gennosuke looked at him. "What? Is that not what happened?"

But Tsurugu was looking at Orochimaru. "That is what I will report to Minamoto-sama."

Orochimaru bowed to Tsurugu and turned toward the door. Gennosuke yet stood in the way. "Wait," he said to Orochimaru. "What does he mean?"

Orochimaru's expression lost the blank passivity of a servant. "Let me pass," he said, "on the rank of my master."

"Your master is dead!" returned Gennosuke.

"He is not," interrupted Tsurugu quietly. "Makino was never his master, despite what Makino thought."

Gennosuke's eye twitched. "A shadow? For which lord?"

Orochimaru laughed, a sound so inappropriate for his position that it chilled them all. "My master is greater than yours, and greater than your master's master."

"Greater than the shogun? The emperor, then? Did he send you to find the sword?"

"No, Gennosuke." Tsurugu gestured. "Stop and listen."

They quieted, eyeing one another. Kaworu shifted his weight subtly, ready to pounce.

Orochimaru spoke first, no longer a servant. "Go on, then, *onmyōji-sama*."

Tsurugu inclined his head in gentle thanks. "The Kusanagi was taken from a great serpent in the west," he began. "It was lost again to the sea, also in the west."

Kaworu caught his breath with an audible click in his throat, and he went very still.

Gennosuke, less familiar with the inhuman world, needed more. "I don't understand."

"The eight-headed serpent, the great forked dragon, was called Yamata no Orochi," prompted Tsurugu, keeping his eyes on Orochimaru. "And dragons are creatures of water."

"Gōjun," supplied Kaworu in a breathless rush. "You serve

Gōjun. The Dragon King of the Western Sea." He swallowed. "He sent you for the sword."

"That is true." Orochimaru let his human guise slip away like a dropped *kimono*, and he faced them as an enormous snake. An *uwabami*.

"Two were sent," Tsurugu surmised. "You went to the Minamoto to learn where the sword could be found, and the other killed Fujiwara-dono—and now Makino."

Orochimaru nodded. "The sword was cast into the sea by the imperial family," he said. "They relinquished their claim to it. Before it was theirs, it belonged to Amaterasu, and before it was hers, it belonged to Gōjun. I have only come to reclaim what is his own."

"No one here opposes you," said Tsurugu. "What I said about chaos is true." And they would not open war with a sea dragon.

Orochimaru nodded, undulating slightly.

Tsurugu sat forward and asked, "Could we see it? Just look on it?" Something so sacred and powerful....

Orochimaru considered. "It is not a thing for mortals. It is for gods and emperors."

"We won't touch it," said Tsurugu. "Please."

Orochimaru extended upward, his long, thick body rising and pressing upward on a ceiling panel, pushing into the space between ceiling and roof. He brought down a wooden box nearly as long as Kaworu was tall.

A chill set Tsurugu's hairs on end. In all his long life, he could see this only once, and only by chance.

Orochimaru took human form to work the latches. Inside the wooden box was another box of smooth, carved stone, padded with clay. Within the stone box lay a striated log, rich with red and brown streaks and with a penetrating fragrance. Camphor wood, Tsurugu realized. Orochimaru lifted the log with great care, tipping it upward so that he could reach inside. It was hollow, and lined with gold.

Orochimaru withdrew his hand, revealing the sword.

Kusanagi no Tsurugi was a thing of eerie beauty, roughly the length of a man's leg and with a long, thin blade.

"It's not curved," wondered Gennosuke.

"No, of course not," answered Tsurugu, consciously steadying his voice. "This is not like the *tachi* you know today. This is an ancient sword, nearly two thousand years old."

The blade had a thick raised center which spread into the cutting edge like a fish's spine—or a snake's, Tsurugu thought. The blade itself was a striking silvery-white, and it showed no sign of rust.

Tsurugu felt an overwhelming urge to touch it, to brush the blade, but he folded his hands together tightly. There were many ways to experience a thing without pawing at it, and it was more respectful to gaze upon it and appreciate its beauty than to smudge it with his fingers.

Kaworu, who must also be able to sense the power of the sword, sat back on his haunches and showed no temptation to reach for it. *We all experience power in different ways.*

"What about the emperor?" asked Gennosuke. His voice was thick. "He is still the descendent of gods and the ruler of this land." He looked at Orochimaru. "I serve the daimyō, who serves the shogun, who serves the emperor. This sword belonged to your master, but it was also given to mine."

Orochimaru smiled. "Do you think you can take it from me, human boy?"

Gennosuke's jaw clenched, and Tsurugu spoke before he could answer. "It is not ours to reclaim," he said hurriedly. "It is, as you said, a thing for immortals and emperors. If Amaterasu means for her descendent to bear it again, let her look after it, and it is none of our affair."

Orochimaru nodded, pleased. "It is a question between gods," he agreed. "Thank you for your discretion, *onmyōji-sama.*

We will remember you."

Tsurugu bowed. "Thank you for your kindness."

He rose and gestured for Kaworu and Gennosuke to follow. He had to report Makino's death and somehow explain the sword was gone—perhaps say it had never been saved from the sea at all, that the story was only a story. But there would be peace, among warlords and between dragon king and humanity, if the fate of Kusanagi remained a mystery.

Orochimaru replaced the sword, shrouding it from human sight forever.

Luck is a gift from the gods, but fortune has to be earned.

The Cat of Five Virtues

Richard Parks

Soon after the fall of the Taira Clan, a boy was born to a Genji samurai named Takamasa. As his beloved wife died after giving the boy life, he concluded that the child was unlucky. He named the boy Taro, meaning 'eldest son', in the belief there would eventually be others born of a more fortunate nature. In this Takamasa was mistaken, since in due course a new principal wife and two junior wives all failed to give him any more children. Prayers at the local temple proved ineffective, and so he turned to older means.

"Clearly, I have offended the gods in some fashion," Takamasa said. "And so I must make amends."

The next morning Takamasa set out with two servants bearing offerings of cloth and *saké*. The northern road eventually led them past a hill with bright red torii gates marking the path upward. The path was shaded by maples now showing autumn colors, and the lack of sunlight reminded them of the changing season. Takamasa shivered. It had been some time since he had last visited the shrine. Taro's mother had been a faithful devotee of the gods, but Takamasa preferred temples. The path of enlightenment seemed simple if not easy, and the Buddha either distant or within all, making him less of an immediate concern.

The gods were different. The gods were at once very

powerful and yet far too much like people—easy to offend, often capricious, and likely to have their own interests which either did not or emphatically *did* include you, and it was hard to say which situation could be worse.

They passed between a pair of mossy stone foxes guarding the path and reached the outer shrine. After purifying themselves at a basin of spring water, Takamasa paid his respects to the wizened old priest, who, for the consideration of his offerings, agreed to speak to the *kami* of the shrine on Takamasa's behalf. While the servants waited outside, the old man waved a baton crowned with paper folded in a zig-zag pattern over Takamasa and muttered words the samurai could not hear. After a few minutes the priest opened his eyes, having closed them for most of the ceremony.

"The god has spoken, Takamasa-sama, and I fear you are mistaken," he said.

"I don't understand," Takamasa said. "My wife died giving birth to the child. I have been denied any further issue. How is this not unlucky?"

The priest looked somber. "The death of your poor wife was indeed unfortunate, but it was not the will of the gods. Rather it was her fate, a realm in which even the gods cannot intervene. I fear you are mistaken as to the boy as well."

Takamasa felt his anger rising. "Are you saying the gods refuse to aid me? To relieve my curse?"

"Not at all, young sir, and please calm yourself. What I am saying is there *is no curse*, and the gods have already aided you. Your late wife was a great favorite of this shrine, and out of respect for her the *kami* resident here have bestowed on the boy a gift of good luck which will extend to your entire household. You are, however, cautioned to never question or spurn this gift, or it will be free to depart from you."

Takamasa frowned. "I certainly would not question good fortune, but I have not seen any sign thus far."

"How old is the child now?"

"He turns five years old in a fortnight."

The old man smiled. "The time was not right, but the *kami* of our shrine has foretold this—after the child's coming birthday, you will see proof what we have told you is true. Please return to your home, and wait for the sign."

Takamasa was far from convinced. Even so, he had no other real options and saw no harm in doing as the priest had said. He did resolve to pay the old man a further visit if his prophecy proved false.

When Taro moved through the women's quarters of his father's house, he almost felt furtive, as if he were in the act of doing something wrong. Not yet five, he did understand that he had a birthday coming that very next morning and that meant mostly good things, perhaps a present or two, but it also meant he was getting older, and soon the women's quarters would be off-limits to him. He did not really understand why this needed to be so. He liked his stepmother Akiko-sama and the two junior wives and their attendants—they wrote poetry and told each other stories, and they did not mind when he listened. By contrast his father never had much time for him, and that was unlikely to change as Takamasa was a busy man with many duties.

"When I am older, I will learn the sword and be of service to my father," he said to himself, though he wasn't sure if that would really happen. Perhaps he would be sent to a temple; he had heard Takamasa and his stepmother discuss the possibility, and he was grateful when Akiko-sama opposed the idea. He could not be of use to his father there.

On this particular evening the air had turned chilly, and Taro curled up in a corner of the room as the women gathered around the central hearth and chatted to each other and sang, and in time their songs soothed until his eyelids grew heavy and he fell asleep. When he awoke, it was full night, and the women had withdrawn to their sleeping quarters. This was not the first time such a thing had happened. Taro had learned how to make himself inconspicuous, especially around his father.

"I guess no one noticed me here," he said to himself.

"I noticed you," said a new voice.

First the newcomer was not there, and then he was. A boy about his own age, wearing white clothing as if for a funeral. Taro thought his vision must still be blurred from sleep, because he was certain the boy was glowing. Taro wondered if he should be afraid, so he decided to ask.

"Who are you? Are you a ghost? Have you come to harm me?"

"Of course he's not a ghost. He is a Zashiki-Warashi," said an entirely different voice.

Taro looked around and noticed a female cat lying beside the hearth. At least, he thought it was a cat, but it was like no cat he had ever seen before. It was black and white, with green eyes and a tail forked like the two tines of a fishing spear. On its head was a metal tripod of the sort sometimes used to hold small braziers, which the cat wore like a crown.

"Excuse me, but did you say something?"

The cat let out a gusting sigh, stirring the ashes in the hearth. "Honestly...do you see anyone else here?" asked the cat.

"I'm sorry I was rude. It's just that I've never seen a talking cat before," Taro said. "Or a...what you said."

"Zashiki-Warashi," the cat repeated the term slowly. "I suggest you learn his name and nature. It is important."

The Zashiki-Warashi nodded, looking pleased. "Important," he said, and the cat sighed again.

"He's cheerful enough but rather simple now. That will change in time as he becomes more accustomed to people," the cat said. "And as for me, normally you would not see me at all, though

I've been here since before you were born. I don't like to be seen, as a rule."

"Then why am I seeing you now, Cat?"

The cat yawned. "That is actually a very good question, for one so young. The reason you are seeing me is, like him," it said, pointing a paw at the shining boy, who was now staring, fascinated, at a glowing ember, "I have been given a task by the gods, part of which was to introduce you to the Zashiki-Warashi of this household. It would be very difficult to complete this task if you never even knew I was here."

Taro thought her words made sense. "I think I have been rude again, to call you just 'Cat'. Have you a name?"

"I do," the cat said. "I am Gotaku-Neko, also known as the Cat of Five Virtues. Either of which is a very large name, and so too noticeable. If you must refer to me, 'Cat' will do. Now then, a Zashiki-Warashi is a spirit of good luck."

"So he's lucky?" Taro asked.

"As is the household where one such resides, but in your case it goes beyond that—he is good luck itself, given shape and form. He has come to live in this house as a gift of the gods to you, and as long as he stays here, you, your father and your entire family will be lucky."

"Wonderful!" Taro said. "I can hardly wait to tell my father...." His voice faded away when he noticed both the spirit of luck and the cat waving their hands—or paws—frantically. "No?"

"Never," the cat said. "This good fortune was given to you specifically, so only you can see it or talk to it. Please understand—it's true your father knows you were given the gift of luck, but only you can know the form your luck has taken. If you tell anyone, your luck will leave."

"But why?"

The cat stretched and yawned, showing sharp white teeth. "Another good question. The gods can be kind, but they are fond of rules, so this is the rule of a good luck spirit. I was tasked by the gods to make you understand this so that you would not lose your luck the first day you had it. That is why I allowed you to see and hear me."

"That was indeed kind of the gods," Taro said. "And of you." He bowed to both the cat and the spirit of luck. "I will try to be worthy of you both."

The cat pulled a bamboo tube out of its fur like a person producing something from a fold in their kimono. She used it to blow and the coals and bring them back to a cherry red, as several had been on the brink of going out. "Ffft," she said, as she put the pipe away. "If you are *really* lucky, you will never see me again. My obedience to the gods is my first virtue. My discretion is my second. This is my third."

With that, the cat disappeared.

"She is still there," the luck spirit said.

"I wondered," Taro said. "But I will not bother her. What may I call you? Your title is quite a mouthful for me."

The shining boy frowned and Taro was afraid he had offended him already, but after a moment he brightened and Taro realized he had only been concentrating.

"Call me Luck," the shining boy said. "It's what I am."

Taro smiled. "Thank you."

The day following Taro's fifth birthday, a courier arrived from Kamakura. Taro and Akiko-sama hurried to the small audience hall where they both waited anxiously to discover what the message was about. Such communications were never less than important, and more often than not unpleasant. Only this time when Takamasa finished reading, there was a smile on his face.

"Husband, what is the news?" Akiko asked.

"It concerns Amatoki-sama," he said, naming the holder of

the adjoining fief. "It seems he has chosen to renounce the world and enter the monastery at Mount Oe."

Amatoki was an older samurai whose wife had died the year before, so his decision to essentially retire was not unexpected, but then Akiko-sama asked the obvious question.

"A blessing for him, Husband, but how does this concern us?"

Takamasa grunted. "As Amatoki has no children it seems the Shogun has granted his fief to me. With the addition of these lands, I am now master of this entire valley and will be granted a title and rank in keeping with my new status."

"Husband, this is wonderful news!"

"It is indeed," Takamasa said, but then he gave Taro a strange look that the boy did not understand. It was neither stern in his usual manner nor cheerful. If anything, Taro thought he looked a little frightened.

Later that evening as the sun was setting, Taro found the boy called Luck wandering near the well in their back courtyard.

"Good evening," he said politely.

"The answer is yes. Sort of," Luck replied.

Taro blinked. "Excuse me?"

"Sorry. It was the answer to the question you wanted to ask me, wasn't it? Yes, your father's good fortune was due to your good fortune. I didn't cause it. Say rather it happened because I am here."

It was a little hard to follow all the threads of thought that Luck was weaving, but Taro understood the heart of it. "The Cat of Five Virtues said you were simple. I think you're smarter than I am."

"She also told you that I would change, and she's usually right. It's true, I had fewer words then, but the Cat of Five Virtues did speak the truth in that as well—I *am* simple," Luck said. "That is not the same as stupid. Come to that, neither are you. Stupid, I meant."

"Are such things going to continue? This would be wonderful for my father."

"For him, for you, and for all of your household," Luck corrected. "Your stepmother, your servants...everyone. So long as you are in the household and no one sends me away. I am *your* Luck."

"I would never send you away," Taro said. "though there has been talk of sending *me* away to the temple."

Luck laughed. When he could speak again, he said, "That would be fortunate for the temple, but do not worry. Such talk is at an end. You will soon see that I am right."

"I hope so," Taro said. "I do not wish to be given to the temple. Let us return to the house. I'm not supposed to be out after dark."

Taro did not think anyone saw him as he escorted Luck back into the house, but Takamasa had been watching his son from the veranda for some time. Since the boy apparently had walked and talked with no one, Takamasa was not pleased.

Takamasa told Akiko what he had seen, but she was not overly concerned.

"My brothers, when they were that age, would sometimes do the same. It is nothing. It will stop as he grows older."

But five years passed. Then five more. Takamasa's standing with his overlord and among the Genji did nothing but increase, but still now and again Taro—now called Masatoki, as he had reached his early adult years and been granted a proper adult name—would be seen talking to no one. Otherwise Takamasa had no real cause for complaints, where his son was concerned. First of all, the luck that the shrine priest had promised had come thrice over. Takamasa was now the governor of the entire province, and his family lived in a grand castle some miles from his old home, with many servants and attendants and a garrison of *bushi* at his command. In addition, his son was showing great promise at horsemanship, archery, and the sword, and it was clear the warriors under Takamasa's command were coming to respect the young man. And yet....

My son still talks to nothing. How is he to inherit this?

Takamasa could not picture his son assuming his place, even though it was his dearest wish. His enemies—and he knew he had more than a few—would likely find out and seize on the matter to have his son removed once Takamasa was gone. There was no way to hide the unfortunate situation—Takamasa knew that Masatoki's odd behavior must surely have been noticed by the servants and was likely common knowledge, but according to Akiko, who as mistress of the household was in closer contact with the servants than he was, no one had mentioned it, nor had she noticed anything of the sort herself.

"Surely you must have," Takamasa said, but his wife was firm.

"Never. I believe you, Husband, of course, but in all our interactions, I have never seen it."

"He only does it when he thinks he's alone," Takamasa said.

"But he is not?"

"Well...I've made it a point to seek him out at such times, and observe. He always does it."

"That is very strange," Akiko said. "One might think he understood how strange it would look and was trying to conceal his actions. Have you spoken to him about it?"

"What should I say? 'Son, stop talking to nothing'?"

"I wish I could advise you better, Husband. I can see that this worry is troubling you and likely has for some time. If this continues, it will only get worse."

Takamasa knew that his wife was right, but the guilt and awkwardness he always felt in the presence of his late first-wife's child had never left him. Then he had an idea.

"Wife, will you speak to him? I know he likes you."

"I hope so, but surely this would be best coming from you?"

Takamasa demurred. "I know how to deal with men, and even though Masatoki is almost a man himself, matters have always been—strained, between us."

"He adores you. Surely you must know that?"

"Even so, I would get angry and likely accomplish nothing. I will listen, but it would be best if he does not know of my presence."

"As you wish, Husband, but perhaps it would be better if I spoke to him alone? I could then perhaps soften any blows that need to be struck."

"You know my temper, Wife, so perhaps you are right. But this uncertainty is driving me to distraction. I want to hear the answer directly from my son."

Knowing he would not be dissuaded, Akiko withdrew to the southern veranda and sent a servant to fetch Masatoki while Takamasa concealed himself behind the sliding *shoji* screen that served as the door. Masatoki soon presented himself, bowed low, and kneeled at a respectful distance.

"You wished to see me, Stepmother?"

"I did. Your father and I have become concerned about you."

Masatoki frowned. "Have I displeased you in some way?"

"Say rather that we are worried. You have been observed speaking, so far as we can tell, to no one. This has apparently occurred on several occasions. We—your father, especially—need to know why this is happening."

"Oh."

Looking into her stepson's eyes, Akiko immediately understood two things. The first was that what her husband had told her about Masatoki's activities was absolutely true, and the second was that her stepson was deeply afraid.

"What are you afraid of, Stepson? We only want to know the truth," she said, but Masatoki bowed.

"The truth is that I cannot tell you. I can only assure you—and my father, I trust—that there is no cause for concern."

"Even though you speak to empty air? Surely you understand why this would seem troubling? Why would you speak to nothing?"

"I am not speaking to nothing," he said, though the words seemed to pain him.

Akiko considered. "Then you are speaking to someone we cannot see, but perhaps, for whatever reason, you can? A spirit, perhaps?"

Masatoki took a deep breath. "Yes. A spirit. One that means us no harm."

Akiko hated the fear she saw in her stepson, but there was no choice except to press on. "Who is it? What is it? Surely you must understand that we would wish to know?"

"I do, and in your place I would, but I must beg you, Stepmother—please do not ask me that."

Could it be? she thought, though the question pained her.

"Is it the spirit of your mother?"

As soon as Akiko spoke the question, she realized it was a mistake, but it was too late. Takamasa shoved the screen aside and stormed out onto the veranda.

"Father," Masatoki said and bowed low again. He would not meet his father's eyes.

"Son, answer her. Is it the spirit of my first wife?"

"No, Father. It is not."

"Then tell me who it is. As your father, I command you to obey me."

Masatoki looked up then, and they both were stunned by the look of utter defeat on his face.

"It is my—and our—Luck, Father. That is who I have been speaking to. Only I can—could—see him."

Takamasa's scowl was as dark as a storm cloud. "What do you mean, 'could'?"

"He is gone, Father. Our luck is gone."

Masatoki bowed until his head touched the floor, and he began to weep.

Masatoki searched every room and all the grounds and gardens of the castle, but Luck was nowhere to be found. Masatoki had never really expected to find him, but searching gave him something to do to take his mind off of the bad news he knew would be coming. His Father had not spoken to him since his confession. Indeed, he had immediately left Masatoki and his wife on the veranda without saying another word. Masatoki tried not to worry, but he knew that worry was, unfortunately, indicated.

He searched past nightfall. All the servants had gone to bed when he finally reached the castle kitchens and its large open hearth.

A familiar voice arose. "You can stop looking. Luck has left you. He didn't want to, but rules are rules. He said he would miss you."

There lay the Cat of Five Virtues by the hearth, just as Masatoki remembered her. She yawned as any cat would, but then produced the bamboo tube from somewhere within her fur and gently puffed on the coals until they glowed bright again.

"A larger hearth in this castle and thus more work, but overall a nice thing," she said.

"I didn't expect you to show yourself," Masatoki said.

"Well, it's not as if you didn't *know* I was here. Luck told you. And you've seen me once already, which lessens the mystery. Besides, there was something else Luck told me to tell you."

"I would be grateful for anything. What was it?"

"He said that I must tell you that I really do not have five virtues. It's just a pun on one interpretation of the script for

Gotaku-Neko."

Masatoki frowned. "That seems an odd thing to ask you to say, and an odd thing to agree to say."

The cat yawned again. "Oh, I don't mind. It was a joke, and Luck was fond of jokes. I have at least five virtues. Possibly more."

"I would certainly not doubt it," Masatoki said.

"That is good. So. You had best head off to bed. You'll need your strength for tomorrow."

"Something bad is coming, isn't it?"

"My fourth virtue—wisdom. But then you have a touch of it yourself, don't you? You knew the bad thing was coming. When luck such as you had departs, it leaves a hole in your world. Something will always take the opportunity to fill it."

Masatoki took the cat's advice and tried to sleep, but sleep was difficult. When it finally came, much later in the night, it held him tight until almost mid-morning. When he had dressed and left his quarters he found the castle in an uproar, but no one he met and questioned was entirely sure as to why, only that there was terrible, terrible news. Masatoki went searching for his father and stepmother, and he found them in the audience hall. Strangely, his father was seated in state on the dais with his stepmother beside him, but there was no one else there. Akiko's eyes were red and swollen as if she had been weeping incessantly, but now she merely looked straight ahead, almost as if in shock.

"Son, I was about to send for you," Takamasa said.

Masatoki kneeled before the dais. "Father, what has happened?"

"I have been betrayed," he said simply. "The new steward of our southern estates was in league with pirates, and the entire year's production was being redirected to the coast. The captain of the garrison there spotted the subterfuge, but by then it was too late. At least the steward was caught, but most of the rice and cloth is gone."

"I'm sorry, Father, if only I had been more discreet in my

dealings with Luck—" he began, but his father interrupted. It was one of the few occasions he could remember ever seeing his father smile, only this time Masatoki felt a coldness settling over him like a blanket of snow.

"The priest who informed me of your gift also cautioned me against questioning it. I clearly did not understand what he meant, and if I had not, in my impatience, pushed for an answer rather than consulting the priests of the gods in this matter, I would have been reminded of the fact. This is my own doing, and it is I who must atone."

The question frightened him, but he had to ask it. "Father, what do you mean, 'atone'?"

"That estate's production was held in trust for the Shogun, and through my carelessness it was lost. We have some surplus, but not enough to cover it by half. Yet I am responsible for all of it."

"What must we do?"

"Son, it is what *I* must do. I will ask the Shogun for permission to commit *seppuku*. If he grants this, he will forgive the debt and allow my titles to pass on to you. I was just about to send a messenger to Kamakura."

"Father, please wait," Masatoki said. "There must be another way."

At that Akiko began to weep again, but Takamasa only sighed. "There is none."

Masatoki looked up. "What if I could get our luck back?"

"I have forced you to give up a gift from the gods. They will not bestow it again," Takamasa said.

"Three days," Masatoki said, though he did not know why, any more than he had really believed that he could retrieve what he knew must be lost forever. "Three days, starting tomorrow morning. I know it is a great deal to ask, but please, Father—three days. If I fail, then do what you think best. I could have defied you, kept the secret, and this misfortune would not have befallen us.

Please give me my own chance to atone."

Takamasa looked somber. "You only obeyed your father, which makes you a better son than I deserve. Very well, I do owe you that much. Three days. Not an hour longer. After which, I charge you to maintain my household and look after your stepmother as if she were your own mother. Swear to me."

"I swear I will do as you wish, Father."

"Then we are agreed. I would wish you luck, but I think perhaps now we need something else."

While he wandered the castle in the fading daylight Masatoki finally realized the implications of what he had asked.

If I have only given my father three more days to contemplate his death, I will never forgive myself. The worst part was he still had no idea what he could do. He resolved to visit the shrine where his father had first received word of the gods' gift. He wasn't sure if there was anything the priests could do, but at least it was a direction. He passed through the deserted kitchen on his way to his rooms, and he glanced at the empty place by the hearth where he knew the *Gotaku-Neko* was curled up, probably asleep.

"Good-bye," he said. "Please wish me luck."

"No," said the cat, "you know that is pointless."

Somewhat to Masatoki's surprise, the Cat of Five Virtues then appeared. She was sitting up, the tripod on her head looking even more like a crown.

"Perhaps it is," Masatoki said, "but I have to try."

"I didn't say the attempt was pointless. I said that hoping for or expecting good luck is pointless. Your luck no longer exists."

"Luck is dead?" Masatoki felt a great sadness. "I had thought he would merely move on to another."

The cat looked surprised. "Really? How could he? He was *your* luck, not another's. Luck still exists, of course, but this particular embodiment of luck did not once he left this house, so trying to find him is pointless. Was that clear enough?"

Masatoki found that his legs would no longer support him, and he simply sat down beside the hearth. "Then there is no hope."

"Honestly, do humans ever listen? I said nothing of the sort." The cat took her bamboo tube, but instead of stoking the fire, she reached out and rapped him across his head like an impatient schoolmaster.

"Oww!"

"I take it I have your attention? Good, because there are a couple of things you need to understand, if you are to get through your current troubles. The first is—this is not your fault."

"But I knew never to tell father—or anyone—about Luck. Yet I did so anyway."

The cat's gaze was, if not kind, as least somewhat sympathetic. "Could you really have disobeyed your father? Silly, that would also have cost you your luck, only another way. The fact is, Luck's departure was inevitable. A gift of the gods, yes, but with strictures almost impossible to honor. You always suspected something of the sort would happen, didn't you?"

Masatoki had to admit the truth. "I tried to be careful, speaking to Luck. I could not ignore him but I hoped no one would find out."

"Well, they did. Now then, the second thing you need to understand is related to something we already discussed—when a piece of luck is gone, it is gone forever. You cannot get it back. Good fortune, however, is different. That is the only thing which will save your father now."

Masatoki frowned. "I thought good fortune and good luck were the same thing."

"There is one difference, and it's an important one—luck simply comes to you or it doesn't. Fortune? It never comes on its own. You have to go look for it."

"Then I had best hope it is nearby. I only have three days," Masatoki said.

"You need a shortcut. I happen to have one."

"Is your fifth virtue kindness?" Masatoki asked.

The cat laughed. Masatoki had never heard a cat laugh before. He hoped, after this day, he would never hear that sound again.

"I'm a cat, silly boy," she said after she had regained her composure. "There is not a cat of any kind who considers kindness a virtue. No, my fifth virtue is knowledge. Which I have chosen to share with you."

"Why?" Masatoki asked, and the cat looked as if she were going to laugh again.

"Oh, you do have a bit of wisdom, don't you? I was right about that, but then I usually am."

"Luck said the same thing."

The cat ignored that. "When I first told you about Luck, it was because the gods commanded me, and one does not cross them lightly. I would say it is because Luck asked me to help you, and I was somewhat fond of him, but the truth is I like this household. You always have decent hearths, and the servants leave a bit of fish or something about so I never have to wander far. That is why I'm helping you, as any cat would—for my own benefit."

"Whatever the reason, I am grateful," Masatoki said. "What must I do?"

"For a start, do not bother with the priests. They can only tell you what the gods say, and I know exactly what they would say. No, rather take the southern road toward the coast and go on foot. I know a horse would be faster, but that is not the point here. So. After the first day you will meet someone who will ask for your help. Whoever that is, you must help them. If you do, fortune will come home with you. Now go rest, and leave at first light. You have a way to go."

Masatoki thanked the cat for her help and then went to bed. He slept well and rose early, and before the castle was fully awake, he was on the southern road. He brought the pair of swords his father had given him on his fifteenth birthday and some food and water but nothing else save the clothes he wore.

He set a brisk pace and did not forget to politely greet everyone he met along the way. The cat had said he would not find the person until the second day, but Masatoki didn't see any point in taking chances. He did meet several travelers, but no one asked for his help. He slept under the stars in a meadow near the road the first night and rose somewhat stiff and sore the next morning. He ate a rice cake for his breakfast and started walking. He walked until almost mid-morning, but in that time he met no one. He paused to rest under a spreading ginko tree by the side of the road.

"This is bad," he said aloud. "I haven't met anyone needing help, and if I go much further I won't be able to get home in time even if I do."

"Did you say you were looking for someone requiring assistance? I am such a one."

Startled, Masatoki put his hand on the hilt of his sword, but a quick glance around did not show anyone. Feeling a little foolish, he took his hand away.

"I could have sworn I heard someone asking for help," he said.

"You did, young sir. That was me."

Masatoki got to his feet and took a closer look around, but all he saw when he looked on the other side of the ginko trunk was an old sack made of heavy cloth, tattered and patched, slumped against the roots of the tree as if abandoned there.

"Strange...." Masatoki started to say, but then the bag opened two big black eyes and a rather large mouth and spoke to him.

"Am I really? I had no idea."

To his credit, Masatoki jumped only about a foot backwards, possibly because of his early exposure to such ideas as embodied luck and an invisible fork-tailed cat. Even so, he kept his hand near the larger of his two swords.

"What are you?"

"That is a good question," the bag said. "From my own point of view, I am a person requiring assistance. From yours, I think I must be very different."

"Very," Masatoki said, looking up and down the road. There was a clear view south, and he was certain there was no one else on the road for at least a league. "Then you must be the person I was told to meet. How may I assist you?"

"I have no idea who may have sent you," said the sack, "but I really could use your help. I have a journey north I must make and, well, you see the problem." The sack wiggled its bottom corners. "No feet."

Masatoki could have asked how the sack got to be where it was in the first place, but time was getting short, and he was too aware of its passage. He was content to simply accept the situation as it was.

"I am going north, at least for a while. Perhaps I can carry you at least part of the way."

"That would be very kind of you."

It was with some hesitation that Masatoki lifted the sack and slung it across his shoulders. He had heard stories of *yōkai*, monsters that liked to waylay travelers, and some took the form of blankets which would smother the unsuspecting. He had not, however, heard of any such who started out as plain old sacks.

As he walked, the sack kept up a cheerful conversation. Nor was it especially heavy, so Masatoki felt his mood lightening, even though he felt time slipping away and had no idea how his father could be saved by an old sack, which was likely just some *tsukumo-gami*, a common object rumored to gain life after surviving being used for a hundred years. The sack certainly looked as if it could be that old. Yet he had met no one else.

One choice is no choice at all, he thought philosophically. *I will aid this creature and hope for the best, for that is all I can do.*

As the day progressed, it seemed to Masatoki that the sack was slowly getting heavier, yet its shape had not changed in the least. He attributed this to the fact that he was tiring as evening approached. He walked until well after dark, and when he could walk no farther, he found a stretch of mossy earth and stretched out there to sleep, with the uncomplaining sack for a pillow. In the morning he offered the sack a share of his morning rice-cake, but the sack said it wasn't hungry, so Masatoki hoisted the sack again and set off.

Try as he might, he could not keep up the same pace as the day before. He found himself growing more and more weary, and the sack, though obviously empty, felt heavier with every step. Masatoki pushed on. He was so bent under the weight of the sack and his own weariness that didn't see the three rough-looking men blocking his path until he was barely ten paces from them.

"That is a heavy-looking burden, young man," said the largest of them. "I think we should relieve you of it."

Masatoki carefully lowered the sack to the ground, a gesture they immediately misunderstood.

"A sensible attitude—" the leader started to say, but in an instant Masatoki's sword was out of its sheath. He held it in a two-handed grip as he had been taught. There were three of them, with swords of their own, and they clearly knew how to use them. Masatoki knew he had little chance of besting them, but he planned to sell his life as dearly as he could.

If I die today, I fail my father, but at least I will have done my best.

The bandits had quickly drawn their swords and were approaching, albeit cautiously, when the sack forced itself upright, opened his large eyes and mouth and spoke up. "Excuse me, but if you kill this young gentleman, which one of you plans to carry me in his stead?"

The effect was instantaneous. Two of the men dropped their

swords in the road, but even the one who didn't immediately took off running with the other two close behind. In a few moments they were all out of sight.

The sack seemed more than a little pleased with itself. "Now that the interruption is out of the way, perhaps we should resume our journey? They might return."

Masatoki, having observed their retreat, rather doubted this, but he was more than ready to leave that place. "Gladly."

He hoisted the sack again, which felt heavier than before, and set out as fast as he could walk. Every time he felt the need to rest, he thought of his father and pressed on. Even so, the sun was setting when his family's castle came into view. He was staggering when he passed through the gate, and it was only then that the sack showed an interest.

"Is this the place?" it asked.

"I'm not sure what you mean or where you need to be, but this is my home. I need to stop here."

"Then this is exactly where I need to be. Well done."

Masatoki had no idea what the sack was talking about, but he had no time to consider it. He burst into the audience hall, where he found his father and stepmother on the dais speaking to a man who was obviously a messenger.

I'm too late....

His father rose. "Masatoki? What is that you have there?"

Masatoki had forgotten he was carrying the sack. He slipped if off his shoulder. It made a very loud clinking sound as it hit the floor.

"Just a sack. I'm sorry, I—"

He didn't get to finish. His stepmother was staring at something behind him. "Husband, look!"

Confused, Masatoki followed their gaze toward the sack on the floor. It had fallen over, and from its top there spilled out marvelous things: slivers of gold, piles of glistening jewels, bolts of finest silk. For a moment all any of them could do was stare at it, then Masatoki understood what the sack had meant.

"Our fortune," he said softly, as if the words might chase it away. "I have brought back our fortune."

Now his father and stepmother were examining what had spilled and what still remained in the sack. The wealth contained there was almost beyond belief. After a long hesitation, Takamasa turned to the messenger.

"I've changed my mind. I will not need your services today."

The man bowed and, glancing in wonder at the sack, left them there.

"Is it enough?" Masatoki asked.

His father grunted. "Far more than enough. Son, how did you get this?"

"I found the sack along the road. Later I met some bandits. Perhaps it belonged to them," he said, knowing it was possible even though he didn't believe it to be so. Nevertheless, he kept as close to the truth as he could. "I drew my sword and they ran away."

"There must be more to it—" His Father began, but his stepmother smiled and touched Takamasa's sleeve.

"Husband, our fortune has returned, and your son brought it back to us," she said. "Perhaps that should be enough."

Takamasa looked as if he wanted to say more, but he glanced at his son and then his wife, and this time he chose to keep his silence.

While Masatoki's luck never did return, the fortune he brought home lasted for the rest of his life. He did visit the hearth in an attempt to thank the Cat of Five Virtues, but he wound up speaking to the empty air and thought it best not to make a habit of it, considering what had happened before. Even so, he knew she was there, and as with the fortune, she never left. He gave special instructions to the kitchen staff as to the tending of the fire and offerings of food to ensure she would have no reason to leave.

In due course he took his father's place, and his fortune and status grew. In time Masatoki was honored with a special *mon* and banner for his service to the Shogun. The design he chose for the *mon* was a simple white circle with the image of a plain sack enclosed.

The banner, however, was far more elaborate. It bore the image of a fork-tailed cat cunningly worked in black and silver thread, crowned with a tripod of gold. Before he showed it to anyone else, he took it to the hearth in the kitchen and held it up.

"It doesn't look a thing like me," the cat said, even though he still could not see her. "I approve."

Masatoki smiled, and he bowed. "I wanted to be sure."

The Boshin War of 1868-1869 ended of the Tokugawa Shogunate and restored Imperial rule. The siege of Tsuruga Castle, the seat of the Aizu domain, was the last act of resistance by the Shogunate forces on the main island, Honshu. Many samurai committed ritual suicide on seeing the castle burning.

The Duty of Birds

Evan Dicken

Part One: 鳥の義理

When I was very young my mother would tell me: "Do not cry, Chie. A samurai's daughter must never show such weakness." But my father cried often—when he fled Kyōto with Lord Katamori; when all the Aizu clan were declared traitors; when he killed a childhood friend at the siege of Tsuruga; when he abandoned his post to lead us from the burning castle.

Before the war it pleased Princess Teru to keep nightingales in the castle garden. At first, she planted green bamboo, thinking they would nest, and they did. The castle echoed with beautiful song through the spring and summer months, but soon autumn came and the birds departed.

Seeing his sister's sadness, Lord Katamori had cages built—delicate frames of wood with painted paper screens made to resemble the manors of the great lords and ladies of Edo. When the nightingales returned in the spring he had the servants capture them, but the birds would not sing. Instead, they fluttered around the cages, scratching holes in the lovely paper walls. Katamori had their wings bound and their legs hobbled with lengths of thin silver chain. The finest trainer was brought from Kyōto, a pinch-faced man with hair like pigeon feathers who lectured the birds on honor, obligation, and their place in things. It took weeks, but at last the nightingales sang, and it was said even the clouds must bow before Lord Katamori's will.

But the songs were not as before. Grief threaded the melody. The nightingales' mournful trills summoned visions of gray skies and cold winter winds rather than bright, burgeoning spring. Princess Teru and her handmaidens wept to hear their song. She ordered the cages smashed and the nightingales released. When Lord Katamori asked why, she said: "Men must kneel, but the duty of birds is only to the sky."

The invaders' cannons did not spare the garden, but we didn't stay to see it burn. Father left his sword at Tsuruga castle and made us dress in servant's robes: rough straw cloaks and heavy bags across our backs like we were porters for some village merchant. We ran north, then west to avoid the fighting around Inawashiro, heading towards Ubagamori and the mountains where my Mother's people lived. There were many refugees on the northern road, all peasants and townsfolk. Samurai were expected to kill themselves rather than submit.

We would have traveled quicker but Father stopped at every rise and hill, staring back at Tsuruga with an expression as if he were walking on knives rather than straw sandals. When he lingered too long Mother would take his arm and pull him on. Just before Tsuruga slipped from view for the last time Father looked to me, eyes red-rimmed and shining in the afternoon light, his voice settling into the familiar cadence of tanka verse:

"Seasons ever change.
Storm winds rage across Aizu.
Even birds must bow.
Proud yet tattered, they wonder:
Is it now spring or autumn?"

We both wept, as smoke spread dark wings above the castle at our backs. I kept glancing to mother, waiting for her reprimand. But she pressed a sleeve to her own eyes and said nothing.

Not all tears are weakness.

Part Two: 蛾は蛾でござる

There was nothing to do but run or die. We left the road and its flood of people just before nightfall, picking our way through heavy brush edged by deepening gloom. When it became too dark to see, we took shelter in a grove of red pine. The ground was hard and rocky, so Mother and I cut boughs for us to sit upon. Although the autumn air was chill, father said we should not make a fire in case there were Imperial troops in the mountains. It was strange to hear him call them that. Just a few months ago *we* had been the Imperial army.

We sat in the cool, humid dark, the forest silent but for the raspy calls of crows drawn to the slaughter. A few perched in the branches above our heads, cackling amongst themselves. Like drunks, crows were always either laughing or shouting.

"There are soldiers nearby." One of the larger crows hopped down, its voice high and gravelly like an old woman's. "Not friends, not far."

I looked to my parents, but neither replied.

"Give us sweet beans and chestnuts or we'll call them down

on you." It stared at us, black eyes glinting in the moonlight.

Father drew his dagger, but the crow only laughed and fluttered higher.

"Go." He said to mother and I. "I will kill any of the enemy who follow."

"Don't be a fool," mother said.

"Please." He turned to her, head bowed. "Let me go. I can't—"

Mother jerked him close and hissed something in his ear. The look on his face was the same as when he'd watched Tsuruga burn, but he put his dagger away.

It might have been the way the moonlight threaded the pines or how the shadows fell across her robes, but when mother stood she seemed taller, her fingers long enough to pluck the crows from their high perches. She made a sound in the back of her throat—not the disapproving cluck I heard when I spilled tea or forgot to bank the coal at night, but the rasp of dry sticks rubbing together. For a moment, the air smelled like our storehouse, heavy with dust, millet, and drying beans. Her hair had come unbound, the long, dark strands waving like spider silk in the sudden breeze.

"Go," the wind said.

The crows quieted, mumbling rusty apologies as they slipped into the air. Mother knelt, resting on her heels, back bent as if she were very tired.

"You promised never again." Father was little more than a vague, dark shape in the moonlit shadow.

"Seasons ever change," Mother said without looking up.

With a whispered curse, Father stormed away.

"Come, Chie, help me with my hair," Mother said after his footfalls had faded.

I wanted to ask what she had done but couldn't summon the nerve. We sat in silence for a while, the soft hiss of my comb like wind through the pines.

"When I met your father, he was a lowly ashigaru." Mother

said as I wound her hair back into a tight bun. "No name, no position, no stipend."

That didn't seem right. We had always been shichū, samurai of the highest rank, just below Lord Katamori's personal councilors. My father had overseen defense of Tsuruga's northern gate. Our manor wasn't as large as some, but it was attractive and well-built—with fresh tatami on the floors and great beams of hinoki cypress trimmed with cedar that made the whole house smell like a forest. We had walls and a garden with a stream and a small stand of magnolia that flowered white-pink every spring.

When I was a child, Father would bring back old lanterns from the garrison. We hung them in the trees, pretending we were courtiers from distant Kyōto out for a moon viewing. The lantern light brought moths, gray, brown, and white. We sat on the porch drinking cool barley tea, the lulls in our conversation filled with the soft sound of dusty wings beating on paper. The moths would fly in ragged, broken circles, diving at the lights until they slipped inside and were burned or fell to the ground, dead.

I asked my father why they behaved so foolishly.

He smiled, tugging at one ear the way he always did when he was happy. "Moths are the souls of the honored dead come back to look upon the living one last time. The light reminds them of the Pure Land and they cannot help but want to return to the Buddha."

The next morning, Mother caught me praying over the dead moths. She took my hand, kneeling down to look into my eyes. "They aren't spirits, Chie."

"But Father—"

"Your father is a fool," she said, smiling in a way that took all sting from the accusation. "He makes castles from clouds."

"And the moths?" I asked. "Why do they seek the light?"

She waved a hand as if brushing away a fly. "Moths are moths, they can't be anything but."

I thought of that as I combed Mother's hair beneath the

spreading pines, imagining we were surrounded by lanterns and laughter and the smell of cedar, instead of darkness and silence and the sharp tang of bleeding sap.

"Go to sleep," Mother said after I'd finished. "We will reach Ubagamori tomorrow."

I wanted to ask her about Father, about the crows, about everything, but it wasn't my place.

In the morning we found father dead. He lay slumped beneath a spreading maple just beside a little stream, belly slit, his cold, bloodless lips pressed into a tight line. Without paper, he had written his death poem into the rocky sand of the stream bank, but wind and the slow rush of water had worn most of it away.

I knelt, trembling, to pray for him. Mother laid a hand on my shoulder, her grip painfully tight even through the thick straw matting of my cape. I thought she would pull me away, but she didn't.

It started to rain. Big, fat drops bled through my clothes to draw icy lines down my chest and back. I kept expecting Father to rise, tugging at his ear to let me know this had been nothing more than a joke.

It was only when we heard the crack of distant rifles that Mother turned away. I heard her splash into the stream but didn't follow. Instead, I leaned in to pry Father's dagger from his iron-cold hands then pressed it to my neck.

When the Imperial troops had invaded Odayama over two-hundred Aizu women took their lives rather than accept defeat—women I had known, women I had practiced spear fighting with, women who had laughed and joked over torn kimono, and kites, and spring plantings. I could feel the weight of their sacrifice pressing down around me like a cold mist. One quick slash and I could join them in eternal honor.

"Come along." Mother kicked a spray of icy water at me. "There will be time to mourn when we reach Ubagamori."

I slipped Father's dagger into my sleeve, stumbling in the

stream on legs that had gone cold and wooden while I knelt.

We walked upstream to hide our tracks even though the cold mountain water made my feet hurt. Before the trees hid him from view, I looked back at Father one last time, not sure whether to feel sad, or angry, or proud. Samurai were defined by their duty—expected to die rather than submit. I'd thought his love for Mother and I made him different, but I was wrong.

In the end, moths are moths.

Part Three: 蜘蛛が巣しか織らぬ

Ubagamori was unlike any other forest. It wasn't the trees—a gnarled mix of ancient cedar, keyaki, honey locust, and pine—but rather a sense of quiet expectation, as if the tangled web of branches above was poised to drop on us like a net.

A knot of gray squirrels watched us brazenly from the shadows, tails twitching into shapes that looked like words but weren't. Hazy forms moved at the edges of my vision, bleeding back into shadow whenever I turned to face them. I could hear the distant patter of rain on the leaves overhead but barely a drop found its way to the forest floor. The air was cold, yet humid, and I found myself sweating despite the chill.

I drew closer to Mother. "This place is haunted."

"It is." She walked on, seemingly unafraid even as the long, red arm of an Akateko reached down from a low-hanging branch to brush the top of her hair. I kept my arms in my sleeves, Father's dagger a comforting weight in my hand.

A brace of seven-tailed foxes loped alongside us, poking their red and white heads around bushes and tree roots to regard Mother and I with canny eyes.

"You're back," said one, just as the other asked, "Is this your daughter?"

"I am, and she is." Mother kept walking.

"So young," said one.

"So curious," said the other.

"So frightened," they said together. Slinking from the shadows they swept around me, tails like silk upon my ankles. Not quite knowing why, I reached down to brush the long, soft fur on their backs. My hand came away bright with blood.

I brandished Father's dagger at the foxes, and they fled between the tree roots, laughing.

"They're only playing." Mother took my hand and held it before my face. There was no blood, just red paint, already flaking away. "Don't fear. You're safer in Ubagamori than anywhere else."

We walked for some time, the forest edging in around us. Gone was the thunder of distant cannons, the shouts of warriors, the cries of peasants caught in the fighting. The breeze came threaded with the scents of earth and dry leaves rather than gun smoke and ash. It wasn't any warmer under the trees, but I realized I'd stopped shivering.

After some time we came to a cave on a hillside shrouded with wisteria and cobwebs. Mother brushed them away then ducked inside, turning to offer me her hand with a shy smile.

To my surprise, the cave was warm, dry, and well-lit, with a floor of hard-packed earth and burning coal braziers set into the walls. I couldn't see the back, but the chamber was large enough for me to stand, even to raise my hands above my head if I wanted.

Mother knelt upon the floor, gesturing for me to join her.

From the back of the cave came a spider larger than a horse, with legs long as house-beams, wide-staring eyes, and a slick black carapace dotted with what I thought to be pale stones but which resolved into grinning skulls as the creature approached.

Mother made a triangle of her hands, bowing so her forehead touched the floor. Not knowing what else to do, I bowed with her. When I looked up, the spider was gone. In its place stood an old woman dressed in fine silk brocade, all knobby knees and crooked fingers, her face dark and wrinkled as a dried persimmon.

"Chie," Mother said to me. "Allow me to introduce your grandmother."

"Daughter." The old woman, my grandmother, knelt to kiss Mother on the forehead. When she pulled back the was a faint shimmer in the air, the barest hint of thin, silvery thread connecting them, gone as quick as a heat mirage.

She turned to me, taking my hands in her small papery ones. I could see her then, woman and spider, images overlaid like a reused handbill.

"We are *tsuchigumo*—earth spiders," she said softly, answering my question before I could give it voice.

"I'm sorry I couldn't tell you, Chie," Mother said. "But I made a promise."

"Minamoto no Yorimitsu was not the first," Grandmother stood. "They have been killing us since the ancient days, better to be secret, hidden."

"Am I a spider?" I asked.

Grandmother gave a little grin. "That remains to be seen."

"And Father?" I asked, hating the tremble in my voice.

"Just a man—a brave, foolish man," mother said with a sad smile. "I wove him castles from clouds."

"Forget about all that, my dear." Grandmother put an arm around her, beckoning to me. "Their world brings only pain, but you're home now."

"I'm sorry," Mother said, voice cracking. "I should never have left—"

"Hush, hush." She cradled Mother, stroking her hair, dimming the braziers, and pulling me close. This surprised me, until I remembered Grandmother had eight arms, not two.

Mother wept then, great wracking sobs that filled the cave until I could feel the sound deep within my chest. Grandmother made sympathetic noises, all the while whispering to me, "I will teach you to weave, little one, to spin and shape. Anything you can dream, anything you want, worlds bound by the warp and weft of your desire."

I found myself nodding along—who wouldn't want to create worlds?

In Edo there are many swordsmiths, some famous, some not. The one who made my father's sword was named Kiyomaro. One could come to his shop near Nihonbashi and pay three ryō to enter into a lottery. Every month Kiyomaro would make swords—sometimes one, sometimes several, depending on how often he was at the forge and how often he was drunk. At the end of the month his apprentice would draw names from the lottery box and those samurai would be given blades while the rest went away empty-handed.

Everything went well until one month, Kiyomaro's apprentice accidentally drew two names from the box when there was only one sword to give. The bladeless samurai was hatamoto to shogun Iemochi, whereas the man who had been given a blade was a low-ranking kashi from the Tosa Clan. Kiyomaro offered to forge a blade for the hatamoto, but the man was incensed, demanding the kashi relinquish his blade. When he refused, the hatamoto grew angry, threatening Kiyomaro.

Tired of the hatamoto's rudeness, Kiyomaro said he had a sword for the man, if only they could step out back of the shop away from the crowd. Although the hatamoto suspected a trick, he was keen to acquire a Kiyomaro blade and confident in his ability to defeat a lone kashi and a drunken swordsmith.

When the three of them went out back, Kiyomaro picked up the pan he used to fry noodles and offered it to the hatamoto.

"That is not a sword!" he said.

"It is," said Kiyomaro, showing him the maker's mark.

The hatamoto drew his blade.

With that, Kiyomaro slashed him across the throat, blood blossoming like spider lilies at the barest touch of the sharp-edged pan. The hatamoto fell to the ground, dead.

Astonished, the kashi looked from the pan to the corpse,

asking how such a thing was possible.

Kiyomaro simply shrugged. "I am a swordsmith. Everything I make is a sword."

I learned much from Grandmother—how to bend my shape to appear as a monk, or a peasant, or a lord; how to draw forms and figures from the smoke by rolling it between my fingers like spun cotton; how to speak in such a way that my words would bind the thoughts of any who heard them. I spent days in waking dreams, flying kites with old friends woven from air and fallen branches, watching the magnolias blossom, hanging lanterns with Father. It wasn't the same, though. No matter how cleverly I made them, the phantoms could only ever do as I wanted.

I crafted our old house from leaves and river mud, weaving light and sound to capture the essence of the place. It took hours, but I even got the smell of cedar and cypress just right.

I brought Mother, thinking it might make her happy again, but it only deepened the lines around her mouth. I tried to have Father tell a joke, but forgot the ending halfway through.

She just smiled her sad smile and cupped my cheek, then walked away.

When I went to Grandmother, she said Mother had become trapped by the world. It would take her a while to forget her sorrow.

Dreams were boring when there was no one to share them with, so I sought out foxes and squirrels and tanuki, and later, akateko and kappa and the other yōkai who haunted the dark corners of Ubagamori. It was satisfying for a time, but the minds of spirits do not flow along the same paths as mortals and I found their games childish, even cruel.

The edges of the forest became like a cage. More and more my thoughts drifted beyond the trees. Grandmother warned of dangers outside—men with blades and torches and great smoking cannons that would make a ruin of Ubagamori as they had Tsuruga. Why seek such pain when you could create whatever you wished?

I tried to explain, but she didn't understand. She offered to spin dreams for me, magical worlds peopled with characters that would surprise and delight, entire lives woven from whole cloth. By then I knew better than to accept her offer.

Grandmother was a spider. Everything she made was a web.

Part Four: 井の中の蛙

"The world is changing," Kenjiro said, eyes bright in the afternoon light. We sat upon a low hillside, shaded from the summer sun by the branches of an old and twisted cypress. He'd brought me kozuyu, walking for hours with a heavy iron pot full of the rich, salty stew. It was a meal meant for celebrations, which was how I knew he was working up to something.

"The Aizu have been given permission to continue as a clan." He bent to ladle out steaming portions thick with carrots, mushrooms, ginko nuts, and other delicious things. The stew smelled of home, and yet I couldn't seem to take my eyes from his thin, long-fingered hands. Kenjiro said he'd been a member of the Byakkōtai, that he'd fought in the siege of Tsuruga, but he had a scholar's hands.

That was what had piqued my interest when I'd found him at the edge of Ubagamori, carving a poem into the trunk of a cedar tree. His composition wasn't very good and his imagery a bit clumsy, but his verse had an earnestness I found appealing.

He'd fallen to his knees when I'd introduced myself as the daughter of Commander Nakagawa, pressing his forehead to the grass. That was how I'd learned the clan believed my father had died in the siege, bravely defending the northern gate. It made me happy to hear the lie. I think it would've made Father happy, too.

After Kenjiro left I'd stood for hours running my fingers over the poem etched in rough bark, eyes closed, drinking in the smell of fresh-cut cedar. There had been many, many meetings after that. Just as I'd wanted, he'd brought gifts of fruit, sweets, and now, kozuyu.

"Aizu is to be given a small fief in northern Mutsu," Kenjiro said, holding the bowls out as if asking me to choose. "They want our clan to fade, but we will rebuild, we will grow, we will show the emperor we are not traitors."

I smiled, not so much at his words but the passion with which he spoke them. Kenjiro was like the kozuyu—so rich, so real—and I was starving on a diet of silken dreams.

Our fingers touched when I took the bowl from him and for a brief moment there was a shimmer between them, the shadow of a thread drawing taut.

Kenjiro stared at me, open-mouthed.

"This is delicious." I said, and I wasn't lying.

He blinked. "I hoped it might remind you of home. I know my family is only middle-rank, but the world is changing, and I thought, well, perhaps you might..."

He flushed.

We finished our kozuyu in silence.

I could see the question lurking behind his nervous smile. We had been meeting like this for months, long enough for me to bind him tight. There was nothing else he could want.

"Many lords died in the war." Kenjiro's words tumbled into the anxious hush. "There will be opportunities for men of talent and intellect to advance themselves."

And there would be. I saw it then, filaments trembling with promise. I could make of Kenjiro whatever I chose. I could bind myself to him and weave a future for the Aizu, a story of redemption and glory—of fire, and steel, and ash.

Nothing is easier than showing men what they want to see.

"Forgive my presumption." He bowed low, mistaking my silence for displeasure. "It was foolish of me to come here."

"Foolish...and brave." I laid a hand on his arm, his shoulder, his knee, his cheek, and I kept them folded in my lap. I had so many hands.

"I will stake my life to—" He blew at a moth fluttering around his face. It circled about then came right back. "I will—"

I wanted to devour him. Instead, I stood, ducking out from under the tree. "Give me time to consider."

"Of course." Kenjiro bowed. When he rose, the hope in his eyes was almost too much to bear.

"Tomorrow?" he asked.

"Perhaps." I walked away, hating the part of me that enjoyed ensnaring him.

Ubagamori was not far and I had plenty of time. For all her cunning and craft, a life of lies had made Grandmother strangely trusting. I'd fashioned another me from moss, rocks, and a twist of vine—a dutiful granddaughter to care for, to laugh and scheme with, a girl who would never leave her side. My only concern was Mother, who would see through my ruse in an instant.

So it was I found her standing at the edge of Ubagamori, half-shadowed by the fall of branches.

"You caught a boy." It wasn't a question.

My stomach clenched at her words, and I reached, as I always did when I was nervous, for father's dagger.

"Did you—? Is Kenjiro—?" I asked. Grandmother's lies were wild, grandiose things, the work of a spider who caught moths but could never understand them. Mother's lies were small and careful, threaded with just enough truth to make them believable.

"He's real." She stepped from the shadows. "As real as anything."

We stood for quite some time, sweating in the hot summer sun.

"Your grandmother is right," she said, at last. "He will bring you sadness in the end. Even your happiest memories will turn sharp as a new blade."

"Perhaps not. The world is changing."

"Seasons change, the world does not. Finally, I understand why your Grandmother was so afraid." She sighed. "Will you go with him?"

The choice sat like a stone in my stomach, perhaps the first real decision I'd ever made.

Our lives are not our own. We are born into obligation—to our family, our lord, our clan, our class. Some take to it, clinging like a child to its mother, comfortable in the path it has laid out for them. Others struggle against their duty and become bitter and cold like tea steeped too long.

The weight of obligation pressed in on me from all sides. I could be a moth or a spider, and yet I felt as a frog in a well, unaware of the great sea that swirled just beyond my gaze. How could I chart the heavens when I saw but a small part of them?

And there it was. The answer came soft as a summer breeze—unexpected, quiet, but oh so welcome.

I drew Father's dagger. Mother took a small, worried step towards me, then paused as I held up a hand.

With a quick motion, I turned to Ubagamori and swept my arm in a circle like I was winding loose silk. There was a brief sense of resistance when I brought the dagger down, as if I were drawing the blade through water rather than air. To be honest, I didn't know if it had worked until I saw Mother's surprise. She looked from the forest, to the knife, to me, eyes wide and unbelieving.

Not giving her time to speak, I turned and chopped the blade towards Aizu, towards Kenjiro. It went quicker this time, and after a moment's work they were free.

"And me?" Mother said with a sad tilt of her head.

Not knowing what to say, I took three quick steps forward and drew her close. She tensed at my touch: only small children hugged their parents like that, but I held tight until all propriety drained from her.

"What are you?" She shook her head, finally returning my

embrace.

"We are birds." I brushed her tears away, then pressed Father's dagger into her hands, leaning in to whisper. "And it is spring."

Sōhei, warrior monks, arose in several orders of Buddhist temples. They defended the temples' territories, maintained the temples' independence, and furthered their sects' political interests. The monks were highly trained fighters, and could fight either against or alongside samurai, depending on their circumstances.

Japanese calligraphy is an esteemed art form, instilled with Buddhist spiritual ideas.

The Three

Will Weisser

In the early spring of their pilgrimage, Seibo, a warrior monk; Hidemori, an artist; and their hanger-on came across a village beset by grave misfortune. The first clue was the smell of rot, the sort all fair spirits avoid. Even the wind which blew down the forested mountainside seemed to halt at the village's borders, as if offended by the odor.

Seibo advanced slowly down the main road, his motions subtle despite his imposing size. "Listen." He stopped and raised his hand. In the stillness, the cries of women and children drifted on the edge of hearing, bitter tears wept behind ramshackle wooden walls. "What happened here?"

Hidemori trundled up, one hand on his pack to keep his calligrapher's supplies from clanking. "I don't know," he whispered. "But we should leave before it happens to us. One temple isn't worth risking our lives."

"Leave?" The Musician hefted his samisen on his shoulder

like a spear, a faint clang emanating from its empty soundbox. He ambled past Hidemori and slapped him on the back, eliciting an angry hiss. "I'm no stranger to running, but I prefer to know what I'm running from."

"You can stay if you wish," Hidemori grumbled. "Neither of us will stop you, just as neither of us asked you to follow us in the first place."

"But what's the point of following a *futarimusha*, if a man cannot count on them to secure food and lodging?" The Musician sniffed, caught the foul scent in the air and startled, but regained his composure quickly. "A dour place, to be sure. But nothing a little song couldn't fix, eh?"

Hidemori scoffed and hurried onward. The houses on the main road were shuttered, and no children greeted them in the mild spring evening. The still feeling was more intense here, and Hidemori, whose training had made him sensitive to disturbances in the *hou-no-michi*, squinted into every shadow, wary of demons.

A temple, one of the thirty-three they had pledged to visit, stood in the woods just beyond the village's opposite side. Before they reached it, Seibo stopped again and pointed to a patch of black earth. No, not black, Hidemori saw, but dark red. A pool of blood, dried into the soil.

The Musician gave a low whistle. "Unpleasant."

"Can you tell what happened?" Seibo asked.

Hidemori shook his head. The *hou-no-michi* was tangled here, a knot in the threads of reality, but that was all he could see. Seibo paced across the empty street, searching for clues. The Musician turned his back to the dried blood and began idly picking his samisen.

The door to the house closest to the temple slid open, and an old woman came out, carrying a pail. She saw the three men and quickly went back inside.

"Wait!" Seibo called.

The door snapped shut.

Seibo grunted in frustration. He approached the door and knocked, but no response came. "Open this, please. We only want to talk."

"Seibo, enough," Hidemori said. "We should go."

Seibo's replied by rapping harder. Again, his efforts were in vain.

The Musician snorted. "You two! Utterly hopeless." Having attracted Hidemori's angry glare, he responded with a smile of crooked teeth. "Watch and see how it's done."

He leaned against the doorframe. "Hey! *Obaachan!* Where's the hospitality of this place, eh? These men come on religious orders, and I'm here to entertain. At least tell us why you won't come out."

The door parted a crack, and one cataract-ridden eye peered out. "Lies. Those two are a futarimusha. You claim they're holy, but they're pledged to service for war. We've had enough soldiers in this village."

"Ah, but my Lady, these two have just started their pilgrimage. They're pledged to Lord Nobunao, far to the north, and won't be of any bother to you. I've kept their company now for some days, and can report in absolute truth that they're harmless. True, the small one passes gas too much in his sleep, but that also serves to prove he's human and not a shapeshifter, eh? Come now." He plucked a chord. "This is Lord Hatano's domain, is it not? Was it his soldiers who were here, then?"

The door slid open, revealing the woman hunched in the doorway, framed in the light from a fire pit inside. Around it were two young children, knees clutched to their chest, tears glinting in the orange glow.

"Still that instrument," she said. "Unless you know a song for a funeral. Even then, we'd have no one to perform the rites." She turned back to the hearth. "Minae! Go fetch the water."

A little girl ran past them, wooden pail dragging a line in the dirt.

"Your daughter is quite beautiful," the Musician said.

The old woman cracked a rueful smile at the flattery. "She may as well be my daughter, now. I don't expect her father to return—my son. Nor any of the other men of this village."

Seibo stepped forward. "All of them? They took all the men?"

"Conscripted." The woman bowed her head. "Even the old weren't spared, as long as they could hold a spear."

Seibo muttered a curse under his breath, then turned to his counterpart.

"Lord Hatano must be desperate," Hidemori said, shaking his head. "But what about the blood in the road?"

"The monk of our temple..." The old woman's voice became choked. "He came down to speak with Hatano's samurai. The monk pleaded with them to only take the fittest men, explained that this village could not survive. Their leader, with the crest on his helmet...he..."

She began to weep. Seibo knelt beside her, his arm around her shoulder. He did not flinch when the woman wiped her face on his sleeve.

"Even the undertaker is gone. I had to take care the monk's body myself, but I did a poor job. His spirit will haunt this place, I'm sure. I shouldn't have burned him like that, I shouldn't..."

Seibo shushed the woman and whispered a blessing. Hidemori covered his nose with the back of his palm. The stink which had lingered in the background seemed more bothersome now that he knew it came from the back of this woman's house.

The old woman's weeping might as well have been a beacon to the tiny village. Seeing the strangers giving comfort to their neighbor, women and children emerged from houses all around, surrounding the three and offering their own versions of the story. Some asked Seibo for a blessing, and he obliged them. Hidemori snuck out and waited near the dried blood.

Eventually, when the excitement had passed and the old

woman returned to her home, Seibo came to meet him.

"Do you think the monk's spirit will haunt this place?" Hidemori asked.

"He sounded a decent man in life. I do not think he will hold the improper burial against her. But untangling the *hou-no-michi* would help to release the pain stored here. Can you do it?"

Hidemori grumbled. Of course he would have to try, after what they had just heard. But he still disliked the breezy way Seibo made the request. Untangle the *hou-no-michi*—as if anything about the unseen world were so simple.

"Very well." He unstrapped his pack and put it aside. He wouldn't need a brush for this work. Better to write it in the dirt, using the line from the pail if possible. The little girl's mark, intentional or not, was an expression of her pain, and what was the art of calligraphy but pure expression? He fetched a hefty stick from the edge of the wood and paced out the work area, then narrowed his eyes and visualized the *hou-no-michi*—the invisible lines that tied objects together, that connected the past to the future. No need for a long piece, a single character would do. As long as he brought forth the shape honestly, as a reflection of the dharma, the *hou-no-michi* would follow its new course.

Ready to begin, he made one last check of his surroundings and saw Seibo heading away. "Where are you going?"

"We came to visit the temple," Seibo's voice faded as he entered the wood. "Empty or not, I'm going to pray."

Hidemori grunted and looked back to his work. It was just as well he wouldn't be disturbed. Holding the stick waist high, he closed his eyes. The motion had to be relaxed, free, but with precision and purpose. He pressed his whole body into the first stroke, and cut into the fabric of reality as it dug into the road. Only when the stick was free in the air did he allow himself to tense, change angle, then release again for the second. He added four more strokes in the same way, sweeping, turning, rising and falling. He landed on one knee, panting and brow beaded with sweat, over an enormous kanji meaning "harmony" traced into the dirt.

He pulled a cloth from his kimono to wipe his face, then sat back to catch his breath. He looked over the completed piece with disdain. It was good, yes, better than many of his peers would ever do. But as ever it lacked perfection, if such a thing were attainable in this life.

He heard muttering from a few of the villagers, watching him in the distance. Otherwise, he was alone. Where had that pesky Musician wandered off to? Perhaps if he fetched Seibo quickly enough, they could finally rid themselves of his presence—that would be worth cutting short his rest.

Moss-covered stepping stones led the way to the temple. Beyond the heavy timbers of its curved roof, its silent halls smelled of burned-out incense. Across the bare wood floor, Hidemori found Seibo kneeling, forehead down, before the statue of Kannon.

"You finished the piece?" Seibo said upon hearing him approach. "Will it work?"

"Perhaps the *hou-no-michi* will heal, perhaps not. It was the best I could do under the circumstances." Hearing his own words, Hidemori became gruff, as if responding to unheard criticism. "Look, I tried, all right? Now, we should be off. It's not fair to ask this town to feed us, after what they've been through. If we hurry, we can make the next temple by dawn."

He turned and headed outside, only to stop and slowly turn when he realized Seibo was not following. "What is it?"

Seibo sat up and placed his hands together, a string of prayer beads dangling between them. "I'm not going to the next temple."

"What?"

"There are children here without fathers, families without sons and brothers. I cannot go until I relieve their suffering."

"Eh!? What are you babbling about? Don't you think I know the suffering of these people? I've done my part for them."

"It's not enough." Seibo returned the prayer beads to his robe, then clapped his hands. "Not until the men of this village are brought back, alive."

"What?! How do you propose to do that? You can't just follow after them, kill the guards and set them free."

"That is exactly what I propose."

Hidemori was struck dumb for a moment. "B...but they're three samurai...riding horses...armed and armored! You're one man, with nothing!"

"With your power, I could do it."

"Impossible. They're a half-day ahead—we'd have to run the whole way just to catch them. To produce a piece like that, I would need time to prepare, to scout a suitable location."

Seibo sat and stared at the statue, unmoving.

Hidemori stomped his foot. "Have you lost your mind? Certainly, I wish the men of this village could return, but you don't see me getting wild ideas like this. The purpose of this pilgrimage is to build our spiritual acumen on the way to meet our patron, not to get ourselves killed for no gain at all."

Seibo answered by raising a finger, pointing at the far corner of the temple. Hidemori peered into the shadows beside the statue. There were two white spots there, floating in the dark. The spots blinked, and Hidemori hopped back in surprise.

The shadows moved, and from behind the statue appeared a little boy, no older than five. He bowed deeply and muttered a polite greeting.

"The undertaker's son," Seibo said. "His family was not welcome in the village, and his mother passed years ago, so he came here when his father was taken. The brave face he wears brought to my mind another boy, of the same age, whose parents had recently died. His grandparents were too elderly to care for him, so they took him to a temple. The monks there saw he was strong of body, and sent him to Ichijo to begin training as a fighter for a futarimusha."

Seibo paused, remembering, then shifted to face Hidemori and beckoned the boy. The child curled up, tucked like a newborn in his thick arms.

"You spoke of your purpose in coming here. But I believe each of us must decide the purpose of our own journey. Just now I have determined mine. Before I pledge myself in service to Nobunao, I will devote my pilgrimage to serving the common people."

Hidemori grumbled and paced. Insanity. Pure insanity. He hissed between clenched teeth, "Regardless of your feelings, you must put them aside for duty. I cannot appear before Nobunao alone; you must come with me."

"I have a duty to the temple and to Nobunao, but my first duty is to the dharma. I cannot work against my own nature, any more than I can turn back the sun or the tides."

"Then we're stuck." Hidemori sat on the floor across from the big monk and stared at him crossly. "If you will not give up this foolish idea, then I will stay here until the men cannot possibly be rescued."

"As long as a slim hope of their survival remains, I will not move," Seibo replied.

And so the two men sat gazing at one another. Seibo breathed calmly, rocking the boy to sleep, while Hidemori fumed, both waiting for the other to give in.

A thump of sandal on wood and a drunkenly-hummed melody brought the Musician into their midst.

"Hey! I looked all over for you two!" He sauntered between them and peered back and forth. "Nice kid you got there. Hey, why so down? I told you this place wouldn't be so bad. Mountain people—once you get them talking, it turns out they have sake stashed under every floorboard." He tapped his foot to fill the silence. "What? You fellows having a spat? You never acted like this before."

"Silence, you idiot," Hidemori said. "This is none of your

business."

"Hah!" The Musician slung his samisen around to his chest and sat down beside Seibo, resting his back on the offering box. "So rude. You know I came here to offer you something: a little piece of information I came across in the village." He waited for an invitation to speak. Hearing none, he continued anyway. "I told the grandfather who took me in that we would set off down the road tomorrow, toward Hatano Castle. He said the road curves down the mountain like so, alongside a treacherous river gorge until it meets a bridge, whereupon it runs back up the other side. But here's the secret: the villagers put up ropes between two sturdy trees just over the ridge there, nearer the river's source. Cross them, and you'll save a whole day's walk! Not bad, eh? And here you thought the Musician was useless. No better news than getting out of Hatano as fast as…possible…hm?"

He wrinkled his brow in confusion at the monk and the calligrapher, who stared at each other meaningfully, engaged in silent conversation.

"What?" the Musician said. "What is it?"

"With a day's advantage, we'll have the drop on them." Seibo traced his finger along the wood floor. "We'll find a good place, with room for you to work."

Hidemori growled and shook his head. "You talk as if the matter were as simple as cooking rice. To weave the *hou-no-michi* like that is *dangerous*." Seeing Seibo's resolve, he let out a resigned sigh. "I will prepare it as best I can. But you will do the rest alone. Agreed?"

"Agreed."

The Musician nodded thoughtfully. "I see now. A battle, eh? Very brave of you, Seibo. If you weren't so stubborn I'd surely try to talk you out of it myself—you, alone, against three samurai!"

Seibo and Hidemori shared a long, knowing glance, and when Seibo spoke, it seemed that for the first time that day, the two companions shared one mind.

"You're wrong, Musician. I won't be alone. You have a very important role to play in this endeavor."

Sakuma Seiji pulled the reins to slow his horse, despite that they were behind schedule, and night had already fallen. The animal kept rising into a trot, wanting to return home and eat. Sakuma didn't blame her. His own stomach was empty, his limbs and neck sore from the weight of his armor and helmet. But there was no way to go faster; the twenty-two men walking behind him weren't up to it, and Sakuma lacked the heart to threaten and beat them until they increased their pace.

They would learn true hardship soon enough. There would be crowded barracks infested with lice, marching and drilling with spears on too-small rations, and then these men would give their all in one final charge across a blood-and-gunpowder strewn battlefield, or else die trapped in a burning stone fortress. And when the time came, Sakuma would die with them.

That was good. He was not yet thirty, but his affairs were in order, and he looked forward to dying in service to his daimyō. He hoped the villagers would come to feel the same, before the end. They were not samurai, not bound to his code, but they were still bound to service for their lord. The same even applied to the monk, the one Sakuma had unfortunately been forced to strike down. Every man had his place—that was the way of things, the order of the world. To let a man—even a holy man—openly defy Hatano would be to let the very foundations of his universe crumble.

His horse nickered and bowed her head. Sakuma patted her neck to quiet her. But she did not quiet. As they made their way around a bend in the path the mare whinnied and became more difficult to handle, until she began to buck.

"The horses!" called Karada, his first lieutenant, from behind the recruits. His animal had grown agitated as well, and he dismounted, tugging the reins to keep her from bolting. "What's gotten into them?"

The villagers shuffled back and forth, nervous. What was happening here? Sakuma's mind touched on possibilities, but if the word "sorcery" drifted through his thoughts, perhaps muttered by one of the men behind him, he did not lend it any special significance. They were far from any battlefield, and no spy would waste their time this deep in the wilderness.

Sakuma hopped down from his saddle, and signaled to his second lieutenant to do the same. Without a rider, the animal calmed enough to be led, though her ears remained pricked, nostrils flared. The light from the lantern on his banner barely penetrated the surrounding forest, showing only that the road widened ahead, running through a grove of cedars, dark shadows etched in lines on their trunks.

With a whistle of command, Sakuma moved forward, and the others followed. Soon, they entered the trees. But as the cedars passed on both sides, the animals became disturbed again, until the three samurai could barely hold their bridles.

Something was wrong with this forest. The village men knew it too, and they made fearful noises as they shuffled along. Sakuma felt the hair on his neck rise.

In the center of the grove, the light of the lantern fell upon a man sitting cross legged, facing away from them.

Sakuma's hand went to his katana. "Who are you?"

"A Musician." The man plucked some strings on an unseen instrument, but they jangled terribly, as if they were barely tightened. Surrounded by the darkness and the eerie sounds, the man's long, stringy hair falling over his back made him look like a demon.

Sakuma gripped his sword tighter. "Your name—I order you to give it."

"Why are names important, eh?" The Musician's voice was

calm. "Everyone thinks they can tell so much from a name. Take my friend, Hidemori, for example. With a name like that, you'd expect a brave man, always willing to stand up to danger—and yet, even as we speak, he's off cowering somewhere in these woods, too afraid to move a muscle!"

"Enough nonsense!"

"Sakuma-sama!" Karada yelled. "The trees!"

Sakuma's horse reared, and in the swinging light he saw the lines of shadows on the cedars were not shadows at all. Each tree had a single character slashed across it in black ink.

"It's cursed!" Sakuma yelled. "Fall back!"

But the villagers were too confused to respond, and the horses only kicked the dirt and bolted.

Sakuma's second lieutenant screamed. He had stumbled backward into what looked like a stone, but when his leg drew near, the stone had reached up and grabbed him. Before Sakuma's stunned gaze, the form of a man rose from the earth. The figure pushed the second lieutenant down into the hole he had left, and the earth seemed to swallow him up, covering his face-down body with soil.

The figure stood then in the open, and Sakuma saw it was a real person. A man, tall, head shaven like a monk, with the character for "ground" painted across his bare chest.

Sakuma drew his sword. "Kill the musician!" he shouted to Karada.

The monk charged. He started five paces away, but he moved at inhuman speed, ramming Sakuma and wrapping with his arms before his blade left the scabbard. Sakuma shifted his weight and pressed forward, gripping the monk's loincloth and attempting to toss him down. But the monk felt anchored to the ground—no, more than that, as if he and the ground were the same object. Sakuma strained, but the monk kicked out his legs and he clattered to the ground with his attacker falling over him.

Sakuma struggled, attempting to push the monk off, but once

again the effort was futile. The monk's body flowed, pressing down as if it wished to rejoin the earth from whence it came. Desperate to breathe, Sakuma pushed on the monk's face to claw his eyes, but his hand was shoved aside and then the monk's arms clasped around his neck. Sakuma gagged and scraped with his nails, but the pressure increased, until he saw spots, then black.

As soon as he heard the lead samurai call for his death, the Musician leaped to his feet and scrambled away. Seibo had told him that if such a thing were to happen, he should run as far as possible. But the musician had other plans, and they didn't include stumbling alone through a dark forest with an armed man on his tail. Instead, he found refuge behind the thick trunk of a cedar and waited for his pursuer to approach.

The second samurai stalked forward, footsteps inaudible above the sound of Seibo and the leader struggling. The Musician peeked out just enough to see the moon glowing on the katana, then glanced at the writing on the nearby trees, hoping he could read them correctly. He had paid close attention when Hidemori explained their purpose to Seibo, but now, in the gloom with his heart thudding, the characters all blurred together. He remembered something about connecting one thing to another, the past to the future. Yes, that was it, that one—the tree with "sword" written on it, low branches spread wide.

The samurai was close. The Musician held his breath and stepped out into his path, holding the samisen up like a shield.

"Please! Just listen. There's something you must know about me!"

His shouting made the samurai hesitate, holding his sword before him, confused. The Musician smiled, nodded, and dashed away toward the "sword" tree.

The samurai followed after, grunting in anger, and swung as

the Musician ducked into the branches.

It was death, of course. What else could occur from such a strike, performed by a man who had practiced them all his life, with nothing to stop it but some flimsy twigs? The chance that the samurai would make a slight error, that the sword would happen to cut just a bit too deeply into the wood and become stuck, was miniscule indeed. But it could happen. And on that night, the samurai's blade carved not into the Musician's flesh, but deep into the bough of the pine, as if drawn toward it like a compass needle.

The Musician stumbled as the samurai tried to pull his sword out. But instead of continuing to run, the musician stopped, and as calmly as he could manage, turned and approached his enemy, still holding his samisen before him. The samurai did not look particularly worried. Why should he be, when his opponent was clearly mad, and another hard tug would free his sword and end it?

The Musician pulled the neck of the samisen out from the body, revealing the dagger embedded within. Before the samurai could open his mouth to yell, the Musician stuck him through the throat.

The forest had fallen silent again. Seibo approached the cut tree, his gait slow, carrying a pair of swords. He surveyed the pool of blood and the Musician sitting, dazed, beside his fallen foe.

"Nicely done," Seibo said.

"No more of this, 'Stop following us,' stuff," the Musician sputtered. "Even that sour calligrapher can't say I haven't pulled my weight now."

Seibo examined the samisen, tested the hidden blade, then laid it back on the ground. "And you still maintain you're just a wandering Musician?"

The Musician huffed. "A man needs protection on the road

in times like these. That's the reason I joined up with you fellows. A lot of good it's done me!"

They both turned at the sound of the lead samurai coughing and scrambling to his knees.

"I thought he was dead!" the Musician shouted, jumping to his feet.

"I released the stranglehold to come help you."

The samurai stood, rubbing his head. He stared at his fallen colleagues, the crowd of villagers who had not fled, the monk, and the music player. Then he crossed the grove and knelt before Seibo.

"Which daimyō do you work for?" he asked.

"None, yet," Seibo answered.

The samurai shook his head. "Ambushed by a futarimusha on a routine errand—no soothsayer could have predicted such an end for me. But it does not matter now. Finish it, please."

Seibo looked down at the swords in his hand, as if he were noticing them for the first time. He began to walk away, his steps labored.

The samurai looked up and growled, "What are you doing?!"

"Leaving."

"You cannot. Have you no humanity? To leave me with this shame would be worse than death."

Seibo halted and looked over his shoulder. "I am not a samurai. I will not take a life without cause, nor will I be your second for seppuku. If your shame brings you suffering, go to a temple and become a monk instead."

One by one, he pulled the katana and the wakizashi from their scabbards and tossed them into the woods. Then he went on his way with the same plodding steps.

The samurai roared, "Fool!"

He leaped for the samisen, snatching it away before the Musician could grab it. Seibo slowly faced his opponent, and his hand touched his chest for a brief moment. The Musician noticed then the condition of the mark Hidemori had given him. The lines were smeared, broken, a mockery of what the "ground" character should have been.

The samurai tore apart the samisen, severing the loose strings, and advanced. But Seibo could barely move. The ground which had once been his ally now seemed to hold him down, as if his feet were sinking in mud. He lost his balance as the samurai charged, toppling like a child learning to walk. The first slash cut him across the side, and then the samurai stood above him and raised the dagger high.

Another blade came down on the samurai's back, and he fell, shouting surprise. In his place stood Hidemori, a katana shaking in his grip.

The Musician rushed up and snatched the sword away, then held the point above samurai's face, poking it forward until he laid back and dropped the dagger.

"You bruised him," the Musician scolded. "Dented his armor. You should have aimed for the neck."

"I'm lucky to be alive!" Hidemori shouted, his voice shrill. He faced Seibo and threw up his hands. "Why would you throw a sword, you oaf? It nearly sliced me in half. I told you this idea was dangerous!"

Seeing the blood on his comrade, he bent to help, and was nearly knocked over by the crowd of villagers rushing in to surround the samurai. Shouting angrily, the peasants kicked away the dagger and began to strip the man's armor, striking him wherever they exposed flesh.

"Wait!" Seibo shouted, though the effort clearly pained his wounded side. "What will you do with him?"

An older villager spat before the samurai. "We have no choice but to kill him. If Lord Hatano learns of our treason, everyone we know is dead."

"He will find out eventually." Seibo struggled to his feet and took a deep breath. "We have saved your lives, but your village is no longer safe. Take your families and flee into the mountains. Times will be tough. Bandits roam the roads, and wherever you settle may yet be torn apart by war." He bent his head. "We did what we could. I am sorry."

So chastened, the villagers set about somberly binding the samurai's limbs, then one by one they lined up to give thanks to the futarimusha and their companion.

"Do not return here," Hidemori said as they passed. "What I have done will leave this place tainted for many years. The plants will turn brittle, visitors will become ill. Ghosts, and eventually demons will make it their home."

Finally, after many thanks and goodbyes, the three stood in the grove, listening to the chirp of insects and the hooting of a distant owl.

"Well, Seibo, I hope you're happy," Hidemori said. "Two men dead. Probably three."

"They were warriors." Seibo clutched his side and winced. "The dharma flows, and each creature lives according to its nature. By your actions today, you have put an unnatural evil in this place. But perhaps we have balanced that by setting others upon their natural course." He stared into the night, toward where the villagers had gone.

"Tell yourself whatever lies you need." Hidemori produced a cloth from his kimono and carefully wiped every trace of ink from Seibo's chest. "There. You should be able to walk well enough to reach the next temple. Once we're comfortable, I'll see to making sure that cut doesn't fester."

He headed off to search for his pack, and Seibo followed after.

"Where are you going?" the Musician said, pointing with the katana at the samurai he had killed. "He has more swords. You know how much these are worth?"

"We're wanted men, now," Seibo called back. "Carrying those swords would mark us for death. Leave them."

"Then who's going to pay for this?" the Musician grumbled, picking up the broken pieces of his samisen. He spun to find himself alone in the dark wood.

"Wait for me!"

The Japanese aesthetic of *mono no aware*, literally "the pathos of things" or "the 'ahh-ness' of things", is an awareness of impermanence or transience of things, conveying both a gentle sadness at their passing as well as a deeper appreciation of this state being the reality of life. Awareness of the transience of all things heightens appreciation of their beauty. It is an important concept in much Japanese literature and tradition.

Ieyasu and the Shadow

Mike Adamson

In the ninth year of the Ōnin War, the young samurai Asahi Ieyasu was a troubled man.

Too soon had his father, the mighty Asahi Takeshi, fallen; yet still he clung to a thread of life as doctors and mystics fussed over him in the high royal chambers of Mabuno Castle, on the slopes of the mountains which rose inland from the wild coast of Toyama Bay. Hope remained, if only in Ieyasu's stout heart; but with a warrior's fatalism he forced himself to consider his actions if the gods should take his father and the line should pass to himself. Twenty-one was too young for other clannish lords to take him seriously as daimyō of Mabuno. In a feudality, when a decade of war had sapped the power of the Shogun—such that the ruling lord took no part in the struggle but contented himself with the arts—the rival daimyō of hundreds of scattered clans no longer looked to central authority. They eyed each other with suspicion and venality, and the only security lay in the power of one's own loyal retainers and the fine steel at one's side.

Ieyasu needed peace in these turbulent moments, and loved to find it in the gardens of the castle. Lanterns swayed gently in the scented night breeze, casting soft illumination over the manicured flowerbeds, decorative walkways, and the red-lacquered bridge over the koi pool. Amid the soft rustlings of night birds, Ieyasu walked the garden in the trance of meditation, hands folded before him, aware of every soft rustle from his silk kimono, and the weight of the magnificent katana in its black, gilt-worked sheath in his belt.

How hard it was to live up to expectations in this life, he reflected. What weight was placed upon each individual to give of his or her best, to make a difference in their world at any cost. This was Bushido, the code by which they lived; Ieyasu felt its burden in each breath he drew.

Outwardly calm, the young samurai walked with silent tread, circling the garden by this path, then that, crossing the water here, then there, and always in the same number of steps. The observant would note that each foot was placed exactly in the spot it had occupied previously, and in this way the precision of his nature was manifest. Each stride was as poised, as balanced, as his breathing, an outward expression of control which fostered the inward mastery so sorely needed.

After his twenty-fifth circling of the garden, Ieyasu paused and looked up at the lights of Mabuno Castle. The great keep with its gabled floors rose against the stars of the soft evening. *Let my father not succumb to his wounds*, he thought, the words forming like a mantra in his heart and soul. *The Asahi need their lord as they need air to breathe, and I do not believe this is his time.*

The breeze fluttered the leaves around him, and sweet buds promising new harvest mocked his hopes. That harvest lay hidden in the veil of time, and he could not know what shape the life of his clan would hold when the blossom came forth. So again he walked, hearing the quiet murmurs of voices beyond the garden wall as guards made their patrols. The divine peace of this place had always been his retreat when reality clamoured too loudly and the demands of the battlefield overcame all the enthusiasm youth could bring. Blooded at just sixteen years of age, Ieyasu was one of the finest archers and swordsmen his clan had ever produced. Part of him, the frustrated part, desperate to act, felt a burning guilt. He had not been at his father's side when he was needed.

Many would tell him the guilt was pointless: the fortunes of combat could be neither second-guessed nor controlled. But the feeling of being a plaything of destiny was alien to him. For all the deep learning he had amassed—of Shinto, of Bushido, of the martial arts and the philosophies underpinning them—he could not change what *was* by any feat of will he possessed. To understand that these things were *meant* to be beyond mortal man was cold comfort.

Thus, he walked.

In the deep places of meditation he searched for an alternative. He did not believe eternity could be bargained with, but he was willing to entertain any idea. His instructors had spoken of the great depths to which meditation could take a man, and he sought to glide into the cool, liquid space where the mind could rise above the body, take advantage of enhanced perspective and seek out answers. Stride after stride, circuit after circuit, Ieyasu walked deep into the corners of his own being, and reached out to the world around him.

What would the night bird do in his place?

What would the flower do?

What would the golden carp in the pond do?

The bird could fly from danger, but could not take with him his injured kin.

The flower must endure whatever happenstance brought to its rooted nature, yet might regrow with resilience unknown to humans.

The koi may not swim beyond the confines of its pool, yet in its way bring forth a multitude, so koi might go on forever.

Deep, regular breathing was the only sound but for the rustle of the breeze in the trees, and again Ieyasu looked up at the castle. If it must be his father's time he, himself, had a choice. Fly like the nightbird from all that would destroy his inheritance...but this was to forsake honour itself. Endure like the flower, and regenerate his spirit and his fortunes when the time was right. Or manoeuvre like the koi, take advantage of all circumstances and be productive for his clan in whatever ways were possible.

In these notions were plans for the future, he realised, but no morsel of wisdom appeared by which he could take control of the present. It was confounding, and he walked again in the smooth, cool silence of solitude. But at his fiftieth circuit no fresh insights had reached him.

He let himself be aware of the garden through his mundane senses once more, and felt the beating of his warrior's heart. *What must be, must be*, was the only thought repeating in his mind, and he had more or less reached equilibrium between his desires and his fatalism when he saw the lights.

Softly glowing spheres of blue radiance hung among the boughs of an ancient cherry tree, and for a moment he thought they were lanterns, but these were drifting quite independently of the breeze. They moved as if with conscious will, and never left the confines of the cherry boughs.

His breath caught for a moment and his heart raced from its steady, controlled pace. What could he be seeing? What could explain this? He did not allow himself to rise out of his meditative state—perhaps his perception depended upon it—and contented himself to move with great caution toward the straggled, gnarled boughs of the oft-pruned old matriarch of the garden.

And then he remembered...his mother, taking him by the hand twenty years ago and leading him to this tree. She had told him it was ancient beyond knowing. It had existed on this hillside long before Mabuno Castle, the garden had been created around it; this tree was special. Wandering wisemen spoke of the *kodama* spirits, strong in its wood and flesh, the spirits of the forest whose abode was the dark, wild places where the wind and rain were lord. Often *kodama* trees would nestle together in valleys and gorges; their antiquity made the very air around them feel different, remote from human knowledge. They were the holders of high things and home to the *kami* of the woods. The Asahi were blessed to have incorporated a revered *kodama* tree into their most protected garden, and the veneration of the spirits who dwelled in this place had been the labour of generations.

Ieyasu put out a hand and saw the blue light reflected upon his skin. No sound came to his ears, as if he walked in a space between one moment and the next, suspended in a dream. He closed his eyes, spread his hands and spoke with his heart. He told the spirits of the tree of the dire times in which men lived, of the misfortunes of battle and the uncertainties of war, and he felt they listened with sympathy—not for the politics of human doing but for the need in the human heart. When he opened his eyes he saw the blue glimmers all around him as the spheres alighted upon his shoulders and outstretched hands, and hovered close around his head. He was unafraid; indeed, he felt blessed, and the weight of the world was lifted from him to be so touched.

The ghost lights, outward presence of the tree spirits, were the real owners of this place. With humility Ieyasu thanked them for allowing humans to dwell alongside them, in reverence of nature. The *kami* of the wilds were superior to the youthful ways of men, and the wise warrior strove for harmony with the world such as he might never win with his peers.

After a time he felt they had a message for him, but couched in terms he could not readily understand. No words came to his mind, but a feeling of warmth permeated him, as if some divine essence flowed through his veins. Peace, rest from his troubles. This seemed to be their wish, and the young samurai luxuriated in those feelings as he stood in the mild night air. The ghost lights, little by little, drew away from him, back into the boughs, and began to fade.

Revelation came in many forms, and Ieyasu pondered upon his gift as he completed one last circuit of the garden, then he settled upon an ornamental boulder near the gates and let his eyes rest upon the ancient cherry tree. In the shallower levels of meditation he let the depredations of time wash by him like water, leaving him untouched, the rock in the stream, shaped but slowly by the rushing years. In this perpetuity, he saw the security of his clan and no longer feared the burden he was destined to accept.

Come what may, he would do only what was right and best for those he had the honour to serve. This was Bushido, and in the certainty was peace which allowed him to step back, disengage the self, and find meaning in the difference he could make to others.

With a deep breath, Ieyasu let his eyes drift from the garden to the keep; then his precognitive sense warned him sharply and he turned on the rock, hand going to his sword hilt. The entrance to the garden was a walled walkway, and torchlight made a golden scatter across the stonework. Extending along the wall was a shadow—the dark mass betraying a living body eclipsing the torches. In his semi-trance, Ieyasu knew only a split second of real time was going by as the shadow grew inexorably along the path, reaching for him like a black cloud. For a moment he entertained the thought that death itself had come—whether for him, at the stroke of an assassin's blade, or for his father, from his wounds.

Need this be so? As he questioned the fear rising from the depths of his being, he rocked forward onto the balls of his feet and the thumb of his left hand on the sheath clicked the blade free of its seating. Razor-honed steel began to appear, gleaming dully in the torchlight, extending inch by inch as the sword glided free. Now the shadow had reached the midpoint of the path and he was in the process of drawing the first breath that presaged explosive action, though his mind remained calm. The darkness of the shadow was not absolute, he realised: the edges of stones were limned with warm lamplight, and quartzite in the gravel of the path glittered like stars. No news was ever totally bad, just as none was ever completely good. Friend or foe, it made no difference, just as life and death made no difference—except in the value for which each was given or won.

Part of him expected only the worst. He fell easily into the warrior mindset, which placed his back figuratively to life's wall, and stood his ground. The affront that this place of peace might be invaded by someone of malicious intent itself demanded justice, and he was calm in his acceptance of responsibility.

As the shadow neared the end of the path he resolved to defend himself and his kin in whatever way was necessary or possible. The tip of his blade cleared the lacquered wood. The sword began its pivot action in his right hand as his left released the sheath and transferred to the cord-bound grip. Lamplight flashed softly on the magnificently worked steel, and now the flapping robe of the oncoming man was visible. Just a stride or two more...

Ieyasu rebalanced his weight, came forward one pace and dropped onto legs like coiled springs, ready to react to his foe. All the deep reflection had flown now, placed into the background by the moment's necessity. A clear head, unfettered by thought, was imperative in battle: only actions mattered.

Arms tensed, he drew back fractionally as the katana completed its positioning action into *chūdan-no-kamae*, and Ieyasu adjusted his balance for the forward thrust which would end his assailant's life.

Torchlight outlined the running figure, his wide robe and ceremonial headgear. A moment later, the lamps of the garden revealed a seamed, elderly face, a wisp of beard at the jaw, and an expression of elation turning to terror as he saw the sword's point aimed at his heart...all in the languid slow motion of a dream, the elastic stretching of time which allowed the samurai to evaluate his actions and respond to his foe, committing to a reasoned course of action with the advantage of seeing a split second into the future.

Ieyasu transferred his intent from defence to evasion, and flicked the sword up into the vertical guard position as the old man teetered upon the toes of his court slippers, almost tripping in his haste. The samurai released the sword with his left hand, reached forward and steadied the old man by the shoulder.

Now he snapped into normal time and exhaled softly, still in total control as his grip relaxed on the gleaming weapon; he gently thrust the old servant back a step and breathed one word. "What?"

Old Fujioshi caught his breath, folded his hands, and put aside the fact he had almost died a moment earlier, to bow deeply. "Asahi-sama, your noble father, Asahi no Kimi, has regained consciousness and commands his son and heir to his side."

The smile with which it was said seemed to bode well. For Ieyasu it was as if a waterfall swept through his mind, clearing away the growth of dark notions. He relaxed from the inside first, and only when his heart was at peace did he lower the sword and perform the ritual action of resheathing. The sword clicked into the scabbard. He drew himself upright for a single deep breath, regained composure, and turned to the gate. He paused, and with the ghost of a smile acknowledged the old retainer with a nod of thanks.

The last thing he saw before hurrying to his father's side was the cherry tree. In the silver wash of the rising moon silhouetting its branches, the many buds had been spontaneously replaced by the first pink petals of the season.

The ancient *kodama* tree was in glorious blossom.

Diary literature was an influential genre in the Heian period. Often written by women, it described events in their lives, mixed with poetry and other observations. It helped develop Japanese as a literary language; men usually wrote in Chinese, considered the educated language, while women wrote in their native tongue. *The Pillow Book* of Sei Shōnagon became famous for her description of life at court as well as essays, lists, and poems.

Skull Pillow Diary

Jaap Boekestein

Dark clouds still above
Our already doomed world,
Will there be showers?
—Shinkei

The sun sets, and we appear. We never see the sun, ours is a land of darkness, of fog and toads and lost souls. Our guests are guided to the *baishun-yado* by strings of colored lanterns, or brought by boat by one of the *amanojaku* ferry-men.

Whoever reaches Red Cloud House is a guest, as long as they can pay, of course. The *ponbiki* Hayate welcomes them, bowing and sucking up: "Welcome! Welcome! You honor us with your presence *o-kyaku-sama*. Welcome! Welcome! We have rice wine and girls, music and dice."

Long before the first guest arrives, we are ready, prepared

and all. Every night I have the same ritual. Carefully I select the whitest maggots and put them on the naked bone of my skull.

"Behave, behave, dear brothers and sisters," I sing, and they always do. The living flesh forms a beautiful face, and many a customer has complimented me on the warmth and softness of my cheeks. Of course only maggots are not enough. My ruby red lips are two fresh chicken hearts, my eyelashes are the most elegant of caterpillars, black and lush. My eyebrows are hungry leeches and my hair is a collection of the finest of spider webs. Only my eyes are mine, and my teeth, but I paint those black with charcoal. My eyes are already perfect: big, shiny, lake twin moons reflected in a midnight lake, a poet once said. I was famous for my eyes. Long before I became famous for my betrayal.

There are a dozen or so, of us, the *shofu*. Sometimes a few more, sometimes a few less. It is hard to be certain in this place.

My name?

Call me *Yoru no himegimi*, night princess. Pay me, and you can call me *inbaifu*, whore, if you want. Please me, and I whisper my lover-name in your ear, just before you fall asleep. It is Jade Butterfly. *Shhs! Sleep!*

Daimaō Furui calls me by my lover-name.

> An icicle forms,
> Night through a frame of glass;
> Time without measure

The gate creaks wider:
Red rust flakes; each grating thrust
Bleeding black dank dust.

Tonight it is busy, a group of samurai brags about the big battle they have been in. How they killed the Mongol invaders in the woods around Hakata Bay. How they all were heroes who saved the islands.

Liars, they all are, every last one of them. Of the humans only the doomed, the cursed, the traitors and the cowards find their way to Red Cloud House. All dead, by the way. I wonder what those warriors' crime was, all those centuries ago. Did they abandon their lord on the battlefield, did they betray their comrades to the foreign devils, did they run and die without honor?

I decide I don't care. Old lies of old ghosts. Let them sing, let them be merry, let them laugh their hollow laugh and spill the rice wine that never quenches any thirst and never dulls any memories. This is Red Cloud House, and it is said no human will ever find solace in the house of the thousand delights. *Oni,* *tengu* and other *yōkai,* yes! Of course. But not those who ever were mortal, those who died.

They say a lot of things about Red Cloud House. A lot of stories are told about us. Maybe they are all true, maybe none of them are. My favorite is that they say the love of a mortal can free you from the bonds of Red Cloud House.

I sometimes dream about that tale, when my fingers run the strings of the *koto.*

Yes, the instrument is just a little out of tune, for ever and ever.

Those thoughts make me melancholic, which is a bad trait for *shofu*. But I guess every one of us girls is sad or melancholic under our sculpted faces. Bad drinks, bad food, sad whores. That is Red Cloud House.

It is all the doomed have.

Oh, why does that dream of being freed by the love of a mortal make me sad? Because I want it to happen. I want to be free. To really die and become part of the Big Wheel, so I can be reborn as a dog, a fish, a snail, anything!

But there are no mortals in the Red House. Demons, trolls, ghosts, the damned... Anyone, except mortals.

There are so many shapes, so many kinds of beings, even I don't know them all. Some of them are truly horrible, some of them are truly beautiful. And lovers... Big or small, dead or demon, fearsome or pitiful, they are all different, all the same. You want to know a secret? A woman's secret?

In bed I master them all. They want their pleasure, their one eternal moment of Heaven. They need me, I have the power to give them what they want, or to withhold it by being clumsy, or unresponsive, by crying or laughing.

"*O, I am so sorry. So very sorry. Don't worry, next time, yes?*"

I am their mistress, no matter how short. Peasant, priest, warrior, shogun, bow for me, pay me tribute!

Ah, the silly dreams of a silly girl.

Still, this dream makes me laugh.

Will *daimaō* Furui visit the Red Cloud House tonight?

If he does, he will ask for me.

And if I am not available, he will wait, drinking, gambling, watching the performers, listen to the tales and lies.

I am much honored he chooses me. He is a big lord, and a sweet lover. He has a white goatee, and a row of small spikes growing out of his back, which only I am allowed to see and touch.

I wish he wasn't a demon.

I don't need a demon's love.

Don't need it, but I do like it. I am much honored.

He is not here. So I sing, I smile, I fill drinking cups and try to sell my body. *Touch the sweet rotting flesh under my kimono. Mount me and my yellow bones will embrace your man-thing. Kiss my bloody chicken lips.*

It is a slow night, the men and non-men like to sit and drink. They sing and joke and gamble. They don't lust for flesh and bones, yet.

The door opens and the red bearded giant enters. Ugh! He is an ugly devil! So big! Pink skin, hair growing everywhere, a face that is huge and strange, with everything twice as big as it should be. And his eyes! His eyes are terrible! They are... round, like they can pop out of their skull at any moment, but that is not even the strangest thing. They are blue.

Blue! I am not lying. They really are blue. Like a clear sky just after a storm. That kind of blue. Very strange.

But somehow... attractive.

Shame on me. I have strange tastes.

Even for the Red Cloud House.

One of the ferrymen must have brought him to the Red Cloud House. The giant stands in the door opening, taking it all in for a moment. It is his first time here, I am sure of it. I have been here all eternity. He wears strange clothes, ugly. Where does he come from, the mountains? From under the mountains? What is he?

I have no idea.

He sits down in a corner.

I am the first of the girls who dares to approach him. No, we can't die, but we can be hurt.

He looks at me, with those strange blue eyes. Like holes in the sky, ready to suck out your soul.

"Saké!" he says with an atrocious accent. He puts down some coins.

I beckon one of the serving boys and he brings a whole jug.

This giant looks like he can drink jug of sake, or maybe more. He stinks, I suspect he is filthy.

"Your name?" He says.

How uncivilized! I amazed the thing can talk. It can! Barely.

"Yoru no himegimi," I reply.

"Yoru." He smiles.

No! I smile, I pour him a drink.

He takes the jug and gulps down the saké. With his hands he gestures I drink from the cup.

This creature is as uncivilized as a beast. No! I have seen dogs with better manners!

The red haired giant drinks some more, and order another jug, and one more. He empties them all. I barely have touched the saké from the cup. He empties another two jugs, earning him the respect of the serving boys.

And me, I have to admit.

"Yoru, you fuck?"

I can't make out if he is drunk, or if he only knows a few words.

But can I fuck?

Yeah. That is my fate. For ever and ever. But I have never felt so low. This creature treats me as a piece of cattle. I suspect he usually fucks pigs in the middle of the night, or something. He smells like it.

"I would be honored," I reply with carefully veiled sarcasm. "But if I might suggest a bath first to heighten your pleasure, my dear guest?"

I don't think he understands me, because he looks at me with those blue eyes. "You fuck, yes?"

I take him by the hand and he rises.

My, he is big!

He is drunk, but big. Men get out of his way.

Smiling I take him to the back, to the baths.

It takes a while before he understands what I want him to do. Only after I slip off my clothes, clean myself and sit down in the hot water, he understands.

He gets out of those stinking clothes.

My, he *is* big!

He doesn't clean himself first. No! Slowly he goes down in the water.

Utterly aghast I watch the man-mountain settle in the bath. He likes it, he says something I can't understand.

I smile, that usually works.

Is there a place where he doesn't have any hair? Incredible! I start to wash him.

He laughs, he is gentle and curious, he let me go on.

I scrub him like would scrub a blood soaked kimono in a mountain stream.

He starts to whistle, the hairs in my back rise. Is he cursing me? Doesn't he know it is bad luck to whistle?

Apparently he doesn't care about my luck, or his.

My hand touches him down there, that will make him shut up.

It does. It also does other things.

Now, this is my terrain. Here I am in charge.

I smile, the ugly giant looks at me, mouth half open, eyes half closed. Still the piercing blue is visible.

Play, play, play. When I feel like it, and the customer lets me, I can tease him for hours, in a thousand different ways. With all eternity at your disposal, you learn a few things.

This time I don't play, not for long. Get the thing in the mood, fuck it, smile and leave.

I do just that.

I climb out of the bath.

I... It wasn't as bad as it could have been. No teeth in strange places. Yes, I don't lie, I have seen that, and worse.

Without looking back I dry myself. I know he is still there, dirty beast thing, sitting in dirty water, smiling. He is still drunk.

"Yoru, thanks."

I turn my head, completely surprised. Did he really thank me just now?

He waves lazily.

I leave quickly.

In the main room my *daimaō* is waiting for me. My hearts blossoms with joy. My demon lover! Refined, tasteful, *civilized*. Dressed in a night lacquered armor. Yes, you I will gladly sleep with.

I am happy we retreat to the best room of the inn before the red haired giant returns from the bath. I don't want *daimaō* Furui see with whom I just have been.

We stay there all night.

When I dwell on things,
Such as flowers and phantoms,
And how they differ,
My heart, all of a sudden,
Shatters into a million pieces.
                    —Shinkei

Storm from a clear sky;
A stranger comes,
An unexpected lover

The next night he is back.

No, not *daimaō* Furui.

I mean the red headed giant.

He stands in the door opening and sees me. "Yoru!" he shouts.

The other girls giggle. They asked me about the gigantic creature and I told them all, and exaggerated a little, maybe. Well, not about *everything*. Now the other girls are glad the giant wants me instead of them.

I have no choice, I sit with him. I smile while he drinks jug after jug. He doesn't say much, I think he does not know how. "From far away," comes out of his mouth, his arms swing wildly. "Long time, wife, not seen."

I wonder if she is as big and hairy as he is. "Missing her. I took ship and left. Was not a good day to leave. Day... Day our Lord died."

Or at least, I think he says that. I can hardly understand him and even make less sense.

"You fuck?" I ask him, using the same kind of broken speech he does. I want it to be over as quickly as possible. Screw good manners!

"Yes."

We skip the bath—Hayate was very upset when he heard what the giant had done—and take one of the rooms. At least he doesn't smell so bad this time.

We fuck.

It isn't bad. He is big but very careful with me.

And afterwards he says, "Thank you," again.

I have had worse lovers.

That night *daimaō* Furui does not appear.

I sit and sing. The girls ask me if he hurt me and I tell lies, which make them whimper and roll with their eyes. Inside I smile. How nervous will they be next time the red headed giant choses one of them!

Night; and once again,
while I wait for you, cold wind
turns into rain.

—Masaoka Shiki

Cat sits in a doorway
Can't decide, go in or out;
Thorn on a bush
catches at my kimono;
We are torn.

"Yoru, I like you."

It is the fifth night. Every night he has returned. Every night we have slept together.

You get used to such a thing, can even start to look forward to it.

I... Never mind.

It is the very first time he says this.

He has his arm, massive, big, heavy, around me. I can't escape. His sweaty, hairy body lies against mine.

How awful! How disgusting!

How... comfortable.

He is so big, so protective. Nothing can hurt me when he is around.

I must be drunk. Have I sipped too much sake? What a

strange thoughts!

Blues eyes look into mine.

"Feel good," I reply. "Very good." I am not even lying.

Sometimes I amaze myself. I am a silly girl.

"Yoru, I will miss you."

"You leave?" I ask. It is the logical thing to ask.

"Yes. On ship. Long way back. Storms."

He is an uncivilized giant, a hairy ape. He is nothing compared to *daimaō* Furui. But one gets used to being fucked nicely, to being thanked afterwards, to lie in his big, big arms. I suddenly feel sadness, for the coming goodbye. I hate goodbyes.

There is also something else. Something gnaws at the back of my mind. Something a guest told months ago. It was a fresh ghost, a servant who took his own life, his heart filled with hate for his master. Wasn't there something about barbarians coming from far way? By ship? *Chikushō*, the ghost called them. I couldn't remember much. Our guests come from all places and times, some from very long ago. Which emperor currently rules in the land of the mortals? Which things happen outside our nightly existence? I really can't tell. Maybe I will learn one day, maybe not, it really doesn't matter. The affairs of the mortals have very little influence of our world. There will always be wars and ghosts, violence and doomed souls.

"I will miss you," I reply. I will, much more than I want to admit.

We lay in silence on the mats. Yoru and the giant.

Finally it is time to get up.

Because it is our last time, everything feels strange. I dress slowly. Do I want it to last a little bit longer?

Silly girl. You have forever. Will you remember this hairy ape in a century? Doubtful. But is has been strange, and yes, sweet. And now it is over.

"You will return?" I ask.

He grins, his big monkey grin. "I hope so. Rich. I buy you,

yes?"

If things were that easy.

"Yes," I reply.

We return to the main room, where *daimaō* Furui is waiting for me.

He is pleased to see me. He is not pleased to see the red headed giant. Why? Maybe because the strange giant has his hand on my shoulder. Or maybe because he grabs and embraces me in public. Oh horrible uncivilized ape! I... I... Secretly I love the attention. I have strange tastes. I struggle for appearances sake.

Wet lips on mine. He likes the way I taste, he says. *Like blood.* My giant kisses me, for everyone to see!

It is too much for *daimaō* Furui. Everyone knows I am his favorite. By insulting me, he is being insulted.

He shouts and attacks.

He doesn't honor the giant by killing him.

The *daimaō's* sword only cuts his cheek, ever so slightly. It is a warning and an insult.

The giant swoops me aside, standing in front of me. Protecting me.

Protecting me?

Yes, really!

His hand goes to his cheek, it returns red.

Blood red.

The red blood of a mortal.

A mortal!

I am not the only one that notices. Everyone in the inn looks at him. Completely surprised. A mortal, *here*? But he looks like a demon! An ugly one!

It doesn't matter. *Daimaō* Furui will kill him now. His sword his ready, his anger is huge.

My red headed giant–He can't be a mortal! Where do people like him live? At the end of the world?–doesn't have a sword. He carries a crude knife, but that will be useless against a demon's *katana*. He is dead.

"I will kill your for the dog you are," my *daimaō* calls out. He insults the red giant even more by not stating his name and lineage. Dogs are not worthy. He raises his sword.

From his belt the giant pulls a short stick. He points it at the demon lord and...

Flash! Smoke! A sound like thunder!

Every one shouts! Every one flees from this mighty magic. All the guests of the Red Cloud House are cowards.

Daimaō Furui is dead. His head is torn open. Brains and black blood are splattered all around.

I didn't flee. I am frozen in terror.

My giant turns around. His face is sad. "I go now."

I know he can't take me with me. Don't believe silly stories. None of them are true.

I look at him. I feel so much pain!

How can pain be so sweet?

"What is your name?" I blurt out. "My name is Jade Butterfly." I give him my lover-name. Why?

I...

Neh.

"*Willem van der Decken*," he replies. I have no idea what it means.

"I return. One day," he promises.

He leaves in the night.

I remain.

Tonight as I sleep alone
I am on my bed of tears,
like an abandoned boat
on the deep sea.

Cursed are those, who have lain with ghosts and drank the wine of demons.

Hell takes its revenge.

They say the Flying Dutchman can be released from his curse if he can find a woman who loves him enough to die for him.

He has no use for a dead woman.

Sadly.

Never seeing you,
I live on like the ancient
bridge of Nagara,
and now long years have gone by,
all spent in ceaseless yearning.
                              —Sakanōe

Do I forget my big hairy giant?
No.

He won't let me.

Every few years I receive a letter, delivered by a dead seaman or a drowned traveler.

I've learned to read Dutch, you can learn a lot during the centuries.

He writes he will be back for me, one day.

I know he will.

I will be waiting.

The Japanese-speaking Yamato people were not the only people on the islands of Japan. After the Yamato dynasty was formed in the 6th century, they gradually absorbed or conquered most of the other groups. The Ainu people of the northern island Hokkaido were not fully incorporated into the Empire until the 19th century. In the centuries before, there were several conflicts and revolts by the Ainu against Japanese authority. The Ainu had an extensive oral culture and prized storytelling.

The Greatest Victory

Lyn Thorne-Alder

It is said that the greatest of soldiers stands backed by every soldier in the army, and every soldier who came before.

It is said that the greatest of politicians stands backed by their entire district and their entire nation.

War is not won by generals, they say; countries are not made great by leaders. And yet leaders and generals are the ones written of in all the tales.

Consider the story of General Tsukushi Tada, who held off an entire army with the strength of his voice alone. Or so it is said.

"I need your help." The Ezo drums had been echoing up the pass for hours when the general barged into the Yamaguchi Bath

House. "I need to stall them." He pulled off his sandals and clogs hurriedly. "The Ezo will be here in an hour. The Emperor's Army will be here in four hours." He took the warm cloth from Kazue, whose turn it was to greet visitors to Yamaguchi House.

Kazue had served generals before. Located as Yamaguchi House was in a mountain pass on a contested border, the men of the Emperor's Army often spent time in the bathhouse's facilities and with their hosts and hostesses. This general was different. He was still wearing his full battle uniform, his sword and short-sword hanging by his side, his helmet in his off hand.

"The Pass of Yamaguchi is narrow, but I only have my unit. Even if the Pass were the width of a single soldier, a unit would not be enough." He frowned at Kazue. "But it is possible I could slow them down for a short while. If the house could pour tea for them, and play the samisen. Perhaps one or two of the hostesses could dance. The Ezo like dancing girls and singing as much as the Yamato, don't they?"

Kazue bowed deeply to the general.

Yamaguchi House overlooked Ezo territory in many places, and the Ezo men were every bit as common attendees of the baths as the Emperor's fighters. Lately, however, business in Yamaguchi House had diminished to a trickle, and those that did visit were close-lipped and tense, their swords as close to hand as House etiquette would allow.

"The Ezo do like tea, Your Greatness. They enjoy dancing." She peeked up at him from her bow.

He was studying her with a look like a child gives a bug: she had interesting colors, but he didn't quite know what to do with her. "You would know, would you?" Before Kazue had opened her mouth to reply, he answered himself. "Yes, you would. And what else do the Ezo value?"

Kazue dropped her bow into a kowtow. With her head pressed to the floor, she spoke carefully. "The Ezo like to talk, mighty general. They like talking, fine talking, more than any drink, more than the finest food our chef can prepare."

"Talking?"

"Orating, sir. They won't interrupt a man speaking, if his language is fine enough, not for anything. They have songs and legends about it."

"I'm no sort of pretty speaker. I can give a speech to the warriors of the Army, sure, but I am not a politician."

"Say what you mean, sir, and I'll make it pretty." Kazue dared a look up at the general. "I have served as a translator for Yamaguchi House before."

"Help me stall the Ezo, young lady, and you can serve as a translator for whomever you wish. I give you my word on it."

The center of Yamaguchi Pass had a flat space just large enough for a tea service and six people, smoothed out of the granite. It was there that Kazue found herself pouring tea for the general and three leaders of the Ezo army. Behind her, the mistress of Yamaguchi House herself played the samisen. She had chosen a quiet and sedate song, appropriate for a day of philosophical discussion and debate. The tea, too, was a calming brew, picked from leaves found only in the far North, deep into Ezo territory.

Kazue poured the tea slowly, each movement as precise as if she'd been in the middle of Yamaguchi House. She presented it to each Ezo with their traditional blessing, and to the general with a short verse of honor and thanks.

The general responded back with an aphorism on the beauty of spring held in the leaves of autumn. He bowed to Kazue, to the mistress of Yamaguchi House, and finally to the Ezo soldiers. He tasted the tea, let it roll around in his mouth, and gestured that the Ezo do the same.

When he had drunk of the brew—too tannic for Yamato

tongues, with a strange, dusty aftertaste—and the Ezo had done the same, the general cleared his throat.

"We have a saying, that any endeavor that begins in tea and ends in rice wine cannot be altogether bad, whatever happens in the middle. I like to think that any discussion that starts with such a strong brew will have strong results."

He continued: soldier's words, polite but without much poetry to them. When he paused, Kazue would translate, adding flourishes where there was room and twisting phrasings to echo Ezo songs whenever possible.

It was thirsty work, and the general drank quite a bit of tea as he spoke. He presented a philosophical question to the Ezo: can anything be considered truly bad that has a good beginning or a good ending? It wasn't a concept Kazue had ever heard from Ezo soldiers, but soldiers, even soldiers in bath-houses, were not known for being the most philosophical of sorts. Sometimes his words rambled; Kazue did what she could to bring them back into line. Sometimes his metaphors stumbled; Kazue's translations held them up. She poured tea while the general spoke, but the Ezo drank none. They were listening.

"I was in the middle of the worst battle of my life," the general told them, "when—" The dusty, bitter tea caught in the general's throat. He began coughing and did not stop.

Kazue poured him water from her pitcher and translated anyway. "—when the clouds parted," she improvised, "and the sun shone through like fingers from the heavens, brushing across our faces and blessing us." She thought fast; it couldn't be a battle against the Ezo. That wouldn't please them as good oratory at all. But there had been a period, when the general would have been a lieutenant or a captain, when they had allied with the Ezo against the Jhendo. "The clouds fell on the Jhendo that hour, and the day that had begun in misery ended in joy. It was a good day, my friends, a good day."

She paused to allow the general to pick up his story. He

had caught the word Jhendo in her speech, at least. He could improvise from there.

"However—" the general began, but his voice was a croak, a ragged, broken sound. He could not tell a pretty tale like that; he could barely convey a dinner order.

"However," Kazue translated, "the opposite can be true as well..."

The general's voice was gone. Three more times she stopped to allow him to pick up his story, and three more times he could manage only a croak. Kazue translated his croaks, building around them whatever stories she could guess at or create. She made as if his gestures were directing her, cuing her to different parts of her tale.

Nearly four hours had gone by when the general knocked over his empty tea cup. Kazue jumped. She had been so far into her narrative that, for a moment, she forgot she was supposed to be translating the general's words.

Silence hung in the air. The general carefully righted his cup and scraped out a sound. This time, not even a single word was discernable. Kazue found herself going cold. She looked between the Ezo and the general. She could not pretend to translate when he could give her nothing at all to go on!

The Ezo field marshal laughed. "Finish your story, honored hostess. Or should I say... honored enemy?"

"Sir." He must have meant the general. "He calls you honored enemy, mighty general."

"No." The field marshal's Japanese was rough and thickly accented, but it was clear. "No, hostess of Yamaguchi House, I speak to you. Finish your story."

And so it was. Kazue, a junior hostess in the Yamaguchi Bath House, held off the troops of the Ezo with the strength of her voice and the melody of her poetry. The Imperial army arrived, and the Ezo were repelled once more.

The greatest of generals stands backed by every citizen, and the greatest of tales begins with a single cough.

In the later half of the 19th century, Japan realized it had fallen behind technologically, and resolved to catch up. With the Meiji Restoration in 1868, the new government aggressively promoted industrialization. New industries using western technology grew rapidly, and within 20 years, Japan had become the industrial leader of Asia. These developments brought new opportunities to the people, but destroyed much of the traditional, feudal culture.

✐ Snag of Dewclaws

Josh Wagner

When Akemi brought the iron spike to his grandfather, the first thing the old man did was stick it up his nose.

"Yep," he said, "that's the smell."

Akemi, wobbling on his heels, said, "What smell? What *is* it?"

"You can't tell?" The old man traced the spike's smooth surface with the crumpled flesh of his middle finger. "Don't you have eyes to see?"

His grandfather's own eyes were pale as milky pearl. He handed the heavy iron wedge back to the boy and went about feeling around for his teacup on the wooden table beside him.

"I have eyes," the boy said softly.

Akemi had discovered the spike early that morning after his mother sent him into the forest to gather firewood. He was wandering down by his favorite spot, where a narrow stream slithered through a crescent of cedars. Here he knelt on the bank and swished his hand in the water. Akemi loved to stir up the minnows and count how long it took them to recover formation. When he'd grown bored with this game he stood up and brushed himself off. That's when he saw it, half sunk in the damp grass.

"Ringo-chan!" The old man shouted, slapping the table's surface.

Akemi heard his little sister's stifled laughter as she scampered out from behind their grandfather's chair. She was holding his wooden cup with both hands and spilling tea all over the floor.

"Give it back, Rin," Akemi said, exasperated as only an eleven-year-old boy with a little sister can be. "It's not funny."

"Don't be so hard on her," Grandfather said. "Such mischief only proves my suspicion. The poor girl is clearly under its influence."

And perhaps Akemi was as well. He crossed his arms and refused to say another word. Lately he'd been feeling particularly impatient with the evasive and circuitous manner in which grown-ups seemed to delight in speaking. This time he would wait it out. His grandfather would either decided to tell him or would not.

After a short silence the old man sighed.

"What you've brought into our house," he said, "is a dragon claw."

"No." Ozuru said. "It's not."

There were only seven or eight hairs above the boy's lip, but he referred to them as his mustache. Ozuru was the oldest, so when he made a call the argument was as good as over. His habit of contradicting whatever Akemi said without pause had been getting worse lately, so Akemi thought twice about showing him the spike. But what else was he going to do? These were his friends. You don't just find a dragon's claw and not show it to your friends.

"But his grandfather said!" countered Jiro, second oldest of the group.

Akemi could always count on Jiro to leap in and defend the most fantastic possibilities. Jiro's eyepatch, which he'd worn ever since a pernicious firebrand accident three weeks before, gave him an extra edge of authority.

"Yeah," Hachiuma said, because he liked to back Jiro up...but then he said, "Except maybe not," because he liked to back Ozuru up, and finally, "Hmm... well... I don't know," because he needed to find a way to stop talking. Hachiuma was scrawny and pigeon-toed, with a bit of an overbite. The way his face got all twisted around you could tell he was trying really hard to put everything together. No one else in the group had really listened to him for the past few years.

"Akemi's grandfather is wrong," Ozuru said.

The boys were gathered in the clearing near the woods outside the village, where Akemi first found the spike. Here wildflowers clustered at the base of heavy old stones thrusting out of the grass like rotten teeth. The boys made a ring around the flattest of these, where Ozuru placed the object for inspection.

Akemi knuckled his hips and stuck out his chin. "Well, what is it then?"

"It's a nail," Ozuru said plainly.

"That's what he said," Hachiuma stuttered. "A dragon's nail."

"Shut up, Hachi."

Ozuru knelt. He dangled the spike between his fingers, tip down, flat head up.

"Look," he said, "you hit it here with a big hammer."

"Why would anyone need a nail that size?"

"Breaking up rocks, binding steel, all sorts of stuff. But a dragon? Come on. It's just a hunk of iron."

"What was it doing out in the forest then?" Jiro said.

Ozuru aligned his posture and scratched between the two faint wings of his mustache.

"Is there a quarry around here somewhere?"

No one replied. They all held their collective breaths as seven frenzied eyes bounced back and forth.

And then they ran. As only boys chasing down the fire of the unknown can run.

But even after hours of methodical zig-zagging through a forest whose other side they'd never seen before, still they found no quarry.

What they *did* find was the forest's other side.

The boys tumbled out of the woods into a grassy field near the base of a quiet hill where a razor ridge of rock cast hedges of shadow on the empty slope. Their first thought was why they'd never bothered to explore this area before. Events in time often seem to arrive too late or too soon, particularly to boys their age, until frustration inspires the invention of reason to account for the precision of fate. The reason here was obvious. Akemi had found the spike, opening the gates of the forest to a new mystery—in this case, what appeared to be the spike's source: a strange path of crushed stone and wooden planks, bound by two parallel iron rails spaced a little farther apart than Ozuru's wingspan. The path had no visible beginning or end. It flowed around the base of the hill, past the boys, and straight on alongside the diminishing forest's edge until both dwindled into a space where eyes could not follow.

It felt familiar somehow, though they'd never seen anything like it before. Hachiuma was the first to touch the metal, as the others stood soaking up the thrill and kinetic illusion of its vanishing point. Gradually they all began tapping, pushing, kicking, and tasting. Akemi struck one of the rails with the spike, and a sweet echoing chime exposed an alliance between them.

"Look," Ozuru said. "Your dragon claws are everywhere."

Each of the planks has been pierced by an identical spike, which bound wood to rail with identical iron heads.

"Dragons have, what—three claws per foot?" Jiro said. "That's a lot of dragons."

"I think it's five," mumbled Hachiuma. "Or maybe four?"

"Guys!" Ozuru's voice aged by years. "It's just a nail."

Akemi wanted to argue but couldn't see the use. Nor could he have found the words. But he was too angry to stand still. He started to fidget behind his back, and hoped his Grandfather would have some answer to offer him.

"Definitely five," Hachiuma said.

"Let's go back and ask around," Ozuru said, "then meet here again in the morning."

The plan seemed reasonable. It was getting late, and though each boy felt the same compelling urge to follow this path, to get sucked down along the converging rows and discover how far the strange road goes, they agreed to call it a day. Their disappointment was tempered by a sense of relief, as if knowing these rails must go on forever...that one does not follow a road like this and expect to return.

"Well of course," Grandfather said, unfazed by the challenge to his explanation. "As dragons run along the dragon road they sometimes leave a claw or two behind, stuck in the wood. It's only natural. Add up all the dragons over time and you've got a lot of molted claws."

"Molted?"

"Cast off. Discarded. Things fall apart, Akemi. But sometimes they grow back."

"Dragon claws grow back?" Ringo said from the corner of the room.

"Of course! Like your own fingernails."

"Ozuru says it's just an iron tool," Akemi mumbled.

"If you could gather dragon scales from the caps of waves, would you not weave them into armor?"

Akemi wondered if he would.

But it doesn't really answer the question either way, he thought. And for the first time in his life the boy truly feared his grandfather might not know as much as he'd always believed.

In the morning Akemi holds Ringo's hand as the two of them walk through the old woods. His mother insisted he take the girl with him so their grandfather could have some peace and quiet. Ringo was ecstatic but Akemi hasn't stopped feeling anxious since the night before. He's afraid tell Ozuru what his grandfather said, certain the boy will dismiss every word.

It takes them longer than it should to get through the forest. Akemi feels like he's always either chasing Ringo down or encouraging her to keep up. At one point she sits in the dirt and demands her brother carry her.

"You're too big for that now," he says.

"I want to ride a dragon," she says.

When they finally make it through the woods the other boys are already there, waiting by the rails. Akemi immediately notices a double dose of smugness in Ozuru's face. He's clearly holding back some secret.

"Does it seem different to you guys today?" Hachiuma says.

"Different how?" Akemi asks.

Hachiuma shrugs. "I don't know. Just... not the same."

Akemi tries to match Ozuru's eye contact, but he feels burdened, oppressed, defeated. His hands and shoulders are lead weights. He speaks without conviction. "Grandfather said it's a dragon road. It's natural there'd be so many claws left behind."

Of course he expects to be contradicted, but it's even worse than that. Ozuru only puffs out a chuckle. He kneels down and stretches his neck until his ear rests on one of the rails.

"What are you doing?" Jiro says.

"Listening. You can hear when it's coming."

Akemi wants to throttle him. Ozuru is clearly dancing around his point, withholding vital information and staging a dramatic delay just to drive him crazy. *You'll make a fine grown-up*, Akemi thinks, and determines not to give him the satisfaction of any further questions. He wanders a ways up the track, pretending to study it closer. Hachiuma and Jiro mosey around like grazing sheep, flinging stones at nearby trees. Little Ringo-chan walks over to Ozuru and mimics his pose, more squatting than bending, clutching one of the rough wood planks to pull an ear down onto the metal. She mirrors as best she can Ozuru's grave look of concentration. Face to face, sideways eyes.

"It's called a *railroad*," the boy tells her, loud enough for the others to overhear.

None of them have ever come across the word before. They stop to listen. Akemi doesn't turn around. Ozuru sits back on his heels, brushing sand from his knees.

"A cart called a *train* rolls along these metal bars. Big enough to carry fifty people. It's made of iron, like any other tool. And it runs on a fire that the train carries with it wherever it goes."

"Where'd you hear that?" Akemi says.

"From my dad."

"It sounds made up," Jiro says, keying off Akemi's tone of voice and stepping in for support.

"Are you calling my dad a liar?" Ozuru clenches his fists.

"Whoa guys, whoa," Hachiuma says.

"No, no," Jiro backpedals. "I just can't picture it."

Ozuru gestures wildly. His arms seem to elongate with each movement.

"They're like big ships but they go on the land," he says. "And way faster."

"It's singing," says Ringo, whose ear still touches the metal.

"My dad knows these things," Ozuru says. "He works for the government."

Akami's grandfather might be older than Ozuru and his dad put together, but the government is the will of the Emperor and the Emperor is *kami* and *kami* are older than everything. Akemi sighs, knowing he will eventually have to admit he was wrong and Ozuru was right after all.

Then he hears a familiar voice trickling out from the forest.

"Ringo-chan! I found you."

Akemi turns to see the rumpled form of his grandfather step out from between two trees, sweeping his bamboo cane over the ground in wide arcs.

"Oji!" The little girl hops up and sprints toward the old man in a frenzy. He swoops her into his arms as the others gather around, cheering and bouncing, trying to show him what they've found. All chattering over one another, as only children bursting at the stitches of understanding can chatter.

Akemi doesn't laugh or smile. When he looks at his grandfather he feels betrayed, broken and embarrassed. How could he not know something even Ozuru's stupid dad knows? Or was he lying? And is that just what grown-ups do?

"Akemi? Where are you, boy?"

"It's a *railroad*, Grandfather," Akemi says bitterly. "Made of iron and spikes. There's nothing to do with dragons."

"Oh?" Grandfather seems surprised but interested. Curious, even.

"It's for a boat on the land," Ringo says. "Filled of people."

"Is that right?"

As if in answer to Grandfather's question, a new sound stutters softly from over the hill—a viscous whistle on the wind.

"What's that?" Jiro says.

"How did you find us, Grandfather?" Ringo asks.

"I followed my nose," the old man says.

"I do that sometimes," Hachiuma says. "For sure."

They hear it again, a bit louder this time, complicated now by another deeper, rattling sound. *Like an animal in pain*, Akemi thinks.

"What is it?" Hachiuma says.

"Shh," Grandfather says. "What do you see?"

The boys turn in circles, glancing in all directions, but they can't find the source of the sound. Not until...

"Smoke!" Jiri shouts.

A billowing black plume swirls into view from behind the rocky ridge.

"It comes!" Grandfather proclaims.

On the tail of his voice a third shriek strikes the air. The blue sky seems to shudder and melt, radiating into a weave of translucent worms as the great beast breaks the bend of the hill to bear down upon them. Its jaws thrust forward in a perilous sweeping wedge. A full muzzle of steel teeth gnashes at the dusty ground. One glowing gimlet eye, a molten diamond. Talon by claw, over and under, left to right, the creature drags itself forward on multi-jointed arms, somehow crouching and galloping at once, warping space in rainbow loops while tiny flashes of lightning erupt and crackle back into the great puffs of storm veiled upon its horned snout.

They are all too stunned to move. The ascent of its terrible wail encloses them in an envelope of vibration. Its body impossibly long and twisting. Coils and rivulets of black ribbon. Lucent scales that splinter the sunlight into a chaos of falling stars.

Every stray thought in Akemi's mind unifies under the banner of a great warning that the end is near. This is it. They'll all be killed or eaten or ripped to pieces any minute. When it finally tears by, Akemi feels a cyclone rupture through the cavern of his body, abducting his dreams or evicting his soul. Rigid as stone he waits for the plated tail to wrap him round, to snatch him up in a snag of dewclaws and whisk him away into endless clouds.

He hears his grandfather's voice booming: "Do you see it?"

"We see it!" Jiro and Hachiuma shout.

"We see it!" Ozuru and Ringo cry.

And Akemi sees it too, eyes shut, hair tousled, teeth clenched, his feet already inches off the ground.

At the Battle of Midway in World War II, the US Navy surprised the Japanese Navy and destroyed 4 aircraft carriers. After that, the Japanese military was slowly pushed back to the home islands and eventual surrender. Perhaps more costly than the loss of ships, was the loss of many skilled pilots. Some only survived with a little supernatural intervention...

eMidway

Alice Dryden

Counting kept the fox in its place. Takeo had learned that trick as a small boy, when he first had to go to school with a fox cub's skinny tail wriggling indignantly in his shorts leg. Later, he discovered that aviation manuals and technical specifications quieted the animal inside him, too.

So as he hurried across the carrier deck, Takeo counted off the aircraft already in the sky and heading towards the enemy fleet. Ten B5N torpedo bombers and four Type o fighters, plus his own and Nobu's still on the deck. That made sixteen; two eights. A lucky number.

An hour before, he had counted off eighteen of the Type 99 dive bombers and six Type os; three eights. Lucky again, although not for the ones who hadn't returned.

He ran his gloved hand along the rim of the cockpit, caressing it, as he climbed in. The Zero-fighter was a sleek, cold tube. Men had designed and built every part of it. It had no spirit, until it swallowed its pilot.

The canopy slid shut, muffling the noises of a big, busy ship in motion. He heard the crack of the starter cartridge, and the propeller blurred. Straight away the plane tried to pull itself forward along the deck, but he held back, waiting for the signal to take off.

Once he was cleared, there could be no hesitation. Throttle open, he pointed the howling plane at the spot where the grey deck stopped dead. Before he reached the void, his Zero wobbled into the air and began to climb steadily. The fox gave an anxious wriggle.

"My plane has a skin of aluminium alloy," he told it. "It is powered by the Prosperity engine of the Nakajima Aircraft Company."

The fox settled.

Takeo had not dreamed that he would love to fly. Joining the Air Service of the Imperial Navy had felt like a matter in which he had no choice, but he soon understood that the choice had been right for him. The higher he climbed, the lighter his heart. Concentrating on the controls lulled his fox, and he took pride in being one of his squadron's best pilots. After a lifetime spent longing to be ordinary, the desire to excel had surprised him during his training.

The sky, with its few high clouds, had a liquid clarity that made him feel closer to the unseen stars and gods. He thanked them both when he saw that Nobu had also completed his takeoff successfully, and was rising to join him.

Takeo got on fine with the rest of the squadron. They teased him, not only about his need to count everything, but for the way Hana, their mascot, barked and growled when he came near; his pointed face, said to be the shape girls found most attractive; his bottomless appetite for fried tofu. Takeo recognised it as their way of showing friendship, and it pleased him. They might call him a prude because he always insisted on bathing alone, in private, but a prude was better than a coward. Either was better than a demon.

Nobu, though, quietly religious in an old-fashioned way, and quick to blush... Nobu was special. His home village was close to where Takeo had grown up, and Nobu's discovery of the fact early in their training had bonded them. Wherever Takeo flew, Nobu took up the wingman's position, just astern and to the side. The urge to look after Nobu was a pull in Takeo's stomach sharper and more painful than the pull of gravity in a steep dive.

They formed up with the rest of the fighter escort, above the slower B5Ns with their torpedoes slung beneath them. Takeo had eaten before takeoff, but he was already ravenous again. The carrier shrank in the distance, a toy boat on a painted ocean brushed in long strokes of blue and white. He unwrapped one of the rice cakes Mother sent him as often as she could—something else the other boys teased him for—and munched it as he steered one-handed. Nobu bobbed up on his right wing, pointing and laughing at his greedy friend. Takeo waved and turned the Zero's nose towards the horizon, and the unseen enemy.

The flavour and texture of bean paste in his mouth recalled Mother so strongly he could almost hear her voice, the day he left for training.

"You could live to be a thousand years old. You could learn to make the foxfire; you could talk to gods and stars. You could fly with no need for a plane, if that's what you want. But you're going to war," she said.

"With everyone else in my class. I want to be like the others." She knew he had to go; she, too, would have felt the tug that summoned him. But mothers had to protest, and she wanted to be an ordinary mother as much as he wanted to be an ordinary son.

"You're not like the others, Takeo-baby. You realise that once you leave home, you can't just be the fox whenever you want?"

"I can't do that now."

"You've always had a safe place here. Out there in the world, you'll be concealing yourself from everyone. You'll sleep alone; bathe alone. There's no going back, once you make the choice.

Man or fox."

She had made that choice once, when she fell in love with Father. Takeo tried to picture her as a playful cub herself, but she had worn the disguise for so long that it was impossible. She wouldn't even show him her tail, now, though he had played with it long ago, shifting from cub to toddler as he rolled and bit.

This was the first time she had ever seemed unhappy with her decision.

He didn't tell her that he had said goodbye to the fox earlier that day, as he scampered through fields with the wet grass brushing his belly, rolled in the dappled sunlight of the woods, and ate a fresh offering of hot fried tofu laid on the mossy stones of the ancient shrine. Then he locked away the swiftness, the keen senses, the lithe little four-footed, furry body.

"I've made up my mind," he said, fiercely. "Like you did."

She leaned close. "Are you sure you wouldn't be more comfortable as a girl?" she whispered. "You could still switch. If you do it now."

"Mother!" He turned his head away to hide his pink cheeks. "A girl can't be a pilot!"

"Exactly," she said.

She knelt to hold him tightly, her arms squeezing his shoulders and waist. No—it was the harness, holding him back in his seat as the plane turned, and Takeo was at war.

He counted the aircraft as they began their diving run. The eight–nine–ten torpedo bombers went in low and flat, vulnerable to the anti-aircraft guns of the fleet. Nothing Takeo could do about the flak. The fighters' job was to defend the slower bombers from the enemy in the air.

Flat, matt and angular, the aircraft carrier was difficult to differentiate from the one Takeo had left behind. He could almost believe they had been tricked by a mischievous spirit into flying in a circle. But there were the American fighters, looking like koi carp with their plump bodies and short wings. They were moving, trundling along the deck, but so slowly. Takeo could have dived down to pick them off—but that would expose him to the ship's guns, and it was not his job. He counted them off as they lifted, forming groups of four. Nosing past the carrier was the white wake of a torpedo gone wide.

The fifth bomber had now released its load, and was climbing as quickly as it could. The sixth was holding its angle bravely, but the ship's guns tore it to pieces before Takeo's eyes. One wing, then the other, fell blazing to the sea, and the fuselage hurtled low across the deck to cartwheel into the water and sink.

The American fighters had gained height, now, and were pursuing the bombers as they climbed away from the fleet. Takeo signalled to the rest of his unit, and they dropped like falcons on pigeons.

Everyone knew the Grumman was no match for Japan's Type o. A tight turn delivered the first one into Takeo's sights, and he shot it down methodically, with the minimum of ordnance. Three squeezes of the trigger; three five-second bursts. The next plane flashed its vulnerable underside to him as it turned to flee. He placed bullets along its belly, and shot away part of the tail. That was two.

He turned and twisted, never staying in one line of flight long enough to be a target. His view grew confused, with the horizon rolling and planes crossing his vision faster than he could count them. He looked for his wingman, but could not locate him.

Always, when he was anxious, the fox rose in him. He felt it surge through his veins, trying to sharpen his teeth and nails for a fight it couldn't understand. Fox breath whined between his teeth.

There was Nobu—the way he crouched over the controls, intent, was unmistakable. The fox hunkered down, only to surge up again as Takeo saw the Grumman lumbering up behind his wingman, who was too focused on his own target to notice.

"Nobu! Look out!"

Takeo was already diving to chase the American away. He saw Nobu jump at the anguished voice over his radio, and glance over his shoulder. Now he was flicking his plane from side to side, but the American was too close to be shaken off. One of the Zero's cockpit panes starred and went white, like ice, and Takeo closed on the Grumman. The other pilot chose to escape by a steep descent. Takeo let him go. Kills were important—he mouthed a silent tally of his score so far—but Nobu more so. He moved up to his slot ahead and beside the other pilot.

As he dropped into position, the Zero shuddered under a succession of hits. Takeo had left his own tail vulnerable. The rudder went wrong, so he had to stamp down hard to stay level. The smell of fuel was sudden and startling to heightened senses.

"Wingspan twelve metres!" he yelled, tearing his oxygen mask away from his face so the radio would not broadcast his panic. "Length nine metres!" He prickled under his flightsuit as fur licked along his arms. The tail, outraged at its confinement, plumped up and thrashed. Clapping the mask back over his nose and mouth, Takeo breathed deeply. His heart pattered, like a small, trapped animal's.

"Empty weight... empty weight, um..." He imagined the fox loose in the cockpit, struggling in the heavy folds of the flightsuit. Tiny paws scrabbling at the release lever as the flames rose. Charred fox bones in a cage of twisted metal at the bottom of an ocean, for a thousand years. As far as one could be from the stars and the gods.

"Takeo? Takeo!"

A shrill whine was all the answer and reassurance he had for his wingman. Nobu. Nobu must be saved. But Takeo, who had not lived long enough to grow wise, could not even save himself.

Smoke streaming along the wings. Fuel slopping over his feet. The fox keening, struggling to break free. *Count.* Counting always helped. Ten, fourteen, twenty bullet holes in the cockpit. Four, three, two—the reading on the altimeter falling as the minutes of flight left to him ticked lower with every spurt of fuel.

He had no strength left to hold the fox back. Well, then, let it enjoy the heights, briefly. Reaching up with his left hand, he loosened his oxygen mask.

The muzzle poked free, black nose questing at the thin air. The prickling of his forearms became unbearable, and he pulled off the gauntlets to reveal smooth fur. In Takeo's vision, the sunlight grew brighter, the shadows deeper. Where there was movement his eyes snapped to it, and he could follow the planes that filled the sky as if he were idly watching so many flies crawling on a wall.

Rubbery pads took the stick in a sure grip, and a claw rested on the fire button. The heavy boots slid off his feet, and paws kicked the rudder pedals. Fox reflexes spun the Zero. An enemy fighter plunged into the sea.

Takeo's tail thrashed again, but this time he recognised the motion as communicating excitement, not terror. The fox he had kept shuttered down all this time—the fox *wanted* to fly! Of course it did—it was part of Takeo, after all! His mind, his body, overlaid with fox.

He aimed and fired ahead of one of the Grummans, watching the arc of bullets curl backwards and strike perfectly along the fuselage. The American planes could take a lot of punishment, more than the Zero, but they had limits. Flame lit the sea-grey body, and the aircraft plunged. Takeo slung his own plane sideways and down through the gap it left.

"Nobu follow me!" he barked into the mask slung from his neck. His voice was hoarse and thick. Nobu lined up on his tail, obedient, unquestioning, like the good wingman he was.

Takeo's eyes flicked and darted as he sought a path through the dogfight. He tipped the wing, rolled the Zero on its axis, soared past, above, between the turmoil. Nobu's plane seemed stuck to his own, just the way they had trained together. He turned away from the sun, to where the fleet must lie.

The battle faded behind them, so that the two aircraft, and their shadows on the water, were the only moving objects from horizon to horizon. The clouds sulked, motionless, and at this height the sea seemed frozen. In the cockpit, the needle of the fuel gauge moved steadily down. The beat of the engine was sound. There was no threat in sight.

Takeo remained half-fox.

Ravenous again, he ate the last of his snacks; studied his compass, hoped that it was reading true. The sea crawled by. Takeo gazed down at their two shadows joined tail to nose as they bumped across the waves.

For a long time there was no change, then the shape elongated and separated. The rear portion grew larger. The other Zero was dropping behind, losing height almost imperceptibly as it lagged.

"How are you doing, Nobu?"

The answering crackle was faint. "My eyes... blood, I think..."

"Can you still see me?"

"Just."

"Then follow. And keep your nose up."

Ten more minutes, and still only open water below them. Surely they should have reached the carrier by now? He scanned the horizon with a predator's eyes, and made out the floating speck that meant safety.

Safety for Nobu, at least. Takeo could not walk among the other pilots like this, and he had no idea how he might transform back. He could circle for a while to buy time, pretending there was a fault with the landing gear, but he had too little fuel to do so for long. Perhaps if he ditched, he could paddle the life raft to some secluded island and live on crabs and fish until he changed back, or forever. Perhaps he would sink to the bottom of the sea still strapped in with his secret.

"Takeo?" The voice in his ears was faint.

"You land first. My plane's in better shape than yours."

"I can't see! It's all dark!"

On the deck of the carrier, they were making ready for the two planes, creating space among the battered survivors already landed. Takeo lined his nose up and dropped his landing gear.

He would not lose Nobu to the sea now, nor to a crash on the deck. He would *not*. He bristled, his fur standing on end. Electricity crackled in each hair, and the needles on the cockpit dials swung back and forth. His trapped tail writhed against his leg. Claws gripped the stick.

Yet the picture that came to him—in the middle of the spinning, the sickly fuel smell, the noise and smoke—was of the little, mossy shrine, and the fresh offering upon it.

Foxfire filled the cockpit with a bright, white glow.

"Can you see me now, Nobu?"

"Yes! Yes, I can!"

"Good." Takeo shook himself from nose to tail, and his forepaws on the stick guided the Zero down to the deck of the carrier.

The two young men lay side by side in the bath, their bodies blurred beneath the foam. Beyond the door were all the sounds and smells of a busy hospital, but the scent of soap and the splash of water blocked them out for now.

The deep cuts above Nobu's eyes were healing and he had been passed fit to fly, but he was unhappy. Takeo saw it in the set of his mouth. He knew the disgrace of the lost battle, a defeat which had been reported in no news broadcasts or papers, was weighing on his wingman.

Takeo had not even been allowed to contact his mother. She

knew he was safe; would have sensed his death. That was some comfort to him, but no contact meant meant no food parcels, and he was faring badly on the hospital rations. He felt a pang that might equally have been hunger, an uneasy fox, or homesickness.

Entirely human ears would have missed the quiet sigh beside his ear, but Takeo turned his head. "What's the matter, Nobu?" he asked.

"I had an interview today. They're reassigning the survivors to new units. What if they split us up?"

That was Nobu's worry? Takeo felt his body flush with proud, embarrassed heat, like the needle stab of fur.

"They won't split up two pilots who work well together," he told Nobu. Somehow, they would not. The fox would find a way. "There'll be other battles, and we'll be in them. Together." He did not promise they would win.

When Nobu still frowned, Takeo splashed water in his face to make him blink and laugh, but the other boy would not be distracted.

"Takeo? When I followed you back to the carrier, you were sort of glowing."

"You were half blinded," Takeo said. His tail stirred beneath him and he plunged his hand below the surface to still it.

"And after we landed, some of the crew said you looked strange," Nobu continued.

Takeo's spine pricked. But by the time they had forced the cockpit open and pulled him out, there had been nothing out of the ordinary to see. Anything glimpsed as he landed part-transformed would have been a brief, strange sight indeed, and impossible to corroborate. He was safe.

"One of the doctors here was asking me questions, while you were asleep." Nobu poked him in the ribs. "He said you fought when he tried to undress you. Are you really so shy, Takeo?"

That was a bold question from someone who was shy himself. Takeo let the water lap at his chest. His limbs began to tingle, and his lips moved as he recited lengths and widths like a prayer, and counted blossoms on the tree outside the window. Yet, here he was, sitting naked next to his friend. He would not have arranged this if he did not feel safe. He relaxed against the tiled edge of the bath, as if he was settling into the cockpit.

"Nobu, listen. Before you joined the military, you prayed at your family shrine for divine help to protect you."

Nobu's face was already rosy from the hot water, but now he flushed a deeper pink. "How do you know?"

"Because I am the help you prayed for." He took his friend's hand and guided it below the surface, closing it around the damp cylinder of his tail. "My family has been tied to yours for a long time."

Nobu's eyes widened, but he didn't speak, and he didn't let go of the tail.

Relaxed by the water, and Nobu's trust, Takeo allowed his ears and face to lengthen. Fur bloomed along his arms and legs, to sway like waterweed in the warm current. Nobu's face was a perfect mix of amusement and wonder. Takeo wriggled his tail, enjoying the sensation of another's touch upon it, and grinned with pointed teeth.

He was a fox and he was a fighter pilot, and he was both together. He had made the foxfire, and now he would practise until he could make it at his own will and control its power, as easily as he fired the Zero's guns. His cockpit radio brought him voices as remote as gods and stars. He might not yet have a thousand years' worth of wisdom, but he could fly without magic. No matter what the rest of this losing war brought them, he would keep Nobu safe.

Koi are a species of carp, bred in Japan as an ornamental fish and found in many gardens. They are a symbol of perseverance in the face of adversity, wisdom, and transformation.

Foxes are important figures in Japanese folklore, and indeed there are several flitting through this book. They can transform themselves into human form. They may be protectors, servants of the goddess Inari, or tricksters.

The Emperor and The Fox

Frances Pauli

Rie held her skirts down until the breeze passed and squinted at her face in the glass bubble. She inserted a coin into the narrow slot in the metal, turned the handle, and a small hatch below the globe rattled as fish food overfilled the compartment.

Bits of it rained to the gravel around her feet. Rie hurried to cup both hands together, to catch as many of the smelly koi pellets as she could hold.

"I'm next." A boy's voice mingled with the shuffling of many shoes against the gravel.

"Hurry up."

Rie's classmates pressed her to finish, and she closed her fingers tightly around the food and held it to her chest like treasure. She stepped away from them, her hair flying free of the braid on one side and making a mask across her eyes. The line surged forward, and she shuffled aside.

"Careful there." A soft hand brushed at her forehead,

revealed a pointed face. A strange man leaned down to gaze at her with even sharper eyes. "Don't want to tumble into the pond."

"Thank you, Sir." Rie dipped politely and spilled a few grains of food across her shoes. The pond was closer than she'd expected, and she'd wandered farther from her class than she'd have guessed possible in so few steps. They still crowded around the vending machine, but Rie could barely hear their chatter now.

The man who'd stopped her hunched beside the path. He wore a long coat and carried a pole which he leaned on. He squinted at her and something swished behind him, a flash of red. "The emperor is hungry," he said.

"The emperor?"

"The oldest fish in the garden." His eyes flashed once, like the scales of a great fish. "They say he was here before they built the paths, and that he's more than a hundred years old."

Rie tightened her fingers, spilled more pellets and tried to imagine what the emperor looked like.

"You'd like to see him?"

"Very much, please." She nodded, and the man's eyes flashed again. The food in her hands shifted, turned dense and heavy.

"Then hold onto that," he said. "When the emperor comes for it, don't let go."

Rie nodded again. The man smiled. His lips curled at the edges, made his face even stranger, longer and even more pointed. Behind her, her class had noted her distance. Wooden soles pounded against gravel, and she turned on reflex.

"Fox!" The boy who'd pushed her in line arrived first. His name was Eiji and he skidded to a stop beside Rie, showering her feet with gravel. "Did you see it?"

"No." Rie meant to ask the man where to find the emperor, but when she looked back, the path was empty. No one stood beside it. The pond shimmered in the afternoon light, and a swirl of white petals floated on the glassy surface. "Where'd he go?"

"Darted in between the bushes."

"What?"

Eiji shrugged and pointed at the plantings, a narrow gap between a miniature maple and a rhododendron. "How come you didn't see it? It was right there."

"I was talking." Rie hugged her fists against her chest and felt the weight in her hands, the absence of raining crumbles.

"To whom?"

The rest of the class joined them, bringing a chorus of voices and a jostling chaos that forced Eiji to shift away. Rie had a handful of koi food only moments ago, and now it didn't feel right at all. She squatted and turned her back to the press of students. Teacher Shimizu called for them to line up, and Rie risked opening her fingers a little.

Something silver inside. She closed her fists again and stood to attention. How had her fish food changed into that? Where had her pellets gone? She'd used her only coin in the machine, and now she had nothing to feed the pond's denizens.

You'd like to see him?

Rie heard the strange man's voice and tightened her fingers on cold silver. He'd done it. Somehow, the man had switched her koi food for something else. He'd played a trick on her and then vanished without anyone else noticing.

She stamped her foot, remembered she'd dropped a few pellets, and squatted again. The class moved away slowly, following Teacher to the wooden bridge where they could feed the koi their treats. Rie opened her hand in the shelter of her skirts. A silver pendant rested on her palm. It flashed like the man's eyes, shaped like a koi and etched all over with squirmy lines.

Hold onto that.

Quickly, she pulled the chain over her head, dragged her braids free of the necklace and then sifted through the gravel around her feet. She managed to recover a few pellets, half squished to powder but better than having nothing. With the sad morsels clutched in her fist again, Rie scrambled after her class.

She caught the tail of the line before the first students began tossing their food for the fish.

The pond surface transformed. The mirror reflecting the arch of trees and blossoms shattered in a frantic flashing of scales and fins. Round, rubbery koi lips broke through the water, begged for the food and thrashed from side to side to collect it before their friends could.

Rie's class rained pellets from the bridge, and the koi gobbled them up. The water turned white and red and golden yellow as the rounded bodies squirmed after the food.

The emperor would not play such games. How Rie knew that, she couldn't say, but her hand tightened, and her feet stalled just short of stepping onto the bridge. A clump of thin bamboo gathered beside the path, and behind that, the water lapped right up against the gravel.

She shuffled back a step, watched the students crowding to hang over the water, reaching to tap any koi head bold enough to thrash into reach. Rie ducked from the path. She slipped behind the bamboo, and stepped alongside the pond in the shelter of the grass.

The water lay dark where it met the gravel. Only a series of slow ripples gave away the frantic scene around the bridge. Rie squatted and stared into the pond. She looked past the flat reflected sky, squinted, and saw the shadows of deep rocks and waving, bladed plants.

She watched them dance while the air around her echoed with laughter and her nostrils filled with the soft scent of jasmine growing somewhere nearby. The ripples slowed. The surface shifted from flat to deep to flat again as Rie adjusted her vision.

Something moved in the water, not thrashing or writhing as the hungry koi had done. This rolled across the bottom and between the shadows, a dark oval shape growing larger. Rie leaned out just a little. The slope forced her heels to dig in. Gravel crunched beneath her toes.

A round shadow rose from the deep. A great dome, wider than Rie's head, broke the surface, popped, sent out a dance of ripples. The bubble burst, emitting a sharp note. The water in the pond splashed toward her toes, and Rie reached her hand out, opened her fist and rained a pathetic powder of old crumbs into the bubble's wake.

The locket swung away from her shirt, dangled over the pond's lip and cast a silver glow across the ripples. The little metal koi flashed sunshine, and a rubbery black mouth appeared below it. The water gurgled. A scaled head followed the lips, huge plates around a big round eye. Rie reached her fingers, leaned forward and heard the gravel crunching.

It *had* to be the emperor. The black koi's head was almost as big as she was. The shadow of his body wafted away below the water, so long that she couldn't find the end of it. His mouth stretched open, twin silvery pectorals churned the surface, and the ripples washed at her shoes. She slipped an inch closer, reaching her arms out from her sides for balance.

The emperor lunged up. Rubbery lips latched around the silver necklace, devoured the metal koi and tugged at the chain around Rie's neck. Her fingers grabbed for the treasure, locked around the chain and held tight. She meant to scream, but the strange man's words echoed in her thoughts and drowned out the urge to make a sound.

Don't let go.

Rie held fast to the necklace and the great koi jerked hard. She fell forward, smacked into a chilly surface. It gave way and pulled her down, down until the world above closed over her head. Her hands refused to release the chain. She kicked her legs, but that only aided the emperor's tugging.

Rie sank into the pond, too deep, deeper than the shadows on the stones had suggested. She held her breath, but felt her chest tighten around the need to inhale. The water turned dark all around. The black shadow of the emperor loomed before her, flashing scales and huge glowing eyes like underwater moons.

"Just let go." His voice came from everywhere. His whiskers twitched, though his lips remained sealed.

Rie's chest hurt. She pulled as hard as she could, kicked and twisted.

"Let go, let go." Many small voices beat against her. The water changed colors, filled with smaller koi, bullet-shaped bodies that shifted and flashed.

Don't let go.

"Spy." The emperor's mouth opened, but Rie's necklace did not come free. Something round and white filled the inside of his stretched lips. He blew a gigantic bubble with her pendant trapped fast inside it.

The tiny voices echoed the emperor's. "Spy. Spy. The fox has sent another."

Rie needed air. Her eyes burned and even the bright koi dimmed. Their voices stabbed at her head, and each word pushed her farther down into the darkening water. "Spy. Fox spy."

Inside the emperor's mouth, the bubble expanded. The curved surface reached Rie's face, broke over her and swept out still. It closed around her head and grew even more, until her whole body was enclosed in the membrane. Her lungs gave up the fight. She sucked in, expecting water to fill her, to take her like a stone to the pond's bottom.

Instead, a rush of air. Relief. The voices sang outside her bubble, but they felt distant now. Rie twisted, but her limbs felt small and useless. She tingled all over, flashed and changed.

"Fox. Thief. Spy."

Rie opened her mouth to argue, but only bubbles came out. Her body felt light and agile, but when she tried to reach for the necklace chain, her arms fluttered uselessly. The necklace floated in front of her eyes, flashing silver. The emperor's lips closed, releasing Rie from his grip but sealing her inside the orb with the miniature, metal koi.

"So be it, spy." The emperor drifted farther from her bubble. He shrank back, and a mob of colored fish rushed in to fill the gap.

Rie's body tightened. Her legs fused together, and no matter how she twisted, would not part again. The koi all turned their rubber lips in her direction, round spouts to all sides of her. They blew a final accusation, *spy*, and a thousand tiny bubbles flowed from their round mouths. The froth burst against the membrane shielding Rie, popped her shelter, and sent her tumbling free, tail over fin, into the open pond.

Deep in the emperor's caverns, all the magic in the world began. They guarded it in shifts, breathed it in and out through plated gills, and kept the bubbles flowing over the glowing stones. The newest koi swam at the rear of the school, following the fish in front of her down between the plants and into a crack in the stones.

The gash stretched into a tunnel, and that branched and twisted and led them down into the emperor's domain. The school glinted like gathered stars. They turned together, moving as one. Each round mouth tightened. The koi fish flexed their stubby whiskers and held their gills close until they reached the source.

She waited at the rear, threshing her fins through warm water that tingled against her scales. Her tail waved slowly from one side to the other, washing the tunnel walls with a gentle current. The fish in front of her shifted forward, a blur of red and white that signaled their turn to breathe had come.

They swam forward as the previous school evacuated the chamber through vents in the domed ceiling. The little koi wiggled forward, joined the ring of fish surrounding a heap of glowing rock that rose from the chamber floor. All their colors lived beneath that stone, all the magic, all belonging to the emperor.

They exhaled in unison, a great exhalation of bubbles. The air washed over the rock, stirring the magic underneath. Heat radiated from the source. The little koi's body tingled and her school moved up, threshing tails, swimming toward the dome above so that the next group might take their place, tending the emperor's secret power by bathing the source with their life's breath.

The little koi bolted with her school, fit herself into the nearest passage and swam as hard as her tail could push her up into the pond again. Once they entered the shallower waters, the tingles faded. The school scattered, drifting to the tender plants and the shallow places where the mud was thick beneath the gravel and many tiny delicious tidbits could be sucked from the muck.

She swam through the water, letting her whiskers lead the way and listening to the bubble voices of her school. She heard them through her skin, through the way the water touched her scales, and she knew them just as she knew every twist of the pond—in the way of fish, in every movement of the water.

The other koi chattered as they swam, singing of the emperor's glory, of the long history of fish, and of the interloper who haunted the pond's border. The fox. The thief who pined for the emperor's power.

The newest koi sucked at the mud, listened to the stories, and swam until her school's turn came around again. They pooled together naturally, flicked their tails and sank toward the gash in the pond's bottom. The water warmed as they dove, and tingled the closer they got to the source.

The emperor watched over their dance, secreted in the shadow of the bamboo bridge, deep enough that no eyes could see him from above. He owned the shadows and the pond just as much as the warm caverns far below. He was very old and as wise as the wind. The fox may have sent another spy, but she'd been swiftly dealt with.

The little koi listened and swam with her school through the tunnels. She breathed her bubbles to the source of magic, and she prowled the pond until the next turn. Three times she dove and three times she rose, but when the voices of her kin called her to the fourth, something hard slapped against her scaly side.

She righted herself with a flick of her tail. Her school called from the cavern entrance, but when she curved back in that direction, the smack came again. This time it knocked her on the other side, and the little koi fled from it, flipping her tail and using her front fins to swing left and right. Every time she tried to veer back, however, the tapping came again. Something long and hard fell against her scales, driving her away again.

The other fish dove into the tunnels and the littlest koi was forced farther from them, along the edge of the pond to a shallow finger where the lilies choked the water and the gravel thickened, pressing her closer to the surface.

She darted past the little cove, but the thump against her side came again, and she veered from the impact and ended up tangled in the twisting stems of the garden's most prized flowers. She jerked and twisted in panic, but her fins had caught fast. The little koi opened her lips to cry out, but something large and soft clamped over her lips.

"Don't waste it!"

Another blow, harder than before, and the little koi was pressed up until her world broke around her and only cold nothing touched her scales. She flew through the air, landed on something both hard and soft at the same time. Her tail worked side to side, flipped her in a furious attempt to find the pond again.

A soft hand pressed down, pinned her to the grass, and she couldn't quite remember how she knew those words. Hand. It pushed against her side and her lips opened. Glass. Cold and round like a stone mouth pushing against her lips. The little koi flipped her tail, waved her fins, and could go nowhere.

The pressure pumped at her scales, and bubbles spouted

from her mouth. They dribbled into the glass hollow, a rainbow of koi breath, source touched, the emperor's rightful property. She struggled, but the hand pushed again and again. Each time it rose, the little koi's gills fluttered. Each time it fell, she spat her bubble breath into the glass.

Her body twisted and tingled. Her ribs ached and her tail fin felt as if it had been split in two. She flapped her fins, but they'd gone long and gangly, refused to obey her orders. Something heavy dragged at every movement, and a deep chill sent a shiver through her skin.

"Almost there." The man's voice urged her on. His hands pumped her chest, pushed the last of the bubbles free.

The little koi kicked her feet. She coughed when he plucked the bottle away, and when she saw the glass, full of rainbows, she blinked her eyes and remembered the chant of the fish. *Thief. Spy. Thief.* She rolled onto her belly, closed her eyes, and breathed.

In the distance, her classmates chanted her name. Rie pushed herself to her knees and glared at the man. He'd set his pole down, and now he hunched over a glass bottle full of bubbles. His fingers fumbled to get the stopper in, and his agitation sent his fluffy red tail swishing through the grass.

He'd tricked her for certain.

Rie's fingers found the chain around her neck, plucked at the little fish and dragged the necklace off. Her hands shook. She dropped the silver koi charm into the grass and tried to stand.

"I'd go slowly." He didn't even look up from his prize. The bottle neck was wrapped in leather, and he attached a slim belt to it.

Rie squinted at him. The light had fallen; it was much later in the day. Or perhaps another day? How long had she swam and breathed for the huge, black koi?

"It's always a shock at first."

"You tricked me."

"It's what I do." He bowed, finished his task, and slung the bottle of rainbows over his shoulder.

"Who are you?" She sat back on her heels, and the garden spun around her, bamboo and flowers. Her stomach tightened.

"I'm the man who saved you from drowning." He spun toward her so fast she rocked back and had to use her hands to support herself again. He jumped at Rie and crouched, nose to nose. His eyes flashed like knives, and his hand crept toward the necklace she'd dropped. His nose twitched, and atop his head, Rie discovered a pair of triangle red ears. "That's all you need to know."

"You're not a man."

"Not quite," he said. "But then you are not quite a little girl, either. Not anymore."

She opened her mouth to argue, but instead of words a fat bubble pressed between her lips. The fox-man reached a finger for it, and Rie snapped her mouth shut before he could steal it.

"Silly girl." His eyes narrowed, sharpened. He looked like he might dive on her again, drive the very last of the magic from her lungs to trap in his wretched glass. Instead, his gaze dropped to the necklace. His hand darted out and snagged the chain.

Rie lunged for it too. Her fist clamped around the metal fish, and the fox-man tugged against her.

"Let go."

"You said not to."

"Give it to me." The knife eyes turned dark, and the man's lip curled up showing Rie a row of tiny pointed teeth.

Her fingers trembled. The metal slipped. "No!"

She tugged back, tightening her grip and leaning away from a face that looked less and less like a man's with each breath. His teeth gleamed, and the fingers pulling on the chain grew slender black claws. Rie's heart pattered. In the distance, familiar voices chanted her name.

Rie, Rie. Thief. Spy.

"Rie!" When they found her, the fox cringed away. His fingers gave up the fight. He left the chain dangling from her hands, but bounded aside with a low growl and a flick of his bushy red tail. His body shrank. The bottle of magic vanished, and the sharp eyes flashed once as he darted into the bushes.

"Rie! Rie. She's here!" Eiji tramped through the bamboo, shouting her name over his shoulder. "I found her!"

The little fish hung between her fingers, and Rie's body shivered, remembered that it was wet and cold.

"Did you fall in? Are you okay?" Eiji leaned his face close to hers, blinked, and Rie flinched away. "Rie?"

"C-cold."

"They've got blankets." He snapped back up and bounced toward the bamboo. "Over here!"

Rie shivered and watched the koi charm shimmer like water. The pond lapped softly around the lilies, and the sun had nearly set. Did her school dive toward the source even now? Did they blow their bubbles over the stones?

"What's that?" Eiji pointed to the necklace.

"It's not mine." Rie's fingers flexed around the chain. She pulled the pendant closer and looked sideways at the pond, at the mirror surface reflecting sky, trees, bridge. *Thief.*

Eiji's voice scraped against her skin, too hard and full of air. "Teacher's coming."

Rie listened to the voices, the feet, the rustling of the bamboo and turned to face the water. Her skin shivered, scaleless. Her breath whisked out and in without magic. Somewhere in the brush, a fox yipped.

Rie lifted her arm and flung the necklace out and away. The silver koi flew in a high arc. It flashed above the water, silver and magic. The mirror broke. A huge shadow rose from the pond, a black monster with scales as big as her fist and a round, rubber mouth.

Voices chanted her name. Someone wrapped a heavy blanket around her shoulders. Rie shivered. "Rie! Rie."

Thief.

The emperor swallowed her apology and fell back without a sound. He vanished, and the pond fell still as glass, as if he'd never risen.

About the Authors

Mike Adamson holds a PhD from Flinders University of South Australia, where he has studied and taught for some twenty-three years. Mike lectures in anthropology, is a passionate photographer, a master-level hobbyist, and has a passion for speculative fiction, currently appearing in over twenty venues, including *Helios Quarterly*, *Lovecraftiana*, *Zetetic*, and *Aurealis*.

Stewart C Baker is an academic librarian, speculative fiction writer, and occasional haikuist. His fiction has appeared in *Writers of the Future*, *Nature*, *Galaxy's Edge*, and *Flash Fiction Online*, among other places. Stewart was born in England, has lived in South Carolina, Japan, and California, and currently resides in Oregon with his family—although if anyone asks, he'll usually say he's from the Internet. You can find more of his stories at infomancy.net.

Laura VanArendonk Baugh is an internationally-recognized and award-winning animal trainer, a popular costumer/cosplayer, a chocolate addict, and of course a writer. Find her at www.LauraVanArendonkBaugh.com.

Jaap Boekestein is an award winning Dutch writer of science fiction, fantasy, horror, thrillers and whatever takes his fancy. Five novels and almost three hundred of his stories have been published. His has made his living as a bouncer, working for a detective agency and as an editor. He currently works for the Dutch Ministry of Security and Justice. His English publications include stories in: *Cyäegha*, *Nonbianary Review*, *Strange Shifters*, *Lovecraft after Dark*, and *Surreal Nightmares*.

Evan Dicken studies old Japanese maps and crunches data for The Ohio State University. His fiction has appeared in *Flash Fiction Online, Pseudopod, Analog, Beneath Ceaseless Skies*, and *Daily Science Fiction*. You can learn more about him and his work at evandicken.com.

Alice Dryden lives in London and has stories published in *Apex Magazine* and a number of small press anthologies. Outside of fandom, her main interests are aviation, particularly the aircraft and aces of the First World War; touring the UK and Europe on her scooter; and Kenshukai karate.

Harry Elliott is a writer and an actor, but foremost he considers himself a teller of stories. Born in England, Sussex, and then raised in Cyprus, where he experienced military life serving in the National Guard. He eventually returned to his country of birth to pursue his passions, which led him to Kingston, where he achieved a Bachelors Degree in Creative Writing and Drama. He now wanders the land, looking for people to give him money in exchange for pretty fictions.

Steven Grassie is a speculative fiction writer from Glasgow, Scotland. His fiction has primarily appeared in anthologies, such as *Hero's Best Friend* and *Thunder on the Battlefield: Sorcery*. A Japanophile for as long as he can remember, Steven can often be found reading about the samurai, or pretending to be one in the karate dojo.

Alison McBain is passionate about diversity. With dual Canadian-U.S. citizenship, a Japanese-American mother, and a B.A. in African history and classical literature, she has an eclectic background to support it. She is an award-winning author with more than sixty short stories and poems published/forthcoming in magazines and anthologies, including *Flash Fiction Online, Abyss*

& Apex and *On Spec*. When not writing, she puts on her Book Reviews Editor hat for the magazine *Bewildering Stories*, contributes to the international literary collective *Reader's Abode*, or tweets @AlisonMcBain.

Marta Murvosh grew up watching *Star Trek* reruns and grade B monster movies, then graduated to pulp fiction. She was an award-winning newspaper journalist for almost 15 years before earning a Master's in Library Science. She is now a teen librarian working in the Pacific Northwest and continues to write for trade magazines.

Kirstie Olley has been telling tales since before she can remember and the stories have been steadily getting taller as she has. They have long since exceeded her in height. A working mother and JRPG gamer she has an eclectic range of tastes. Over the past four years she has had ten short stories published, many of which have won competitions or been short-listed for awards. To read more of her award winning stories or to find out exactly what it is she finds so fascinating about Bush-Stone Curlews visit her website: www.storybookperfect.com.

Richard Parks is a native of Mississippi, and now lives in central New York with his wife and cats. His work has appeared in *Asimov's Science Fiction, Realms of Fantasy, Tor.com, Weird Tales*, and other periodicals and anthologies. Early in his career, a popular recurring character was Eli Mothersbaugh, a high-tech ghost hunter based in the sleepy—and oft haunted—imaginary town of Canemill, Mississippi. More recently he has found success with his historical fantasies featuring Yamada Monogatari, a demon hunter of Heiji era Japan. His writings have also received nominations for the World Fantasy Award and the Mythopoeic Award.

Frances Pauli is a hybrid author of over twenty novels. She favors speculative fiction, romance, and furry fiction, but is not a fan of genre boxes. She posts free stories, excerpts, serials and previews of the upcoming books on her website: francespauli.com.

TS Rhodes is a professional pirate reenactor, storyteller and author. She is the winner of the 2012 Robyn Harrington Memorial Short Story Contest, and runner up in the IsciFic award. She is also the author of *The Pirate Empire* series, which tells the lively fictional story of Scarlet MacGrath, a female pirate captain, as she fights, robs and loves her way across the Caribbean.

Douglas Smith is an award-winning Canadian author of fantasy, SF, horror, and supernatural fiction. His work has been published in twenty-five languages and over thirty countries around the world. He's won Canada's Aurora Award three times and have been a finalist for the international John W. Campbell Award, Canada's juried Sunburst Award, the Canadian Broadcasting Corporation's 'Bookies' award, and France's juried Prix Masterton and Prix Bob Morane. His books include the novel *The Wolf at the End of the World*, and story collections *Chimerascope* and *Impossibilia*.

Lyn Thorne-Alder is a writer, gardener and crafter who enjoys hiking, wine tasting, and reading. Lyn lives in the Finger Lakes region of New York State with her husband and their three politically-minded cats. To learn more about Lyn Thorne-Alder, please visit lynthornealder.com.

Josh Wagner was living out of his truck in the middle of the desert with his dog Lucyfurr when he wrote his first graphic novel, *Fiction Clemens*. Since then he's traveled all over the planet, spinning stories out of what he finds. Outside of comics, Josh is the author of six books, screenplays, poetry and short fiction. As co-owner of Viscosity Theatre, an experimental theatre company based out of Missoula, MT, Josh has written and produced several plays. In his spare moments he reads too much, gets lost in the woods, and dances until they kick him out of the bar.

Will Weisser fell in love with science fiction and fantasy literature during comics boom of the early 90's and never looked back. Now residing in the fantastic realm known as the Philly 'burbs, he uses his geek talents to program computers by day, while by night he huddles over unfinished manuscripts, attempting to engineer characters who touch the human spirit. In his scant free time he enjoys practicing martial arts (which he is pretty good at) and playing guitar (terribly).

Enjoy more stories
of fantasy, adventure, and magic from
around the world in

Myriad Lands

Volume 1 contains stories based on real cultures (or their magical analogues) traditionally under-represented in fantasy literature from all over our world.

Stories by: Tade Thompson, Mary Anne Mohanraj, Lyn McConchie, Daniel Heath Justice, Dilman Dila, Daniel Ausema, and more.

Volume 2 contains stories set in imaginative other-worlds where society can take many different patterns.

Stories by: Tanith Lee, Neil Williamson, Adrian Tchaikovsky, Phenderson Djeli Clark, Megan Hutchins, Tom Fletcher, Melissa Mead, and more.

Availible from Guardbridge Books.
http://guardbridgebooks.co.uk